SPRING'S RENEWAL

SPRING'S RENEWAL

Seasons *of* Sugarcreek

BOOK TWO

SHELLEY SHEPARD GRAY

AVON
INSPIRE
An Imprint of HarperCollins*Publishers*

SPRING'S RENEWAL. Copyright © 2010 by Shelley Shepard Gray. All rights reserved. Printed in the United States of America. No part of this book may be used or reproduced in any manner whatsoever without written permission except in the case of brief quotations embodied in critical articles and reviews. For information address HarperCollins Publishers, 10 East 53rd Street, New York, NY 10022.

HarperCollins books may be purchased for educational, business, or sales promotional use. For information please write: Special Markets Department, HarperCollins Publishers, 10 East 53rd Street, New York, NY 10022.

FIRST AVON PAPERBACK EDITION PUBLISHED 2010.

Designed by Diahann Sturge

Library of Congress Cataloging-in-Publication Data
Gray, Shelley Shepard.
    Spring's renewal / Shelley Shepard Gray.
        p.   cm. — (Seasons of Sugarcreek ; bk. 2)
    ISBN 978-0-06-185236-7 (pbk.)
    1. Amish—Fiction.   2. Floods—Fiction.   I. Title.
PS3607.R3966S67 2010
813'.6—dc22
                                                                    2009044954

10 11 12 13 14   OV/RRD   10 9 8 7 6 5 4 3 2 1

If you walk with the Lord, you are never out of step.

Pennsylvania Dutch Saying

Great is His faithfulness;
His mercies begin fresh each morning.

Lamentations 3:23

SPRING'S RENEWAL

Chapter 1

"Children, it is time to clean up," Clara Slabaugh said. "We must wash off the blackboards and set our room to rights. Now, who would like to sweep the floor today?"

As expected, a chorus of twenty-four voices groaned loudly in reply. As she looked from one imploring face to the next, Clara fought to keep a stern expression. Sometime near the beginning of the school year, the children had started this game. Each afternoon, they did their best to delay the inevitable.

But she knew better. Clapping her hands together, she lifted her chin a bit. "Come now, it is necessary to keep our schoolhouse neat and tidy, *jah*? One cannot learn if the room is as tangled as a bird's nest."

After another few seconds of protest, ten-year-old Anson Graber raised his hand. "I'll sweep today, Miss Slabaugh."

"Thank you, Anson. Then perhaps Peter would care to help you water the crocuses when you're done?"

"I'd like that, yes," he said, his smile revealing a new tooth gone missing. Peter, too, looked pleased to have the special job of watering the patch of dirt right next to the doorway.

After assigning jobs to some of the oldest students, the rest of the children gathered their things together and pulled on coats. Not a one of them took time to button.

Clara understood why. It was March first, and what a pleasant March first it was! As the saying went, it had come in like a lamb. Outside, the weather was in the forties, and the sky was clear and sun shone bright.

Just as Clara had all but Anson and Peter in line to be dismissed, little Maggie Graber had a question. Clara bent down to her level. "Yes, Maggie?"

"Teacher, how come Anson must water the crocuses? Nothing's coming up."

"You are right, but we must have faith that the flowers will one day come and bloom brightly, just like they do every year."

One of the seven-year-old boys broke from the line to peer out the open doorway. "It's still just dirt."

"There's beauty just underneath," Clara promised. "Under the ground, as under our skin, beautiful things are just waiting to be discovered."

"Even for you?" Maggie asked.

Maggie's sister Carrie gasped. The others were stunned to silence.

Clara's hand flew up to her scarred cheek. The innocent question startled a lump in her throat. "Yes, even me, Maggie. My scars are only skin deep. Inside, I'm just like every other person you know."

Around her, the other children's eyes widened. Clara knew Maggie's question and her answer had embarrassed them. Well, it had embarrassed her as well, to her shame.

She sought to set everyone at ease by ringing the dismissal bell a full minute early. "I'll be seeing you tomorrow, then, children. Do be careful going home."

Ten hugs later, she watched the last of her scholars wander off to their homes, the littlest ones carefully watched over by their older siblings.

When she was finally alone, Clara leaned against the doorframe and breathed deeply. Another day, done.

Her second year of teaching was almost done, too. In a mere two months, classes would end and the joy of her existence would be taking a three-month break.

Clara tried not to care so much about that.

But still, she couldn't deny how hard it was not to feel melancholy some days when there seemed to be so little else to look forward to. At twenty-two, she was well on her way to being an old maid. She had no sweetheart to call her own.

In fact, she'd never been courted.

No, all she had was her job and her mother, who relied on her almost to the exclusion of all others.

Of course, Clara had her dreams, too.

In her dreams, she wasn't bound by a bossy parent's

needs. In her dreams, parts of her face were no longer marked by scars. Neither was her right hand. Nor the rest of her body. No, in her dreams, she was beautiful.

Of course, she shouldn't care about such things.

Feeling shamed, Clara got to work on grading the children's papers. It wouldn't do to stand around and wish for things that could never be. No, she should be counting her blessings—and she had many, she knew.

She had a job she enjoyed. She loved teaching, and for the most part, her students were respectful and enjoyable. She had a bright mind, and a wonderful-*gut* library from which she could check out as many books as she wanted.

And she did have a mother who loved her, no matter what she looked like.

It was only sometimes, in the late afternoon—in the time between her time with students and the work at home—that she wished for something more. For someone to see beyond her imperfections and reckon that she'd make a fine wife.

But here in Sugarcreek, Ohio, all anyone ever seemed to notice were her scars. They'd never taken the time to see what kind of person she was underneath.

Wishing for something different would surely be a mistake.

"Cousin Tim, you're still here!" Anson called out the moment the young boy spied him next to the barn.

Tim grinned at the ten-year-old who was running toward him at breakneck speed. Oh, but that boy always ran like his feet were on fire. "Where else did you think I'd be?"

"Don't know." Anson shrugged as he approached. "Guess I ain't used to ya being here yet."

"Sometimes I can say the same thing." Though Tim had been living in his uncle's home for two weeks, there were times that he still felt taken by surprise.

Anson scampered closer to Tim, his blond hair every which way, and dropped his books on the ground. "Whatcha working on?"

"Oh, this and that. Your father asked me to do some mending and fixing up around the house and barn for a bit. Today I decided that his fence here needed repairing."

Looking at Tim's hammer, Anson wrinkled his nose. "You might be needin' more than that hammer."

The fence did look like it had taken its last breath of air. "Perhaps I should build a new one. Ah, well. I've got time to do that, *jah*?"

Anson nodded sagely. "Mamm says your being here is a real blessing. Daed can't be in two places at a time." Picking up a piece of discarded rotten wood, he added, "Plus, Joshua ain't no help at the moment. Right now, he seems to be more interested in Gretta than anything else."

It took an effort, but Tim kept his expression sober. It wouldn't do for Anson to think he was being laughed at. "Joshua and Gretta are newlyweds. They're supposed to only be thinking about each other."

"Well, I hope Joshua starts thinking about the store

more so Caleb won't have to work as much. Then he could be around here more."

"Is that what you say or what Caleb says?"

Anson shrugged. "Both, I guess. Caleb doesn't like working at the store so it puts everyone in a sour mood."

"I imagine things will settle down soon."

"I hope things don't settle so much that you leave. I like you here," Anson replied, just as he tore off to the house, leaving a cloud of dust in his place.

Tim chuckled as he turned back to the fence he'd been repairing. Anson was right, the fence certainly was in a bad way. The slats were mostly rotten, and it had taken some careful considering to decide whether he should simply repair a few chosen boards or replace the whole fence around the corral altogether.

He'd leaned toward saving Frank a few dollars, but now he wasn't so sure if that had been the wisest decision.

In the distance, he heard Aunt Elsa's merry voice, followed by the three youngest children clambering for attention.

After something crashed and the youngest—Toby it was—started crying, Tim winced. Noise at his uncle's home was never far away.

Most times, it was a constant companion.

It was taking some getting used to as well. Back home in Indiana, he was used to the opposite way of life. After his birth, his mother's doctor had warned against any further pregnancies. So he was an only child.

He'd never minded that.

Actually, most days, he'd enjoyed it just being the three of them. At the end of every day, after his father had read a passage from the Bible, Tim and his parents would read together in their family room. Little by little, the worries of the day would dissipate and he'd be filled with the certainty of God's love. It had been nice.

In addition, over the last year, he'd been seeing Ruby Lynn Kropf. Though he still wasn't sure she was the right one for him, he'd enjoyed the idea of thinking that she might be. Tim had looked forward to one day taking over his father's land and farming it by Ruby Lynn's side. Together, they would raise a houseful of *kinner* and visit with his folks often.

But then one day his parents showed him a letter that had come in the day's mail.

In the letter, his uncle had asked him to come live, for the spring and summer, at his home. With Joshua so recently married and the youngest *kinner* terribly young, they were stretched thin. Uncle Frank wanted his help with the farm, until Caleb, his fifteen-year-old cousin, could take on more responsibility.

Tim's first inclination had been to decline. His parents needed him, and he knew his uncle was well-situated in the community. Surely there was someone else who could help?

When both his parents encouraged him to go, he'd stared at them in shock. "But I can't leave you two alone."

"You'll hardly be leaving us alone, Tim," his mother chided. "We've got many friends here."

"But that's not the same as family."

"We've your father's sisters and brothers, too."

"What about Ruby Lynn? She won't take it too kindly that I'll be leaving her for a few months."

His parents exchanged glances. "She's special to you, we know," his mother said slowly. "But I think that maybe Ruby needs to grow a bit. She's two years younger than you. Perhaps you each could get to know some other people."

He'd been shocked. "I don't want to get to know any other girls."

"Perhaps she might want to meet some other young men? At least she needs to opportunity, *jah*? This separation will give her some time."

In the end, Tim knew he'd really had no choice after all. His parents had wanted him to move to Sugarcreek for a spell, and so he did.

But he was finding it to be a trying experience. At twenty-two, he figured he was a bit old to be helping out like he was.

"You about done for the day?"

Startled from his ruminations, Tim turned to his uncle. "Uncle Frank, I'm sorry. I didn't see you approach."

"I guess not. Your eyes had a look about them that said you were far away."

He smiled at the description. "Not so far. Just in Indiana."

"Ah. You missing home?"

Missing his parents and home sounded too babyish.

"No . . . I'm missing Ruby Lynn. My sweetheart. What else can I do for you today?"

Uncle Frank's eyes twinkled with merriment. "Not a thing. It's time you relaxed. Go on in the house for a while."

Just thinking about the many *kinner* running around made Tim shiver. "*Danke*, but I think I'll stay out here for a bit."

"You know, sometimes, when I'm eager to get away, I go for a walk." His uncle pointed to the faintest of trails that started just a few yards away. "If you take that path, it will eventually lead you down to the creek. It's not a river or anything, but sometimes it's running."

Walking to an empty creek didn't sound terribly adventuresome, but Tim was grateful for the reprieve. Anything would be better than weaving his way through the maze of children in the house. "Maybe I'll go on down there now."

"Take your time, nephew. Elsa will hold supper for ya if you aren't back by the time we eat."

That sounded like too much to ask. During his short time with his aunt and uncle, Tim had been made aware of just how much effort it took Elsa to run such a big household smoothly. "I'll try to be back before supper."

Understanding creased the lines around his uncle's eyes. "I know you will. You're a good man, Tim. But I don't want to impose on you too much. Everyone needs some time to himself every now and then. Sometimes it's a *gut* idea to take a look at the scenery, too. Take what's offered."

With some surprise, Tim understood what his uncle wasn't saying. His dissatisfaction had been noticed, but not necessarily found fault with. "*Danke*, Uncle."

After putting away the tools, he set off on his walk.

The landscape was beautiful. Rolling hills surrounded him and trees dotted the landscape. Most fields were plowed, their rich soil black and vibrant. Every so often he'd spy a jaunty red cardinal flying toward its mate or a ground squirrel scurrying with purpose.

His own path snaked its way through a vivid green meadow dotted with tiny purple flowers just aching for a glimpse of the sky. Caught by the beauty of it all, Tim breathed deep. The land around Sugarcreek was truly one of the Lord's most perfect treasures.

After almost a mile, the ground sloped a bit and grew rockier. And then finally, like an unexpected rainbow, Tim spied the creek.

As waterways went, it wasn't much of one. Only a few yards wide, the creek held only a few feet of water. Underneath the current, the bed was a mixture of rocks, pebbles, and sand. But the water ran clear and the gentle noise of the stream was as inviting as a glass of cool lemonade on a hot day.

He'd never been one to resist a treat.

Bending down, Tim removed his straw hat and ran his hands in the icy cool water. Unable to stop himself, he cupped his hands to have a little taste.

And then he saw her.

"I wouldn't risk tasting that water, if you don't mind me saying so," a girl called out.

Tim straightened, keeping his eyes on her approach. Her skirt was violet, and the black apron she wore over it was in stark contrast to her white *kapp*. A small tremor rushed through him as he realized she was Plain, too. "It's polluted, then?" he asked when she was only a few yards away.

"I'm not sure how dirty it is, but I will say that the Millers' cows have enjoyed the waters enough to make me wary." She smiled.

He flinched in surprise. At first, he'd only been thinking about her eyes. They were light brown and tilted up a bit at the sides, like she was about to break out laughing. But when his gaze flickered to her lips, he noticed only one side of her mouth rose perfectly. The other stopped in a maze of puckered red skin that decorated her cheek. "I think I'll pass on that drink, then. It's better to be safe than sorry."

She stopped. Suddenly looking uncertain.

And it was no wonder. He, too, had heard the strain in his voice. Tim was reminded of a deer in the glade, her stance was so timid, her posture ready to make a quick escape if need be.

Struggling to not stare at the scars on her face, he spoke again. "I'm Tim Graber. Frank Graber's nephew."

Her posture eased. Eyes, brown and expressive, looked him over. "And I am Clara Slabaugh."

"Do you live nearby?"

She pointed to a white house in the distance. "Close enough. I walked to school today. Going home on the road takes longer, so I thought I'd cut through here."

"School?"

"Yes. I'm the area's teacher." She paused. "Sometimes I enjoy walking home this way. It's a lot quicker to take a turn by the creek than to keep to the road."

She said the words almost like an apology. As if she was the one intruding on his time. But that couldn't have been further from the truth. He was the one who didn't belong.

Or, perhaps he was trespassing? "Clara, am I on your land?"

"Heavens, no. I'm not certain who exactly owns this piece of property, if you want to know the truth. For as long as I can remember, all of us in the area have used it. And we all enjoy the creek. Even the Allens. They're your English neighbors, you know."

"I . . . I met them." Even as he uttered the words, he winced. Oh, could any man sound more feeble?

For a moment, her eyes held his. Then, as a faint red flush appeared in her cheek—the cheek that looked as soft and perfect as the petals of a May rose, she turned away. "I'd better be going."

He didn't want her to leave. There was something about Clara that calmed him. He appreciated her serene demeanor. So much so, he yearned to keep her close. "Would you like me to walk you the rest of the way home?"

"There's no need. I walk by myself all the time."

"Ah." Now he was embarrassed. But not enough to not risk getting to know her better. "Are you married, Clara?"

Her eyes narrowed in surprise—and with a bit of distrust. "No."

"Courting anyone?" Oh, but it was a forward question. What had possessed him to ever ask such a thing?

Hurt filled her gaze. "I don't think that's any of your business."

She was right. It was not. He'd been unforgivably rude.

"I must be going." Before even waiting for a reply, she turned her back to him and started walking briskly toward the small white house in the distance.

Too affected by his impertinence, Tim simply stood silently and watched her walk away. Within minutes, she'd gone up and down a hill, then faded from view. "Goodbye, Clara," he whispered.

Then wondered why he was so overcome.

Chapter 2

Had she ever met anyone so terribly direct? Anyone who had ever made her feel so . . . much? Continuing her walk toward home, Clara quickened her steps, hardly noticing that her skirts kept getting tangled in her long strides.

But even the strenuous walk couldn't push thoughts of him away.

Tim Graber had done strange things to her heart. From the moment he'd cast those wonderful golden eyes her way, she'd felt lost in his gaze. Almost like a bolt of lightning had blazed its way into her insides and delivered a mighty shock. She'd hardly been able to breathe, she'd felt so fluttery standing next to him.

But then he'd asked such prying questions. Asked if she was married or had a sweetheart. That had been when she'd known he was no different than any other boy in Sugarcreek.

He'd been teasing her. Of course she didn't have a suitor. In all her years no man had ever thought to look beyond her scars. Clara knew she should be accustomed to it. Hadn't her mother told her time and again that no man would ever choose her over a girl who was unmarked?

Her temper in such a state, Clara pulled open the door and shut it tight—more harshly than necessary. The walls shook, rattling the glass of the front window.

"Clara, is that you? What in heaven's name are you doing, crashing into the house like a loose animal?"

Setting her satchel down, she breathed deep for patience. But yet again, her mother pushed her buttons. "Clara, why haven't you answered me? Can you hear me?"

"I can hear you, Mamm," Clara finally replied.

"Well, then? What are you doing?"

Clara stood for a moment and closed her eyes in frustration. Some days she wished her life was different. If she couldn't have a husband, then she wished she could live on her own. Or if that wasn't possible, she wished her mother was less demanding.

Tears pricked her eyes. Oh, but she shouldn't be letting her temper get the best of her! And she certainly shouldn't be thinking such ugly thoughts. She needed to take time to give thanks for her blessings.

"Daughter, why aren't you walking down here? What are you doing?"

She started. "Nothing, Mamm. I was just setting my things down." Smoothing her skirts, Clara walked into the parlor, where she found her mother sitting quietly in the dim light.

Nothing occupied her hands. No book was nearby, either. As the years had passed, she'd done less and less for herself. In many ways, she seemed to enjoy being fiercely dependent on Clara on many levels. Pointing to the clock on the opposite wall, she said, "You're home late today."

"Am I?" Uneager to tell her mother about meeting Tim, she said, "I must have taken longer cleaning up the classroom than I thought."

"I've been watching the clock for thirty minutes."

Clara knew she had.

For too many years, it had just been the two of them. Her father had died while plowing the fields only a few months before her sisters had gotten married and moved away. Next thing she knew, Clara was living alone with her mother. It had been a big change—perhaps too much of one for her mother. As the years passed, her health had fallen into a decline.

Without ever discussing it much, everyone had just assumed that Clara, with her lack of future prospects, would stay at home to care for their mother.

And so she had.

Sitting down on the edge of a chair, Clara knew her duty: "How was your day?"

"As well as can be expected. I had a headache off and on for most of the afternoon. Your tardiness made it worse. Promise me that you won't be so late again."

"I cannot do that." Realizing she sounded a bit harsh,

Clara amended her words—and continued the lies. "It was necessary to do some extra work today. It couldn't be helped. And I'm sure it will happen again. It is my job, yes?"

Looking deflated, her mother nodded. "I suppose. And we most certainly do need your income. Why, I couldn't survive without it."

Before Clara could say a word, her mother shakily rose to her feet. "Well, let's make supper now. I am terribly hungry. How about we make some chicken and dumplings? That sounds like a good dish for such a dreary day."

It was on the tip of her tongue to tell her mother that it hadn't been dreary out at all. In fact, the day had been a glorious one.

She was tempted to point out that most anyone would suffer headaches by sitting in the dark, day after day. That her *mamm* would feel better if she went for a walk and tended to the garden.

But the conversation that would follow would most likely drain the last of the sympathy she felt for her mother. And if that happened, then she would become depressed as well.

So Clara didn't dare say anything. She followed her mother to the kitchen, each step heavy with wishes that things were different. Praying for guidance. Again.

Lilly Allen knew she was getting fat. Standing sideways in front of the tiny mirror in the women's restroom in her waitress uniform, she examined herself from every angle. "You're pregnant," she whispered. "You're supposed to be getting bigger."

But somehow she looked bigger *everywhere*, not just around her middle. Yep, at the moment, she looked chubby, not pregnant.

And she was five months along.

"I'll feel better when I start to show," she promised her reflection. Yep, she was sure she'd feel better when she was in maternity tops. And maybe she'd feel better when she stopped cramping so much, too.

Lately, she'd been cramping a lot.

Shaking her head, she strode out of the ladies' room and went right back to work. Now that the harsh days of winter were almost behind them, the tourists had started flocking back to the Sugarcreek Inn in record numbers.

Each day she waitressed, the time flew by. Lilly knew she was really lucky to have found a job that she was so well suited for. The tips were great, the other girls who worked there were nice, and the customers were fun. The only negative was that her feet and ankles were sore and swollen at the end of the day.

Racing back to the kitchen, she handed Gretta a new order. "Three slices of chocolate crème pie and one shoofly, please."

"I'll get in a jiffy," Gretta promised with a smile.

Standing beside Gretta, Miriam laughed. "Lilly, I think you could tell Gretta that the customers wanted ten pieces of pie and she'd be agreeable to it. She's walking in a cloud, she is."

· "I can't help it." Gretta shrugged. "I'm just so happy right now."

Though the restaurant was full, Lilly leaned against the counter and gazed at the newlywed. Just a few weeks ago, she'd attended her very first Amish wedding. It had been amazing to watch Gretta and Lilly's next-door neighbor Joshua Graber exchange vows. "Married life is agreeing with you, isn't it?"

"Oh, indeed."

"And you don't mind living above the Graber's store?"

"Oh, not at all. The Graber Country Store is a cavernous place. Our little apartment above the storage area is a right cozy spot for Joshua and me. One day, when we're in a family way, I suppose we'll have to think about getting a home of our own," she mused as she sliced neat portions of the chocolate pie and deftly slid them onto the plates. "A better place to raise our *kinner.* But for right now, I'm appreciating the privacy. If we weren't above the store, we'd be living with one of our families."

Lilly winked Miriam's way. "Who knows? With all that privacy, Gretta might be in a family way sooner than we think."

Miriam chuckled as Gretta turned bright red. "I think I'll go see if anyone would like some coffee."

"I'll be right behind you," Lilly said. After putting the four dessert plates on a tray, she lifted it, then put it right down in alarm. She'd felt a tightening around her middle.

"Lilly, are you all right?" Hands covered in flour, Miriam scurried around the stainless steel counter. "I heard you gasp."

She rubbed her side. "I guess I am. When I lifted the tray I felt a strange pull, but maybe it's just a muscle."

"Or maybe it's the baby moving?" Miriam mused.

"I . . . I bet that's it." She didn't think so, though. The pregnancy books described a baby's movement as a flutter. Not a sharp twinge.

Forgoing the tray, she decided to carry out the plates in her hands. It might take two trips, but at least she wouldn't be lifting so much weight. "I'll just deliver them this way."

"Don't overdo it, Lilly," Miriam warned. "You don't want to hurt yourself."

"I'll be careful. Thanks." Quickly, she carried two dishes out, then turned around and brought the next two out as well.

She was just considering a break when two women entered the restaurant. On the surface, they looked as different as night and day. One woman was dressed in a gray dress, black tennis shoes, and black apron. A delicately pressed white *kapp* covered neatly arranged hair. Next to her, was another woman, about the same age. Earrings and a gold wedding band decorated her ears and fingers. A periwinkle blue sweater complemented neatly pressed khakis and navy flats. Light makeup accented her hazel eyes.

"Hi, Mrs. Graber! Hi, Mom. This is a nice surprise."

The two women looked at each other and grinned. "We've been out at the sales in Berlin this morning and decided we needed sustenance," Mrs. Graber said. "There was no place better for us than here."

Grabbing a pair of menus, Lilly led them to a table at the back of the dining area, right next to the kitchen door. "How about this table? That way Gretta will be able to come out and say hello, too."

"That's a fine idea," her mom said.

Just as the front door rang again, Lilly turned on her heel and then was brought up short. It was a man. An Amish man. Hat in hand, he examined the bright, cheery restaurant with a frown.

She rushed over. "May I help you?"

"I came for lunch," he said, obviously ill at ease in the crowd of women. "Do you serve lunch?"

"We do." She led him to a table by the window. It was a little apart from the rest of the restaurant, and neither near the kitchen nor many of the other customers. Lilly had an idea that he had no need to advertise his presence there.

He sat without a smile and opened his menu without a word of thanks.

Too busy to wonder why he was so grumpy, Lilly went to check on her mom and Elsa. "Do you know what you'd like?"

They were both staring at the restaurant's newest customer with great interest. "Oh, no, Lilly, we don't," Mrs. Graber said in a distracted way. "Give us a minute, will ya?"

"Sure." Reluctantly, she approached the grumpy man again. "Are you ready, sir?"

After a long moment, he looked her way. "I am."

She blinked in surprise. He had the most beautiful blue eyes she'd ever seen in her life. Blue and clear and . . . sad? "What . . . what would you like for lunch?"

"The chicken dinner with potatoes." He spoke every word slowly, like he was carefully measuring his speech.

"I'll have that right out."

He only nodded in response.

Obviously, he'd said all he intended to. As she walked back to the kitchen and turned in her order, Lilly wondered what had made him so unhappy.

And then she wondered why she even cared.

Chapter 3

Tim's boots and pants were caked with mud. His leather gloves had turned stiff, they were so dirty and sweaty. He truly doubted whether his shirt would ever be white again. All of that was a minor discomfort compared to the state his back was in—pulled and sore. The muscles felt like he'd been the one dragging the plow all morning instead of the horses.

Oh, but plowing was a mighty difficult job, especially when he had to do the majority of it all by himself. With no one to help guide the horses or to clean the plow or to set things to right, he had to continually stop and start in order to clear every section of farmland. The constant stops cost precious time and made him eager to be done.

With a sudden ache, he found himself wishing for home again. Every spring, he and his father would prepare the fields together. They'd end the day with hasty showers outside the barn before they dared to enter Mamm's spotless kitchen.

With regularity, his father would attempt to sneak on by, but Mamm would catch him, scolding each of them with a laugh. He and his father were a good pair. They were lucky enough to not only enjoy each other's company, but able to work well together, too. With his father, plowing the fields was far more enjoyable than the same jobs at his uncle's.

Though it wasn't his uncle's fault.

Frank had intended to help him today but a series of predicaments had occurred, making it necessary that he stay at the store. A large shipment that was overdue had come in and therefore all hands were needed. Of course Tim had waved off his apology. He was strong and capable. He didn't have to have his uncle's help to get the job done.

But it would've been easier and far more enjoyable.

After brushing the horse down and cleaning up the lines and plow as best he could, Tim found the outside pump. After priming it, he started washing his hands, arms, face, and neck as best he could.

He'd just splashed a cupful of fresh water on his face when Elsa approached, young Toby in her arms. "Timothy, look at you! If I would've known you were willing to bathe out here, I wouldn't have worried so much about there being enough hot water for you," she teased.

He took the towel she offered and hastily wiped off his face. "It's habit. My *mamm* doesn't appreciate me tracking in mud on her clean floor."

"And you listen to her?" Her eyes widened in mock surprise. "I need to pass that news on to Caleb and Anson. They haven't quite figured out how to mind me yet."

Tim laughed. He did enjoy his aunt's humor. "Please don't share my story. I'm sure my mother could tell you that there were plenty of times when she wished I would listen more."

"Perhaps you are right," she replied, her eyes twinkling. "Listen now, the *kinner* at school are performing a little play about spring this afternoon. Since you have finished with the field for the day, I thought you might like a break. Would you care to join Toby and me and come along?"

"I would." Since moving to their home, he'd gone few places. He'd enjoy seeing more of Sugarcreek, and would like to see the schoolhouse, too. And, of course, he knew he couldn't pass up the opportunity to see his cousins in the play. "I wouldn't miss it. Anson and Carrie have talked of nothing else for days."

"They are terribly excited. Can you be ready in a half hour or so?"

"I can. I'll be all set as soon as I put on fresh clothes."

With a sigh, Elsa looked at his shirt. "It's going to give me quite a time, trying to make that shirt white again," she murmured.

Tim chuckled. "I figured you might say that."

Peeking out through the window, Clara gasped. Oh, but there was a wonderful-*gut* crowd of parents and siblings visiting today! They were sitting on quilts on the grass in the front yard. Sweet Maggie Graber and Jeffrey Miller were walking among them, passing out the peanut butter cookies Clara had baked the night before. She was glad that she'd taken the time to make two batches.

Inside the schoolhouse, the noise level was almost deafening. Her scholars were excited to share the fruits of their labor and continually kept repeating their lines.

Clara knew enough to let them practice for a few moments in their frenzied way. It would relieve their stress and make it easier to be quiet when it was time to begin. Each pair of children was going to recite poems about the bounty of the spring. They were dressed in their finest and looked freshly scrubbed.

But now that the cookies had been passed out and all the relatives were anxiously waiting for the program to begin, Clara knew it was time to reinstate order. "Come now, *kinner*. It is time to get started."

Anxious voices climbed another decibel.

Clara clapped her hands three times. "Now, now. It is time. We must begin, my scholars. Anson, where are you?"

Fresh-faced in a bright white shirt, he raced forward. "Here I am."

She bent down a bit to reach his eye level. "Do you feel ready to introduce your classmates?"

"*Jah*, but I still don't understand why you don't want to."

"Your parents came to see you, not me," she said, knowing deep in her heart that her given reason was only half of it. She'd learned time and again that her appearance could be a distraction.

Of course, there was more to that as well. While she wasn't shy at all around her students, she often became *naerfich* around their parents. "They will be *verra* happy to listen to you. You will do a mighty *gut* job, Anson. I feel sure of it."

He took a deep breath. "Well, okay." And before Clara had time to share any more words of wisdom, he opened the schoolroom door, gave a little whistle between his teeth, and stood at attention.

Clara rolled her eyes as the assemblage dutifully became silent and all faced him. That was not quite the way she'd hoped to begin her program—but she should have guessed that was Anson's way. There was not a shy bone in the boy. And he wasn't afraid to take control no matter how he did it.

As she heard him introduce their program in his clear, bright voice, she noticed most of the people gathered begin to smile. Yes, she had done the right thing by having young Anson begin their show.

Stepping out, she walked to the side of all the parents so she could see the students, too. The majority of them followed her movements, watching her for directions. When she nodded and smiled, they began their song.

The audience listened in rapt attention, then clapped politely when they finished. As soon as all the children came to sit near Clara, Anson proudly walked right back to the front. "And now, here's Maggie and Mary. They're going to recite our first poem, 'Spring's Renewal.'"

Mary held out her hand to Maggie. After seeing Clara's hopeful nod, Maggie gripped her girlfriend's hand and walked out to stand in the position Clara had marked with a taped X that morning.

Anson stood to one side as the girls took turns reciting the poem's stanzas.

Clara listened and felt her chest swell with pride. They were doing a mighty fine job, hardly stumbling over many of the words at all!

Feeling secure enough to scan the crowd, checking to make sure each child had some family present, Clara felt a lump form in her throat. There, right in the midst of the parents, sat the man she'd talked to near the creek. Tim Graber!

Unable to help herself, she craned her neck out a little farther, eager to catch a better look at him. But she was mightily taken off guard when she saw that Tim wasn't looking at Maggie and Mary at all! No, he was staring right at her.

For a moment, she felt spellbound, unable to look anywhere but right back at him. Just like in the field, she was mesmerized by his handsome, easy looks, and his quiet spirit. He surely did not look like he minded sitting on the grass at a children's production.

And, even more surprising, he didn't look like he found anything wrong with her. No, he was staring at her in interest, not shock or distaste. When their eyes caught and held, his lips slowly curved upward.

Afraid someone would notice if she smiled back, Clara looked away.

After four more pairs of students recited poems, Clara tapped Anson on his shoulder. "It's time to say thank you and goodbye."

Agreeably, he hopped to his feet. But then, to her surprise, he reached for her hand. "You come, too."

"No, Anson. This is your time."

"Come, Teacher," he said a bit more loudly.

"Ach, Anson—"

"Go up, too, Miss Slabaugh!" a group of students sitting to her left chorused.

The encouraging words had already claimed a number of parents' attention. Clara knew she had no choice but to follow Anson and quickly say her thank-yous. Otherwise it would cause quite a scene.

As gracefully as possible she rose to her feet and, holding Anson's hand, walked to the center with him. "Thank you all for visiting our class," she said. "I think you will agree with me that our scholars did a fine job."

As everyone clapped, two little girls rushed over and hugged Clara tight. That brought all the other *kinner* over for hugs, too. Laughing, she looked again at the audience, all shyness won over by her exuberant students for a bit. "You may take your children home as soon as you are ready."

As each child slowly drifted away and Clara chatted with their parents, she couldn't help but smile. It had been a wonderful-*gut* program.

When a small hand pulled on her skirt, she turned to the child with a smile. Then saw it was Toby, who was holding Tim's hand.

After greeting the toddler, Clara faced his companion. "Your program was very fine."

"*Danke.* I . . . I'm surprised to see you here."

"Aunt Elsa asked me if I'd like to come. I thought it would be a good opportunity to see your school and your classroom."

"We've been outside." As soon as the words left her mouth, Clara wished she could take them back. She sounded so clumsy and awkward!

"Yes, but now I have a better idea of how you are as a teacher. You're a good one, I think."

"I try my best."

Around them, the area was quieting as more and more children left the area. Mrs. Graber approached with Anson, Maggie, and Carrie in tow. "I thank you for the nice program, Miss Clara," Mrs. Graber said as she reached for Toby. "As always, the children did a good job. You are a teacher we can all be proud of."

"I'm proud of them as well," Clara said, looking at the Graber children fondly. "I need to give some credit to young Anson, here. Because he did such a nice job introducing everyone, I was able to stay in the back and keep the rest of the group organized. Anson, I would have been lost without you."

Anson preened. "I liked being out front and calling names."

Patting his shoulder, Mrs. Graber chuckled. "I would have been fairly shocked if you had not." She looked from Tim to Clara. "I see you two are getting acquainted?"

"Yes," Clara said shyly.

"Actually, this wasn't the first time we met," Tim said. "Our paths crossed last week."

Just recalling how much that meeting had affected her, Clara said, "Yes. I was walking home by the creek and Tim was there. We talked for a bit."

Tim smiled. "You cheered me up that day, Clara. I hope our paths cross again one day soon."

She didn't know what to say to that.

But Mrs. Graber didn't seem to want to shy away from that at all. In fact, a new light entered her eyes. "I see. Clara, perhaps you'd like to join us for supper one evening?"

Maggie cheered. "Teacher, please say yes!"

"I wouldn't want to impose," she said automatically, though inside, she couldn't help but be excited. She enjoyed everyone in the Graber family. And though she was a single teacher, it wasn't often that she was invited to her students' homes for suppers. People knew her mother wasn't in good health and therefore were reluctant to ask Clara to leave her for meals.

Of course, it was fairly obvious that the invitation didn't have much to do with Anson, Carrie, or Maggie.

"One more person won't make a difference at our table. Consider coming over soon. You could bring your mother. We'd enjoy her company, too."

Beside her, Tim didn't say anything, but he did seem to be watching her carefully. "*Danke.* I'll ask my mother soon."

Scooping young Toby up in her arms, Elsa Graber

sighed. "I suppose we'd best get our walk home started so Miss Slabaugh can get home, too."

"Thanks again for your help, Anson," Clara said to the freckled-faced boy.

"Welcome. Bye, Teacher."

Tim stepped forward. "How about I stay and help you clean up?"

Mrs. Graber smiled. "Ach! That's a wonderful—"

"No, no, thank you," Clara interrupted. "I'll be fine by myself." Knowing how she sounded, she softened her words. "I mean, I still have some other things that need doing."

Tim looked to comment on that. But his words were cut off when the children started running off, Carrie calling out for him to join them. "I . . . I guess I better go, too, then."

"Yes, it would be best," she murmured. Though, best for whom? she wondered.

Timothy merely gave her a long look before following the rest of his family.

As the crowd of Grabers soon disappeared over the hill, their exuberant voices faded away, leaving Clara good and completely alone.

But instead of feeling exhausted, she suddenly felt terribly fresh and buzzing. Tim Graber had shown her a definite interest. His steady gaze had made her feel things—made her feel interesting and almost . . . pretty. He made her think about the future she had always wanted. A future that included marriage and children and love.

She held the feeling tight to her heart . . . even though she knew those things could never actually happen. They were only a dream.

Turning away before she caught herself attempting to listen for his voice in the wind, Clara steeled herself to her job. After all, that was what she should be holding close.

That was what was truly important.

Chapter 4

"I'm glad you came along, Tim," Elsa said as they walked along the winding gravel road toward home. "Very glad, indeed."

"Seeing my cousins perform was fun. And speaking more with Clara was nice, too."

She looked at him sideways. "You two did seem to get along well."

"What do you know about Clara, Aunt Elsa?"

"About Miss Slabaugh? I think she's a right good teacher."

"Has she been teaching a long time?" he asked, trying to discover more about her. He wondered what her age was. Clara didn't look to be very old.

"Not so much. This is her second year to teach. I think she's twenty-two."

That was his age as well.

But his aunt knew that. Breaking into a smile, Elsa

said, "She's been a good teacher to our children. She's patient and kind and helps them learn a lot, too. Anson especially likes her very much."

"I noticed that she does seem to have a lot of patience with him."

"She would need it," Elsa joked. "My Anson could talk the ear off a person, he could. But somehow Clara gets him to channel all his energy, such as when she had him introduce everyone at the play today. That was a good thing, that was. If he'd had to sit quietly with the others, he would have been causing trouble in no time."

"The program was nice. She seems nice, too." He frowned. Saying she was "nice" sounded so . . . inadequate.

"She is that. She's done a good job teaching them how to write English. She's taught them many other things, too. Caleb can list all the presidents in order."

"My teacher only had us sit quietly and do our lessons. We did very few programs."

"The previous teacher had events like this, but not as many as Clara. She has the students present several times a year. The Christmas one is especially nice. For that program, us moms came up and made everyone a hot lunch."

Though he'd thought he had seen a glimmer of matchmaking earlier, his aunt now seemed intent to focus only on Clara's teaching accomplishments. He wondered why.

Rather bluntly he said, "Aunt Elsa, how did Clara get her scars?"

"Ah, those scars are a shame, aren't they?"

"What happened?"

She sighed. "Clara was involved in a kitchen accident when she was five or six." She shook her head sadly. "It was a terrible thing. Somehow hot oil from a fry pan splattered on her. It burned her something awful. She was in the hospital for weeks, she was."

Tim was shocked. "That's terrible."

"Oh, it was! Actually, it was much worse than that." Keeping an eye on Maggie and Toby, who were holding hands and trying to skip in the field, Elsa lowered her voice. "Clara got an infection at the hospital and developed a terrible high fever. We weren't sure if she was going to survive. Her mother was in a terrible way."

Looking at him sideways, she said quietly, "I heard it was right painful. She's had several operations. Skin grafts and such. For a few years the poor little thing seemed to always be covered in bandages."

Tim imagined such things had to be very costly. "The community paid for all that?"

"They did, but actually, her father worked for a fencing company and their insurance helped a bit, too. It was a lucky thing, that."

"I feel sorry for her."

"She looked worse, Tim. Now we're all used to it. Besides, that saying about what is inside a person counts is still true. Clara is a beautiful woman on the inside."

To his eyes, she was pretty on the outside, too. Her brown eyes were expressive and pretty. And the rest of her skin was a pale, creamy pink. "Is she courting anyone?"

"She's not." Elsa shook her skirts as they walked to the top of a hill, then started down into the valley that surrounded her home. "I'm afraid most of the men here can't see past her looks. And, well, her mother is dependent on her. Whoever married Clara would have to take on her mother as well."

"That's too bad, don'tcha think? It's like she's destined to be alone for always."

Elsa blinked in surprise. "She's lucky to be alive. I'm sorry to say I've never thought too much about her courting or not. She was always in and out of the doctor's and hospitals, and then her father passed away and her mother's health started failing. Then the teaching job came up and she took to it like a duck in water."

But Tim had seen something in Clara's eyes. Something that said she was more than just a teacher. "Is she an only child like me?"

"No, she has two older sisters. They married but don't live nearby." Looking out in the distance, her voice became reflective. "I guess I've simply been used to her lot in life. She has problems, it is true. But we all have our crosses to bear."

"Hers seem greater than most."

"Perhaps."

Tim glanced her way in surprise. Elsa was being especially close-mouthed. Was it because she didn't think it was any of his business? "Aenti Elsa, I don't mean any disrespect toward her. I'm merely interested."

At first he thought that perhaps she didn't hear him, she took so long to reply. But then finally, she spoke. "I invited her over because I thought you two had formed a friendship. But I hadn't imagined there might be something more between you."

"I don't know if there is. We just met."

"That is true. But Timothy, I thought you already had a sweetheart. Isn't that true?"

"It is, kind of." With some surprise, he realized he hadn't thought of her for hours.

"What is her name?"

"Ruby Lynn."

"And is she special to you?"

"I think so. Maybe." Actually, he was far less sure of how well they were suited. But it wouldn't be fair to her to talk about that. "She's been a good friend to me," he said loyally.

Elsa looked sideways at him. "Most every day, the mail delivers a letter from her to you."

"I write her often, too."

"A woman's heart is softer than a man's I think," she said finally. "It does no good to play with it. This Ruby Lynn—let her be your sweetheart for now."

"There's no chance of a future with Clara?"

"I didn't say that," she hedged.

"But if you were going to make a guess?"

"If I was going to say anything about that, I would mention that Clara's heart might be more tender than most. She's a wonderful-*gut* woman and a mighty fine teacher. But as a girl in love . . . she has no experience. She might expect more than you can give. She's a sweet girl. I'd hate for her to be disappointed."

"I wouldn't mean to hurt her."

"*Jah*, but sometimes we can all get hurt by surprise, yes? Accidents are the opposite of intentional problems, I think. And not all accidents only hurt the skin. Some make scars far deeper, and those are less easily healed."

Tim said little the rest of the way home.

What was making him even think about Clara, anyway? Was he simply bored and trying to pass the time?

Or was there a reason every time he talked with her, interest sparked inside him? Had the Lord guided him to this meeting? Was He bringing the two of them together for a purpose?

"Mom, I'm in trouble," Lilly said outside her parents' door at three A.M.

With a rustle of sheets, both of her parents bolted upright in bed. "Lilly?" her dad said groggily. "Are you sick?"

She folded her hands over her stomach, trying to ignore the pain that rolled forth. "I'm bleeding."

Her mom sat up. "Bleeding? Are you sure?"

"Yes."

In a flash, her mother reached her side and drew a comforting arm around her shoulders. "We better go to the hospital," she said, thankfully not asking any more questions about her condition. "Do you need help getting ready?"

"I'm dressed. Just . . . hurry, please?"

Her parents looked at each other in concern. Lines of

worry flickered across her father's forehead as he darted into their bathroom to change.

Arm still circling her, her mom guided her down the stairs to a living room chair. "Can you sit down?"

Lilly simply nodded as she sat. But inside, she felt as if every part of her was coming undone.

Within five minutes, her dad was heating up the car and her mom was waking up her brother Charlie with instructions to take care of Ty and get him off to school.

The pains grew worse. Every few minutes, her stomach contracted and sharp pulses radiated outward. Lilly clung to her chair for support, then to her mother's hand as they walked into the garage and then got into the car.

Seconds later, the tires screeched as her father pulled out of their driveway too fast.

"Careful, Scott. It's raining out."

"I know Barb." Glancing at Lilly in the rearview mirror, he caught her eye. "Are you hanging in there, Lilly?"

She wasn't. She knew what was happening, what was about to happen. She knew she was bleeding. She knew the pains were getting worse instead of decreasing.

"Just get there, would you, Daddy?"

"I promise." And with that, he pressed the accelerator and they tore off into the night. Lights and stars illuminated their way to the highway, but the fifty-mile trek to the hospital had never been so long.

As another pain rushed forward, Lilly bit her lip to keep from crying out.

"Hang in there, Lilly. I'm praying. You pray, too," her mother said.

She nodded. It hurt too much to reply. She did close her eyes to pray, but she couldn't seem to clear her mind. All she was able to focus on were the cramps and the blur of depression looming over her.

From the front seat, her mother chatted nervously. "Do you think we should have just gone to the twenty-four-hour clinic, Scott? It's closer."

"No."

"Maybe we should have just called an ambulance."

"We did the right thing. We'll get her there."

"What are we going to do if . . ."

"We'll deal with it then," he said.

In the backseat, Lilly continued to let the conversation float over her. There was no sense in taking part in it. She didn't know what the right thing to do was. She didn't know if it was all her fault, either.

For days she'd been feeling funny. She'd had a few cramps, too, but they hadn't been particularly painful. And all the books had said that five months was past the usual danger zone. It had never occurred to her to worry about a miscarriage.

But as her stomach cramped and a flash of pain rolled to her back, she was afraid for the worst. Unable to help herself, she breathed a sigh of pain.

Her mother twisted and looked over the seat. "Don't give up hope, Lilly."

"I won't."

"I know I haven't been the most supportive person

about this pregnancy, but I've been changing . . ." Tears appeared in her eyes.

Lilly knew she was crying, too. Just a few short weeks ago, she'd been fighting with her parents about whether to keep the baby or to put it up for adoption. It had been an incredibly difficult choice to make to keep the baby.

No one had been especially pleased about the news. But then a funny thing had happened. Little by little, both her brothers and her parents had started talking about "Junior" in a positive way.

They'd started teasing her about her changing figure, and even started talking about a future with a little guy in their midst. Lilly had begun to have hope that everything might be okay after all.

And now this was happening.

Finally on the highway, her father moved to the left lane and accelerated. Cars on their right became a blur as he passed them.

"Scott, be careful!"

"I'm careful. We just need to get there."

Leaning back against her seat, Lilly closed her eyes and prayed. She prayed for the baby and for herself and for her parents.

But most of all she prayed for strength. She knew she was going to need it, and everything else the Lord could provide for her.

Because just as she'd thought she could never imagine going through anything harder . . . something more had come.

The moment they stopped at the emergency entrance,

her mother rushed out of the car and inside. Seconds later a team of orderlies and nurses ran out to meet them.

Lilly was barely conscious of strong arms picking her up and placing her on the gurney. Of the cacophony of voices issuing orders and directives as they sailed through the pair of glass double doors.

She was vaguely aware of hands probing her with needles and searching for veins. Of the bright lights shining overhead as a pair of nurses helped her undress.

Of going into surgery.

But she knew she'd never forget the dull, icy feeling that came when the doctor gravely told her that her baby boy had died.

That moment was sharp and real and seemed to last for an eternity.

Chapter 5

"The *Englischer* Lilly Allen lost her baby, I heard."

Clara looked up from the cream-and-violet blanket she was knitting. "Mamm, are you sure?"

"Fairly. I heard it from Francis Miller, who talked to Elsa Graber herself. The Grabers are right-*gut* friends with the Allens, being neighbors and all."

"That's terrible news." She didn't know the English girl all that well, but she'd always been impressed with how capable she was. Clara knew it was hard to make your way in the world when you were different, and Lilly's pregnancy had caused a great many tongues to wag. "When did it happen? Recently?"

"I don't know exactly, but Francis told me it was a sudden thing. That it happened in the middle of the night last week or so." She frowned. "I do feel sorry for her, but she should have expected something like that, I suppose."

Though she should have gotten used to her mother's harsh judgment of others, this pronouncement was unusually callous. "Why do you say that?"

"She wasn't married, you know. I think even the English frown on that. God probably took control there."

Clara disagreed. She'd long since given up blaming God for every mishap—or praising Him for every blessing. She felt his concern and love with her always. But she also thought their relationship was so much more than Him doling out gifts and punishments for good and bad behavior.

But her mother didn't see things that way. In fact, ever since her father had died and Patricia and Ruth had married, she'd been more and more confined to the house—and adopting ever more peculiar notions about the Lord.

No amount of reasoning ever seemed to change her mind. Clara resumed knitting. She was working on a baby blanket for an upcoming auction. The *Englischers* enjoyed paying too much for Amish-made crafts—and the money would go to a good cause: the bills for a local family whose baby needed heart surgery.

Several long moments passed as they continued their projects in silence. As their needles clicked in unison, the strain built up by their earlier conversation began to subside.

"Mamm, your project is looking wonderful-*gut*."

"*Danke*. I think these are turning out nicely."

Her mother was working on a pair of potholders. When she was feeling good, she liked making simple crafts for a few of the art shows. Thankfully, she'd been in good health—and in good spirits—for the last few days.

"I imagine Gretta Graber will be carrying her own baby before we know it."

For a moment, Clara had to place in her mind who her mother was speaking of. She still wasn't used to Gretta's new married name. "Gretta and Joshua just got married."

"Yes, but Francis said they are happy in their little apartment." Her mother chuckled. "I guess that's what is to be expected, though. They are young and in love."

All this baby talk made Clara sad, though she tried her best to not let it show. It was hard to realize that what was happening to Gretta—and even to Lilly Allen—was not something that could ever happen to her.

"I hope Patricia writes soon," Lilly said through clenched teeth. "I think her baby is due within the month."

"She did sound terribly excited about it in her latest letter, didn't she? And it's her fourth. She could probably use some help." Worrying her lip for a moment, her mother finished a row, then arranged the yarn in her lap as she began another one. "It's too bad I can't spare you."

"I'm sure you could spare me if Patricia really did need me. Or, Mamm, I think you should go visit her." Clara knew little about taking care of newborns, while her mother would be a pro. Besides, she had her job. Her students needed their teacher. And she needed them, too.

Thinking on it, Clara warmed up to the idea. "Yes, Mamm, a visit to see Patricia and her *boppli* is a good idea."

Her fingers stopped stitching long enough for her to stare at Clara in surprise. "Oh, I couldn't."

"They would enjoy your company, I think. And holding a new *boppli* would be nice."

"Holding the baby would be a pleasure, but even getting to Patricia's house would be too much for me. She's at least four hours away by a car!" Shaking her head again, her mother resumed her knitting. "Yes, I would have a difficult time. It is already a trial on me just to stay home all day long by myself."

Her mother's list of complaints and excuses seemed to grow longer each week. "Perhaps we could find a way for you to get some help. A nurse or something."

"We can't afford that, Clara. We are on a tight budget, I've told you that."

"Perhaps I could look at the bills? Maybe things aren't as bad as they seem?"

"No. I mean, bill paying is my job, *jah*? No, I'm just going to have to stay here and hope and pray that Patricia decides to visit us soon."

"But with her new *boppli*, it doesn't seem likely."

"Then we'll make do with letters." Her voice firm, she said, "Yes, we will need to simply keep everything just as it is. I will do my best to get through each day, and count my blessings for you. I will always have you, *jah*?"

Clara didn't mind doing her duty. But what her mother was suggesting felt too difficult.

A burst of alarm coursed through her. Though her mother had often insinuated that she hoped her youngest would never leave, it now sounded as if she meant for Clara to stay by her side for the rest of their lives. "Mamm, you can't expect me to always just stay here." For once, she didn't even try to hide her emotions.

Her mother looked at her, surprise evident in her eyes. "You sound as if you don't want to be around me."

"It's not that. Of course I love you. But one day, perhaps I'll want to do something else. Maybe move somewhere else . . ."

"I hope not. Besides, I do believe staying here with me is your calling. Truly, Clara, I don't know how I would survive without you."

"Mamm, you aren't ill."

"But I feel ill. That's what counts, *jah*? Besides, what else you would do if not live with me?"

A number of things crossed Clara's mind. She dreamed of marrying and having her own family one day. If that wasn't her fate, she wondered what it would be like to live on her own, make a home of her own.

But she didn't mention any of that. Clara knew her mother would view those reasons as selfish. "I'm not sure," she said quietly. That, at least was the truth.

"Well, I have a strong feeling about what you were meant to be doing—and that is living here with me. I guess that's why you were marked the way you are. So you'd be able to be here with me until my dying days."

"I can have children, too, you know."

"I know, my daughter. But we can't ignore your scars.

Men would never pick a woman like you over one who is pretty, *jah?* I don't mean to be mean, but it's the truth."

Clara wondered if her mother heard herself. How could her words not be taken as mean? For years now, she'd instilled in Clara her vision of her future. How she should never hope for love and marriage. That perhaps the Lord had allowed the grease to spill on her for a reason—so she could better take care of her mother.

But Clara didn't always accept that.

She was just about to tell her that when there was a knock at the door. Pushing her knitting to one side, she hopped up. "I'll get it."

"I wonder who it could even be?"

The knock rapped hard again. Impatient.

"Yes, here I am," she called out just as she pulled open the door.

To find Anson and Carrie on the other side. "Hello, you two! What a nice surprise!"

"Hi, Miss Slabaugh!" Anson craned his neck forward, just like a little box turtle, all expectant and interested. "Can we come in?"

"Of course." Just as she stepped aside for the two of them, her mother called out.

"Who is it, Clara?"

She answered as best as she could, though she was feeling terribly impatient with her mother. Of course she had to have heard Anson's voice. "It is Anson and Carrie Graber, Mamm."

"What do they want?"

When Carrie's eyes widened, Clara took care to gentle her voice. "Don't let her worry you. She's just curious. Would you two like some cookies?"

"Yes!"

"Anson, we were only supposed to deliver our message," Carrie warned. "Not stay here to visit."

"I know, but cookies do sound good. I'm hungry."

"I'm glad of that. I've got a mighty full cookie jar. My mother and I won't be able to eat them all by ourselves. Come sit down."

Anson followed willingly, Carrie just a few seconds behind him. When they entered the kitchen, Clara was disappointed to see that her mother had left. It was really too bad her mother had retreated into herself so much. It would have been nice for Carrie and Anson to see that she could be a kind woman. And seeing the children might have brightened her spirits.

It was very telling to see both children visibly relax when they saw it would be just the three of them. Also telling that neither child asked where her mother had gone.

"Sit down, you two," she said. "I'll get you a snack while you tell me the reason for your visit."

"We have an invitation," Carrie said importantly. "We've come to invite you and your mother over for supper tonight."

Clara was glad her back was facing them because she was sure she wasn't able to hide her surprise. Though Mrs. Graber had mentioned the invitation, she hadn't thought it likely that one would actually come. After all, they'd lived within walking distance to each other for years but had never before visited for supper. "Is there a special occasion?"

"*Jah*," Anson said. "We have Tim here."

That still didn't make much sense to Clara. Turning around slowly, she schooled her features to remain calm and collected. "Your cousin, yes?"

"Uh-huh." Scrunching up his features, Anson turned to his sister. "What did Mamm say about that?"

Carrie raised her chin. "She said it would be mighty nice if you and your *mamm* would like to join us because Cousin Tim most likely gets tired of seeing only us."

Clara hid a smile. Surely Elsa had been more circumspect than that. "Well, I for one would enjoy your company. If you'll stay here, I'll go speak to my mother to see if she would care to join me."

Neither child looked up as she exited the room, each was already enjoying the snack.

Clara didn't mind. Her mind was already busy, wondering how to best handle the upcoming discussion. Because she already knew that no matter what, she was going. She wanted to go. She enjoyed Elsa's company, and Judith's as well.

And if she was able to see Tim again . . . well, that would be a very nice thing, indeed.

"Mother?" Clara asked as soon as she entered her mother's dimly lit room. "Why did you leave?"

"I wasn't interested in seeing those two."

"They're interested in you. Would you care to join us for cookies?"

"No, I would not." Looking at Clara with a bit of distrust, she said, "Why are they here, anyway? It seems strange that you'd be inviting your students here."

"They brought with them an invitation. They invited us to supper tonight."

"Both of us? To their home?"

"Yes, of course. Where else?"

Suspicious eyes looked her over. "What did you tell them?"

"That I would be pleased to accept and that I would ask you. What would you like to do?"

Her mother's face was so expressive, Clara felt that she could read her mind. She was obviously waging the pros of dinner out and new gossip verses her preference of staying at home and having everyone come to her. "How would we get there?"

"We could walk—"

"I could never go that far."

"Or we could take the buggy of course," she said reasonably.

"The buggy takes almost as long."

Clara fought a smile. Her mother had gotten so good at only seeing the negatives, she didn't realize that her reasonings now sounded almost comical. Patiently, she said, "Mother, they are waiting. What would you like to do?"

"What does that mean? What would I like to do?"

"It means that I've already made up my mind. I plan to go, with or without you. I'm anxious to enjoy some of their fellowship. Plus, I have no intention of turning down such a kind invitation."

Clara could almost see the wheels churning in her mother's head. She looked mighty displeased to be left out of Clara's choices.

"Mamm, I need to get back to my guests. What would you like to do?"

"I'll be joining you."

"I'm glad. I'll go let Anson and Carrie know, then."

As she walked back to the kitchen, Clara felt a curious sense of expectation. It had been so long since she'd felt so excited and fluttery, she treasured the feeling.

And thanked the Lord for giving her such wonderful-*gut kinner* to teach.

Yes, that was what she should be concentrating on. Her students. Her kind neighbors.

Not the man she would be seeing. Not something she had no reason to hope for.

"We will both be joining you," she said with a smile when she sat down across from Anson and Carrie. "Please tell your mother that I'll bring a pie."

Carrie grinned. "You could just bring cookies."

"No, I have some blueberries that have been aching to be used. I think I'll make a blueberry pie. But perhaps you two would like to take some cookies home with you? It's a fairly long walk, *jah*?"

Anson eagerly grabbed another one off the plate. Carrie was far more circumspect, but looked just as pleased. "Miss Slabaugh, you can do everything!" she said around a mouthful.

Clara laughed as she handed Carrie a napkin. "What do you mean by that?"

"You can put on plays and teach us and bake cookies. They are much better than my mother's."

"Oh, please don't say things like that. I'm sure your mother's cookies are just as good. But I thank you, just the same."

Moments later, when they left to go deliver their news, Clara watched their retreating backs and sighed. Wouldn't it be something if she actually could do everything she wished she could?

Of course, there was only one dream that mattered to her. And that was being a mother and wife. And no matter how talented in the kitchen she was, she didn't think it would ever overcome her looks.

A man would want a pleasing face to look at every night at supper. And no matter what happened in her life . . . that would never happen if someone married her.

Chapter 6

"I should probably warn you about Clara's mother, Amanda Slabaugh," Frank said to Tim as they washed up outside of the barn. "She's a different sort of woman."

"How so?"

Frank shrugged, obviously reluctant to talk poorly about his long-time neighbor. "Life has been hard on her. Her daughter Clara has suffered terribly from her burns. Then, about five years ago, her husband died suddenly. I'm afraid he didn't leave her in a good way financially. It's taken its toll on her nerves. At times she's difficult and short-tempered."

"Perhaps she should go to the doctor?"

Uncle Frank almost smiled. "No medicine will cure her, I'm afraid. Only a sunny disposition."

"That would be a difficult way to live."

"I agree. No matter how many blessings a person has, there are always difficult times. A positive outlook and a shining belief in the Lord's work can help a person get through them."

Thinking of his most recent circumstances, Tim knew his uncle spoke the truth. Only after reaching out to his relatives had he found any type of happiness in Sugarcreek.

Constantly looking for the bad was a hard way to live. "From what I know of Clara, I have to say I'm surprised. She seems like such a happy person."

His uncle nodded. "She is. She's at peace with herself, I believe. I have to admit to admiring Clara very much. Her older sisters left and she's alone with the woman all the time. Yet she never complains. Now, if we could only discover what would make her mother happy, too!"

"I'll look forward to meeting Mrs. Slabaugh."

Judith poked her head out. "Mamm wants to know when you two are coming inside. Please say soon."

Wiping off his face, Frank laughed. "Tell your mother that we are coming in right now."

"She'll be happy about that. She expects Joshua and Gretta any moment. And Clara and Mrs. Slabaugh, too, of course."

"Judith, it sounds as if she's gotten herself into a stir?"

"Oh, she has." With a frown, she added, "We just saw Joshua today at the store. You'd think he was our longlost relative."

Frank chuckled. "Tim, we best get inside and do what we can to smooth some feathers."

Tim charged ahead and impulsively flung an arm

around his cousin's shoulders. "Don't worry so much, Judith. You'll get wrinkles early."

While Judith sputtered, Uncle Frank chuckled. "Ah, Tim. I think you are finally fitting in."

Clara had been dreading the walk to the Graber's home. After weighing the pros and cons again, they'd decided that there were little benefits to taking the buggy such a short distance. The walk was less than a mile as the crow flew, and at least triple that if they took the roads.

The only benefit would be that they could ride in the buggy on the way home, when the air turned cooler and the night was upon them. But driving a buggy at night had its own set of problems. Cars and trucks didn't always see them and the horses turned skittish.

She, of course, was used to walking most everywhere. But after five minutes of walking up the first hill, it was terribly obvious that her mother was not used to much exercise at all.

Clara had been mentally preparing herself to listen to a barrage of complaints. But then to her surprise, her mother chuckled.

"Oh, but this reminds me of when I was courting your father."

"It does? How so?"

"He lived on the other side of Sugarcreek, as you know. At first we would only make plans to see each other on Sundays, either at church or at singings. But then waiting a week seemed to be an eternity. So we started meeting each other halfway."

"What did your parents say?"

"They didn't know about it. My father was a very dear man, but a strict one, too. He didn't believe in young women traipsing along the countryside." A faraway look entered her eyes as they approached the little creek bed near the dividing line of their property with the Grabers. "Things looked different back then as well. Sugarcreek wasn't near as big."

"Did your father ever find out?"

"Oh, yes. We had quite a discussion that night! But soon after your father asked me to marry him and everything was much better."

"I'm glad you decided to come with me tonight."

"I am, too, Clara. It does my heart good to see these hills and smell the burst of spring in the air."

Her mother was more subdued when they arrived.

"Thank you for inviting us," Clara said after everyone greeted each other in the expansive great room. "I've brought a pie for dessert."

"You didn't need to do that."

"I wanted to."

Her mother chuckled. "You should have seen her running around the kitchen in a flurry."

"I just wanted to have it be done in time."

Elsa took it from her and handed it to Carrie like a prize. "You may take this to the dining room."

"Oh, it is still warm."

"But not too hot?" Clara cautioned.

"Oh, no. I am fine."

Now that the greetings were taken care of, the talk

became far more loud and boisterous. Everyone started talking at once.

To her surprise, her mother quickly followed Elsa into the kitchen and joined Elsa in insisting that Clara stay with the younger people and visit.

Judith claimed her hand and took her over to where Joshua and Gretta were sitting. They were surrounded by the other children. Gretta was holding Maggie and looked like she'd been a part of the family for years.

A new look of contentment rested on her features. Clara fought back a twinge of jealously. She was certainly happy for Gretta, but would be lying to herself if she pretended she didn't want to be in the same kind of position.

Then she finally caught sight of the one person she'd most wanted to see . . . Timothy. He was sitting with them all, too. But didn't look quite as comfortable as the rest of them.

When their eyes met, he smiled warmly . . . which in turn made her pulse race a bit faster.

"We're so glad you came over," Judith said when there was a break in the conversation. "We never get much of a chance to visit with each other after church."

Joshua looked at his siblings with something that looked very much like exasperation. "It's a wonder anyone ever gets to talk about anything around us. We haven't yet mastered the art of taking turns when speaking."

"I have," Carrie interjected. "We have to be quiet at school when others are talking."

Clara chuckled. "That is true. I'm doing my best to teach taking turns."

Gretta leaned forward. "Tell us how your school year is going."

"It is fine. Your brothers and sisters keep me on my toes."

"I don't remember being too much of a handful," Caleb said with a grin.

"Though I only taught you last year, I must agree. You weren't too much of a handful at all." After waiting a beat or two, she grinned. "In fact, you could be far worse."

Laughter rang out as more and more Grabers entered the conversation. Before long, they were all called to supper and walked to the kitchen with plates. "It's easier to feed our group buffet style," Elsa explained. "Otherwise, the bowls of food get a little too heavy to pass."

"I like this way," Clara said when she found herself at the head of the line. "And everything looks *wunderbaar*," she added as she looked at the array of baked chicken, pasta salad, relish trays, and spring peas. There at the end was her blueberry pie, right next to a cherry cake.

Her mother said nothing, but Clara did notice that she took generous helpings of everything.

After everyone was served and seated around an enormous oval oak table, they all bowed their heads and gave thanks.

To her surprise, Tim chose the chair next to her.

"I'm glad you came," he said quietly. "I was looking forward to seeing you again."

"You were?"

He smiled. "I've been blessed with a wonderful family. But I've also been blessed with fine hearing. Sometimes I yearn to sit near someone who isn't quite as loud."

She felt her cheeks heating. Tim was acting as if his feelings toward her were special. The idea made her flustered, and hope burnished long-ago dreams put to rest.

But she couldn't let him know that. "Now you make me wonder if I should talk at all," she teased.

"If you get too loud, I'll let you know."

She chuckled, then, to her surprise, realized that their exchange had been watched by the rest of the group. Gretta eyed them with speculation. Her students were staring at her with a new awareness.

And her mother looked irritated.

"What will you do when summer comes?" Judith asked.

"All sorts of things. I enjoy my break just like the children do. I try to go on a walk every day and read as much as I can."

"She becomes far too lazy," her mother added with a bit of sharpness in her tone. "I've been telling her to tutor or look for another job."

Judith's eyes widened for a moment before they narrowed slightly. "I doubt Clara will become lazy."

"Yes, all of us need a day of rest," Elsa said before turning the conversation to more general topics.

When Mr. Graber stood up and her mother and Elsa followed, Clara stayed behind to help Judith and Gretta carry the dishes to the kitchen.

"We should plan to do some things together," Judith said. "If you're busy, no one will think you are wasting time."

"My mother, she didn't mean to sound so harsh."

"Even if she didn't, she still probably forgot what it was like to feel young, with the future at her fingertips," Judith replied. "It's up to us to make sure we don't let these days pass us by."

Clara didn't know if she'd ever felt like her future was wide open. Ever since her accident, she'd been so grateful for her blessings that she'd never felt easy about asking for more.

But that said, she would look forward to deepening her friendship with Judith. "I would like to plan some activities with you, if you can spare the time."

"Of course I can."

Gretta glanced at the two of them and grinned. "You two have a look about you that I recognize."

"And what is that?" Judith asked saucily.

"Like you're feeling restless. That's how I was feeling in January."

"And here it is April already."

Gretta ignored Judith's sarcasm. "I know, I know. I sound like I have much to learn. But I also have learned a lot. Joshua and I had quite a time before we reached our agreement."

"I'm surprised to hear that," Clara admitted. "To me, you and Joshua were always so close."

"We had some growing pains. But in the end, we

worked everything out. I'm sure you both will find your way as well."

"If I have a need to find my way," Judith said sharply.

Clara busied herself by putting the leftovers neatly away into the crockery sitting on the counter. The chore kept her hands busy while her mind played over Gretta's statements.

Judith was as opinionated and confident as ever. Clara had a feeling that nothing Gretta was saying would have much of an effect on her. That, Clara supposed, was the consequence of growing up feeling sure of yourself.

She, of course, had had just the opposite type of experiences. The idea that her future wasn't decided was an intriguing one.

When Tim walked into the kitchen, all three girls stilled. "Tim, did you need something?" Judith asked.

"Perhaps. I was wondering if Clara would like to go for a short walk."

While Gretta simply smiled, Judith looked her way. "Would you?"

"Sure."

Something akin to relief flashed in his eyes. "You'll probably want your cape or shawl. After you get it, will you meet me on the front porch?"

Clara nodded. "I'll hurry."

"No need. I'll wait."

When he left them, Judith winked. "I am beginning to think you will not need much of my company after all. You're going to be plenty busy with my cousin."

"I don't know about that. He's just being nice."

"Nice and friendly," Gretta agreed, her eyes twinkling. "Well, you better go get your cloak and meet Tim. Even though he says he won't mind waiting, I have a feeling he just might be anxious for you to join him."

Helplessly, Clara looked around the kitchen. The dishes were only half washed and put away. Two pots still needed to be scrubbed. "The kitchen—"

"I'll call on Carrie to help," Judith said. "You're our guest. Go now."

Fearing that any more protestations would only exaggerate the situation, Clara nodded and left.

Without a word, she crossed through the dining room and right by the front parlor where her mother was looking at quilt designs with Mrs. Graber.

Her mother looked up. "Clara, what are you doing?"

She grabbed her cloak and slipped it around her shoulders. "I'm going for a walk."

"Right now? Why? And with whom?"

"I'll be back soon," she replied, not answering a single one of the mother's questions on purpose.

When she stepped out onto the porch, the cool breeze felt like nature's welcome. So did Tim's smile.

Chapter 7

"Is there somewhere you especially like to walk in the evenings after supper?" Tim asked Clara as soon as they started down the driveway.

"Anywhere is fine. I'm just happy to be outside."

"*Jah*. I feel the same way."

Around them, the air felt breezy and a bit cool, yet everywhere there were signs of spring. Crocuses were beginning to bloom—their tiny purple buds brightening the dark soil surrounding them.

Yes, the early evening was a pleasure, for sure. But none of it mattered to him. His attention was far more focused on the woman standing next to him.

By unspoken consent, they veered left, the opposite direction from the creek where they'd first met. As they walked, they passed a thick hedge. Directly after was the Allens' home. Because the Allens were English, their house shone brightly. Almost every window was illuminated. The faint buzzing of a television drifted out from two open windows. Seconds later, they heard Mrs. Allen calling for something.

Tim shared an amused look with Clara. "Their home is busy tonight, too."

"I would say so. I don't know them too well. Do you?"

"I've only talked with them a few times. My cousins like them very much. Anson and Ty are *gut* friends."

"Yes, Anson's mentioned Ty to me a few times. Maybe a hundred or so?"

He laughed. "That Anson, he's never met a stranger."

"I admire that quality of his greatly." After another twenty yards, they left the Allens' mowed lawn and walked up a hill. There was a well-worn path to the side of the road. "If we continue this way for about five miles, it will lead us to downtown Sugarcreek. About a mile ahead, the Millers have a vegetable and honey stand. Would you like to walk to that?"

"Sure."

"Okay. There are not too many cars, so it always feels safe."

Safety was something Tim never worried about. He felt strong and solid after a lifetime of working hard in the fields. No one would ever mistake him for a weakling.

He imagined, though, that concern for safety was far different for a woman. No matter what the surroundings, it wasn't safe for a woman to walk along the road at night. For a moment, he wished their circumstances were different. He wished he could offer her his protection all the time.

But of course, he was in no position to make such a promise.

So he stuck to safer topics. "Thank you for agreeing to walk with me. I was anxious for a break."

"From what?"

He thought for a moment, wondering if he'd be able to pinpoint exactly what he'd been eager to leave behind. "The noise," he finally said, though that didn't really explain much.

"It's not what you're used to, is it?"

"No. My life at home is far different. My parents and I each follow our own pursuits. It's a much quieter existence."

"Things with my mother are quiet, too. Sometimes too much so. But noise never has bothered me much."

"That's probably a good thing, yes?"

"*Jah,*" she replied with a smile. "Being a schoolteacher would be terribly difficult if I only ever demanded peace."

"Difficult for the children." Tim remembered how rambunctious they'd been at the program.

"And difficult for me! I enjoy getting to know my scholars. I have high hopes for them."

"Some outside our way of life would find that view a little strange. After all, most of your schoolchildren will adopt lives just like our parents and grandparents. They don't need to know much."

"Is that how you think?"

"I'm not sure." After a moment's reflection, he shook his head. "No. Though we may all have much in common, I know we are all individuals. And there's much we need to know both inside and outside of the classroom. Is that what you're trying to accomplish?"

"Yes," she replied with a happy smile. "To my mind, there is nothing 'simple' with wanting to be a wife and mother. Or a farmer. Or a factory worker. All of those jobs take many skills, some more than others!"

"Your words sound almost revolutionary. Some might find them challenging to our way of life."

"Perhaps. But, you know what I think, Timothy? I think each of us is going to follow God's plans for us, anyway. Therefore, we might as well make the best of our days." As if she was embarrassed by her enthusiasm, she looked down at her feet. "I mean, that's the kind of thing I tell my students."

Her enthusiasm for her career—and for their way of life—was infectious. "I would think it would be a wonderful thing, to be a student in your classroom."

"It's where I'm happiest. I truly do enjoy teaching."

They stopped for a moment at the Millers' stand. It was closed, of course, but the tables and striped awning gave promise that new produce was just around the corner.

In agreement, they started the walk back. "I'm . . . enjoying our conversation, Clara. You make the time fly by."

"I feel the same way. I'm sorry if I sounded too excited about my teaching philosophy. It's just a rare thing that anyone ever asks me about it."

"What do people ask you about?"

"Their students. How my sisters and mother are." In the dim twilight, Tim saw a tiny bit of remorse mixed in with her matter-of-fact tone. "I don't mean to sound sorry for myself, but sometimes it seems as if these scars act as a boundary. Some people can never overlook them."

"You're right," Tim said, surprising himself with his blunt honesty. "I mean, they're hard not to notice."

But instead of looking hurt, she grinned. "You, Tim Graber, are exactly right. They are quite noticeable."

"But they're not all of you."

She blinked. "No, they are not," she said quietly. "I can't help the ugliness of these scars any more than Gretta can help her beauty. For better or worse, they're a part of me. But there's so much more."

"Like your views on teaching."

"*Jah.*" She cleared her throat. "Please tell me something about yourself. I don't want to go home tonight thinking that all I did with you was talk, talk, talk about myself."

"There would be nothing wrong with that. I've enjoyed hearing about you."

"I would enjoy learning as much about you," she said shyly. "That is, if talking about such things wouldn't upset you."

Upset him? His first instinct was to tell her that nothing personal like that would ever upset him. After all, he was a man. Men didn't become flustered or bothered quite so easily.

But as he formed the words, he cut them off just as quickly. Perhaps talking about himself, so honestly, so unguardedly, *would* upset him.

Because it would let her into a part of him that he'd kept hidden for so long.

But he had enjoyed listening to her. And it seemed wrong to pry into her life without sharing anything about his own.

Her words had made him feel both proud of who he was yet also question everything he'd ever wanted to be.

As they walked along, their footsteps slowly fading in the dim light, the sounds of the night became louder. In the thicket of trees next to them, a sudden blink of a firefly brought a spark of magical light. Tim found himself looking at Clara quickly, just to see if she'd caught the sight.

She smiled but remained quiet. Obviously waiting for him to share something.

"Clara, there's not much to tell. I'm a simple man."

"Even simple men have stories to tell," she prodded.

"Well . . . here's something—I like to farm."

"Because?"

"Because it's me and the Lord and the ground and the elements. I can work hard and see the fruits of my labor. It's good, honest work, too. I like that. There's nothing sketchy involved. No number crunching. No tricks. Only sweat and muscles and prayers."

"And the rewards when you see a full crop in its glory?"

"Yes. And, of course, the rewards when we go to

market and receive a healthy price for our harvest. That is a good feeling, too. The money earned helps us in many ways. And helps to give us a cushion when times are tough."

"And you farm with your father?"

"Yes. With my *daed* and a few of his neighbors. A few years ago they joined together to form a cooperative. That relationship helped us all work together. Toward our common good."

She smiled.

That seemed to be all the encouragement he needed to keep blabbering away. "I also enjoy the quiet in the fields. I like animals. I like time to think about things . . . I hate to be rushed. Perhaps that comes from being an only child. I'm a selfish man in that way."

"I can't imagine that you are always alone. Do you have a large circle of friends in Indiana?"

Her question gave him a small sense of foreboding. "I do. There's a large Amish population where we live, as I'm sure you know. From the time I started school to most recently, I've been blessed with a good number of close friends. We get together often."

"Is there someone special to you?"

Ruby Lee was. Ruby Lee was someone who he'd always singled out as special to him. Her parents' farm was next to his. Everyone had always assumed that they would one day marry.

Except for his parents, though. They were the ones who had said he needed to get a taste of someplace else. Just to be sure.

And now, as he looked at Clara . . . Clara, who wore her imperfections well, who had so much to give from inside of her that she appeared to shine—so brightly that he was fairly stunned by the beauty. If Uncle Frank hadn't written him, Tim would have never met Clara. Timothy started to believe that his parents had been right to send him to Sugarcreek.

And so, he lied. "No. There is no one special to me."

They were almost to the house. Out front, Tim could see little Maggie chasing Carrie and Anson.

On the front porch swing sat Joshua and Gretta.

To his surprise, a lump of happiness sprung inside of him as he saw their familiar faces. In spite of his protestations, all of them had found their way into his heart.

But Clara didn't look to be concerned with anyone but him. Her gaze on his face hadn't strayed. "Timothy, are you sure there is no one special to you? No girl who is your sweetheart? You act as if there might be."

Before he could reply to that, she held up a hand, looking crestfallen. "Please forget I even asked. Of course your friendships back home are none of my business."

She was right, of course. His relationship with Ruby wasn't her business. Especially since it was so puzzling, anyway.

"We're back," he said instead. "Thank you for walking with me. I enjoyed it."

She blinked. "I . . . I enjoyed it as well," she murmured as they crossed the large grassy area and approached the others. Very properly, she walked by his side. Her hands were clasped in front of her. Some of the light that had shone in her eyes dimmed. "I thank you for it, Timothy."

"We didn't know when you were ever coming back," Anson called out as he ran to meet them halfway. Behind him, Caleb followed at a more sedate pace. "Where did you go?"

"Not very far," Tim answered.

"Just down to the Millers' stand," Clara added.

"Your mother said to tell you that she's anxious to leave," Anson said.

"She's told all of us several times," Caleb added wryly.

Clara sighed. "Yes, I imagine she probably has. It's getting dark out."

As the four of them slowly climbed up the last of the hill before reaching the front porch, Caleb thrust out a letter. "I've been meaning to give you this, too," he said. "I'm sorry I forgot earlier."

Tim stared at the envelope in surprise but made no move to take it. "*Danke.*"

Clara looked at him strangely. "Is that a letter from home?"

"Yes."

"Oh, it's more than that," Caleb said with a too-knowing look. "It's from—"

"My parents, most likely," Tim interrupted. Clara looked confused. Tim didn't blame her, he was acting mighty peculiar about a simple letter. "We best get inside. Your mother's waiting."

She tucked her chin. "Yes. Yes, of course," she said before leaving his side and walking to the front door.

Grabbing the letter from Caleb, Tim glared at him. "What?"

"Sometimes you need to stay out of other people's business."

"But you always like to receive Ruby's letters. What did I do wrong?"

Tim brushed by Caleb's side without answering and hurried to the kitchen. Perhaps he could talk to Clara some? Try to explain things even he didn't know the answer to?

"Good evening, Timothy," Mrs. Slabaugh said without a smile. "I hope you enjoy the rest of your stay in Sugarcreek."

Clara held her mother's elbow as they brushed passed him.

"Clara?"

"I'm sorry. I must go."

"But perhaps we could talk some more later?"

"Maybe we could."

"Clara, let's leave."

"All right, Mamm. Yes. We will go now."

As soon as the door closed he clenched his hands. What had he done?

"Careful with your letter, Timothy!" Elsa exclaimed. "You're about to crush it!"

With dismay, he looked at his right hand. There, in his hand, was the crumpled envelope.

He'd completely forgotten he held it.

Chapter 8

Two weeks had passed. Fourteen terrible, emotional, painful days.

Every time Lilly thought about those hours spent in the emergency room, she relived the pain. Whenever she recalled waking up to the doctor's announcement, tears pricked her eyes. Lilly hadn't known if she'd ever stop crying.

But then, just yesterday, she'd woken and felt a little better. Almost like herself before everything had happened. It was both a blessing and a curse. She was so grateful for the feelings of relief, but also troubled. Somehow, some way, God was enabling her to return to normalcy. It didn't seem right.

Now, in the early morning, as a golden house finch chirped outside her window and called to attention the glory of spring, Lilly sat in bed in the quiet of her room, wondering how much longer she would be able to stay in her retreat, away from the rest of the family.

So far, they'd let her have a lot of time to herself, but last night, when she'd refused to come downstairs to dinner, Lilly had heard a strand of impatience that was new in her mother's voice.

Lilly understood their feelings. After all, the rest of her family had moved on. She heard Ty talking about school projects and his need for a new pair of cleats for soccer. Charlie had met a girl and was now constantly on his cell phone or going to class.

Her parents went to work each morning, seemingly more determined than the day before to accomplish as much as possible in twenty-four hours. Her father had even taken up running.

Only she had been unable to do anything but mourn.

After a quick knock, her mom opened the door and peeked inside. Within seconds, Lilly saw her gaze dart from the pile of clothes and towels on the floor, to the stack of dishes littering her desk, to the partly pulled-down shades, to her daughter.

"Good. You're up," she said as she walked right in.

Lilly pulled up the sheets around her shoulders like a shield. "Not really. I was about to go back to sleep."

With a new look of determination, her mother shook her head. "No, I don't think so. It's Monday morning. A new week. The sun is shining. Ty left for school three hours ago. It's past time for you to start your day."

Lilly had purposely hid her clock. Watching the numbers change had been her sole activity the day she'd come home. It had just about driven her crazy. "Why aren't you at work?"

"I told them I'd be coming in late today because I had a few things to do around here."

"Like what?"

"Like get you out of bed, dear. Honey, I know it's hard, but take it from me. Things won't get better if you only sit and stew and cry."

With a start, Lilly remembered that her mother had had a miscarriage years ago. In her haze of depression, she'd forgotten all about that.

But still . . . she just wasn't ready. Slumping back against her pillows, she made a feeble call for more time. "I'll get up tomorrow. I don't feel well," she said, though to her surprise, it wasn't really true. The pain that had taken hold of her midsection had lessened considerably. Many of her other aches and pains had vanished, too. Now all that remained was a numbness that seemed to constantly float over her mood and her spirit.

A look of concern flashed in her mother's eyes as she approached the bed. "Still sore?"

Lilly shrugged. "Some."

"The doctors said your body should be healed by now." She nibbled her bottom lip. "Perhaps we should go in for a checkup? I could take off the whole day."

The last thing Lilly wanted was to be poked and pulled and inspected again. "I'll be fine. I'm getting better. Like I said, tomorrow's probably the right time to start doing things."

"You know, I don't think so." After pausing for a moment, her mother went to her dresser. After pushing a few bottles of water and a container of painkillers to one side, she uncovered a brush and a hair clip. "As soon as you get cleaned up and take care of yourself, you'll feel like leaving this room."

Before Lilly could defiantly tell her that, no, brushed hair was not going to help a thing, her mom sat right back down beside her, gently turned Lilly so her back faced her, and, with a little sigh, pulled the brush through Lilly's maze of knots and tangles.

"Ouch," she said, though even to her ears she sounded incredibly whiny.

Immediately the brush stilled. "I'm sorry, honey. I didn't mean to hurt you."

"I know. It didn't hurt that badly. I'm sorry." Gosh, how many times had she said "sorry" over the last two weeks? She'd felt like she'd been apologizing to everyone. Her family. To Alec. To herself. To God.

She must have done something incredibly wrong to have miscarried.

Gently, her mother continued brushing again. When the worst of the tangles were combed out, the rhythmic motions soothed her. Over and over the brush went, massaging her scalp, skating through her curls. Taming them.

Little by little, Lilly felt her neck muscles relax. Her shoulders loosen. She hated to admit it, but perhaps her mother was exactly right. Taking care of herself and moving around a bit could only help.

"Thank you," she said as her mom gently clipped her hair back into a ponytail. "I do feel better."

"Brushing your hair brought back some nice memories," her mother mused. "Remember when you were six and your hair was halfway down your back?"

"I do. You'd have to help me brush it every morning. And I'd fuss."

Behind her, Lilly heard her mom's soft chuckle. "How many times do you think I threatened to cut off that hair?"

"At least once a day."

"At least." Squeezing her daughter's shoulders, she said, "Lilly, you have some things you need to do today. You need to call the Sugarcreek Inn and let them know when you're returning to work. They need you."

"But I don't know . . ."

"Maybe after you take a shower and do a load of laundry, you'll have a better sense of when you can help out. When she called yesterday, Mrs. Kent said you could return part-time. But that she definitely does need you . . . or someone else."

"She'd fire me?"

"Don't make this into something it's not. She's given you two weeks off. She's willing to give you a couple of more days. But the other girls have been taking your shifts and, frankly, they're tired."

"I'll call." After she made the pronouncement, Lilly felt like boulders had been placed on her shoulders. Responsibilities threatened to engulf her. Make her weak with it all. She slumped against the bed.

But her mom didn't even notice.

"Good," she said, looking pleased. "As soon as you make that call, I have a project for you."

This all felt like too much. She was going to have to shower, do a load of laundry, call Mrs. Kent. "Mom—"

"We've started a garden."

"What?"

Walking to the picture window, she raised the blinds with a jerk. As sunlight streamed in, she continued. "Come now, Lilly. Stand up now. Do you see it? The garden is right out front. Charlie and your dad and I tilled and brought in fresh soil and planted seeds all weekend."

Getting to her feet, Lilly crossed the room and looked out the window. There, just like her mother said, was a large area of freshly tilled soil surrounded by a little white picket fence.

Her family had done all that when she'd just been sitting in the dark? How had she been so unaware of everything around her? Embarrassment mixed with the fog in her brain. She wasn't quite sure how to climb out of her depression, but leaving the room sounded like a good start. "Mom, what do you want me to do?"

Something flickered in her mother's eyes. Was it approval? Relief? She cleared her throat. "I made a little map on a sheet of paper and wrote down what we grew. I want you to make some signs and stake them in the ground so we'll know what is growing where. And then you'll need to water, of course."

Her mother paused. "Do you think you can do that?"

Was she capable of getting out of bed, getting showered and dressed, making a couple of little signs, and watering some plants?

It was a silly question.

But, unfortunately, it was also a very realistic one.

Inside of her head, thoughts warred. It all sounded so easy.

But right now everything that had seemed easy was now terribly difficult. Maybe too difficult?

"Yes," she began. Ready to explain that she would give the tasks her best shot, but she wasn't completely sure she could do any of it. Ready to talk about how she was still sore.

But before she could form the words, before Lilly could once again say that she wasn't feeling well . . . that she had enough to do without making silly vegetable signs, her mother kissed her brow. "Oh, I'm so relieved to hear that."

"Actually—"

"Thank you, dear. Now, I've got to scoot off to work. Be sure and give Ty a snack when he comes home. I'll be home between six and seven."

She watched her mother walk out the door, leaving it open for the first time in days. Sunlight shown from the window, illuminating the dark walls.

As Lilly blinked and stared at the ray of light, she heard her mother's heels click against the wood floor. Heard her keys jangle.

Moments later, the garage door opened and her mother drove off. She was alone and had promised to finally look forward.

Could she do it?

Closing her eyes, she prayed. *"Lord, I sure need some*

help right now. These past two weeks, I've felt so alone. But now I realize I haven't been that way at all. My family has been on the other side of the door, just waiting for me to reach out.

"And the light streaming in, reminds me that You have been there all along, too. Just waiting for me to remember.

"I need You now. Please help me. I promise I'll do my best not to forget you any longer."

When she opened her eyes, the room looked exactly the same. The ray didn't look any brighter or longer or different.

But she felt renewed. For the first time since that terrible night when she'd lost her baby, Lilly felt God's presence running inside her.

It felt like Hope.

Before she could change her mind, she walked over to her bed, smoothed the sheets, and made it up again—even going so far as to arrange the little teal-and-violet decorative pillows in the middle. She stepped to her dresser and pulled out an old pair of gym shorts. She had no idea if they would fit or not, but they were part of her old life, and she needed the reassurance that somewhere inside of her, she was still the same person she used to be. The sporty girl with plans for herself. The girl who didn't mind getting her hands dirty or her clothes muddy. The girl who would find the idea of her city family planting a garden invigorating. After picking up a pile of dirty clothes and tossing them into her laundry basket, Lilly gathered some of the dishes and carried them into the kitchen. And then, before she could weigh the pros and cons of it, she walked back to the bedroom and opened her bedside table's drawer and took out her digital clock. The green light shone an eerie 10:15. It was time to begin.

Things seemed better after Lilly had showered and slipped on an old T-shirt and those shorts, which miraculously still fit.

Her room certainly smelled better after she'd carried out the dirty clothes and stacked her dirty dishes in the dishwasher. After wiping down her desk and dresser with some furniture polish, Lilly finally felt like her room was back to normal. She'd always been organized and meticulous about her things. It was amazing how the dark cloud of depression could change years of habits.

By eleven forty-five, she'd showered, cleaned, and gotten dressed. Lilly shook her head at how slow she'd become. Back in Cleveland, she used to do all those things in under a half hour.

Almost grateful that her mother had given her a list of things to do, she poured herself a glass of orange juice, and tackled item number four on her mother's carefully printed list: call the Sugarcreek Inn.

After her employer answered, Lilly spoke in a rush. "Hi, Mrs. Kent. This is Lilly Allen. I thought I better call about my job." She braced herself for a barrage of questions—and complaints. She'd been gone a long time and was a new employee, too.

"Lilly, it's so nice to hear your voice. I'm glad you called."

The sweet sound created a lump in her throat. "Thank you."

"We've missed you here. All of us have gotten used to your cheerful smiles and speedy feet. When will you come back?"

It was time to dive in. Staying home in a dirty room was no longer possible. "Right away."

"Are you sure about that?"

"Yes. I mean . . . my mom said that maybe I could come back part-time?"

Mrs. Kent didn't even hesitate. "Yes, of course. Can you start tomorrow? Maybe just come in for four hours? Do you think you could handle that?"

Her boss was like a cyclone. She talked fast and in circles. Lilly could almost see her with a pencil on the calendar, impatiently waiting to either pencil in Lilly's name on the schedule or erase it. "Yes?" she asked, though she wasn't really sure if she was asking her boss the question or herself.

"Good. I'll see you at eleven. Can you do that? Can you work from eleven until three?"

"Yes?"

"Excellent. I'll see you then."

After a quick goodbye, Lilly hung up the phone with a shaking hand. It was done. She was now officially working again and more or less back in the land of the living.

She expected to feel overwhelmed.

To her surprise, it felt good to have something new to think about. Already she was wondering if both Gretta and Miriam would be on tomorrow's schedule. Next, she started mentally cataloging her clothes situation. She wondered which skirts and blouses were clean and which ones still fit.

Maybe her mother had had the right idea, after all.

Yes, being busy was the key to moving forward. Walking to the neatly printed map of the garden, Lilly smiled at the cute water-resistant place cards for plants that her mother had obviously bought at the nursery. Probably had paid too much for, too.

They were brightly colored and in cute shapes. All Lilly had to do was write on each with a black permanent marker and stick the stake in the soil.

Gathering them all in her arms, she walked outside and strode to the nine-by-twelve-foot rectangle. Their new garden. Neat rows greeted her, as did the distinct smell of freshly tilled dirt and fertilizer.

She found herself smiling as she circled it, trying to get a sense of her mother's map. Trying to imagine Ty and her mom carefully planting seeds.

She sat down in the grass and organized the stakes, but then caught herself staring at a robin flying with a twig in its mouth. She watched its flight until it settled on a low branch of a nearby crabapple tree.

In the distance, a pair of cardinals was flying together, weaving their patterns in the sun, like they were playing tag. Their bright red coats shimmered in the sky, making everything they came near more beautiful.

To her surprise, she grinned. "Lord, thank you. This was what I needed," she said out loud. "I need to be outside, where things are fresh. Where new life has begun, and where things are growing and changing. Thank you for giving me the strength to move forward."

Obviously, her mother knew that. Otherwise, she wouldn't have left such a job. Ty could have labeled the markers and popped them in the ground in no time. No one had needed her to do it.

So her mother had known she needed the task. Well, she would just label the stakes, then she would take a little walk. Not far, but just somewhere to get exercise. Her legs would appreciate it, she was sure.

Yes, it was time to move on. She wasn't sure what she was going to do, or where she was going to go, but that was okay. After taking her time and labeling eight stakes, she carefully positioned them, then turned toward the creek and started walking.

To where, she didn't know. She didn't know if it even mattered. All that did matter was that she had returned once again to the living—just like the verse in 2 Corinthians . . . *The old has passed away and the new has come.*

Chapter 9

The sky was a brilliant blue. There was hardly a cloud in the sky.

Altogether, it was far too nice a day to stay another minute indoors.

After quickly cleaning the chalkboards and arranging things for the next morning's lessons, Clara gathered some papers to grade, set them in her satchel, and hurriedly locked the schoolhouse door.

Next, she decided to take the long way home, by the creek. She wanted to enjoy the beauty of the day and the relative peace nature gave her.

She needed some quiet! Oh, but the children had been a handful. She wasn't sure if they were grumpy from their weekend's activities, or merely tired because it was a Monday.

Or they already were feeling a burst of spring fever. But whatever the reason, they had been difficult to control and motivate. She'd sent them home with strict instructions to get some sleep.

That was good advice for herself as well, she supposed. Over the last two evenings, she'd been having trouble sleeping herself. Even that very morning, she'd woken up a bit out of sorts. She'd been dreaming of storms and fires when the alarm clock had shrilly sounded at six that morning. All while she'd hurriedly gotten dressed and packed her lunch, the unpleasant visions that the dreams had brought had seemed determined to sit tight in her brain.

She knew why . . . over and over she kept reliving the conversation she'd had with Timothy on Saturday night. When they'd been walking, everything between them had seemed relaxed and good. But a cloud had fallen over her conversation, too. She knew he'd been hiding something from her.

Oh, of course, she didn't expect him to tell her all of his secrets! But she'd left the Graber's home with the feeling that he'd lied to her about something important.

When Tim had cut off Caleb, he'd looked guilty. She knew she'd stared at him in confusion. What could have caused him to act that way?

Her mother had sure discussed Tim and her visit with him during their long journey home. "Why did you go walking with him?"

"Because he invited me, Mamm."

"It seemed mighty forward."

"All we did was talk. It's a simple friendship," she'd said, doing her best to convey none of the things that had been running through her head. Actually, she'd gone walking with Tim because he'd seemed to actually want her company. He had made her feel like a normal girl. Like a woman who was admired.

She'd wanted to hold on to those feelings as long as possible.

But as her mother walked by her side in the dim light, far more dark feelings floated between them. "Well, of course you're just friends. Elsa and Frank told me Tim has a sweetheart back home. Did you hear she writes him on a regular basis?"

With a sinking feeling, she'd wondered if that was who the note had been from. "No."

Her *mamm* had looked pleased to know something Clara did not. "It's true. Supposedly they are stretching their wings and such. They can visit and go walking with other people, but it's just a formality."

"A formality?"

"Yes. When Tim returns, he and his sweetheart Ruby will take up where they'd left off."

"I see."

"I hope you do, daughter." When they came to the last one hundred yards, the ground turned steeper. Clara had curved a hand around her mother's elbow to give her assistance. Mamm had leaned close and let Clara bear much of her weight.

It was a shame that Clara had not felt any reciprocal support. "Well, I am glad we went to the Grabers'," she chattered. "It was a nice change from sitting together alone in this house. Don't you think?"

"*Jah*. But—I don't think you should make a habit out of going walking with a man who's practically engaged."

"I didn't do anything wrong."

"Perhaps you did not, but we don't want the Grabers to think that you were taking advantage of their hospitality. Making calf's eyes at their engaged nephew isn't good."

"I wasn't making any calf's eyes."

They'd reached their house. Clara lit the kerosene lantern to guide their way inside. But the light only served to highlight her mother's fierce expression. "Just make sure you do not ever do that again. You'll embarrass yourself."

Tears had pricked her eyes when she'd gone to sleep. Wondering how such a good situation had all of a sudden turned terribly wrong.

But now, as she walked by the creek, a sense of fullness came over her. Things always did seem better in the light of day.

There was a chance her mother had been completely mistaken. Perhaps Tim didn't have a sweetheart at all! It wouldn't be the first time her mother had scrambled up gossip.

Feeling better, she sat down and stretched her legs in front of her when she heard footsteps behind her.

Clara turned and quickly looked up. Could it be Tim?

Instead, it was Lilly Allen.

They'd never been formally introduced, but Clara would have known the girl anywhere. Everyone knew about the girl's pregnancy and miscarriage.

Of course, Lilly Allen probably had no idea who she was. As far as Clara had heard, the only Amish Lilly knew were the Graber family and the Amish women who worked at the Sugarcreek Inn.

Lilly nibbled on her bottom lip as she stood rooted to her spot, as timid as a newborn fawn. "Hi. I was just going for a walk," she said. "The longer I live here, the more I appreciate this little creek. It's so peaceful."

"I've stood on its banks many times, just to rest and pray."

Lilly looked around, her eyes widening when she saw Clara's book bag and such. "Do you mind if I stay here awhile? Were you planning to work? Am I bothering you?"

Clara turned her face to look at her directly. "Of course not."

"Thanks. I was in no hurry to wander back home."

When Lilly continued to stare, Clara spoke up. "I'm Clara."

"Lilly Allen," she replied.

Clara shifted nervously. It had been a while since anyone had stared at her so rudely. Entrenched in the Amish community like she was, she rarely came across many English. And most of them only looked as far as her dress and *kapp*.

Lilly couldn't seem to take her eyes off of her face.

Clara felt just peevish enough to comment on it. "The marks . . . they're just scars. I was burned when I was six."

Lilly blinked. "I'm sorry to stare at you like that. They took me by surprise, that's all. Your other cheek is so pretty."

Now Clara was the one taken by surprise. She'd imagined her forthright speaking would have made Lilly turn in shame. Instead, the other girl was speaking to her directly. "Sometimes, they take me by surprise, too. I forget how ugly they are."

"They're not. You're very pretty." Lilly looked her over this way and that. "In a funny way, I think they make the rest of you look even prettier."

"No one's ever said that."

Lilly shrugged. "I used to speak my mind too much. I've been trying to watch myself, but I guess that habit isn't completely gone."

"I heard about your baby. I am sorry for you."

"Thank you. This . . . this is the first day I've come out of my room since it happened."

"I imagine it would be a difficult thing."

Lilly swallowed. "It was. Hey, do you mind if I sit down?"

For a moment, Clara considered telling her that she was just leaving. That she didn't want to sit and talk. But there was something in Lilly's face that struck a chord inside of her. Maybe it was the fierce pain?

Or the feeling of loneliness that emitted from her?

"No, not at all."

After Lilly sat on the rock beside her, she kicked off her tennis shoes and rested her bare toes on the rocks. Clara couldn't help but look at the English girl's long legs. And notice how at ease Lilly seemed to feel with herself.

How must it feel? To be so content with one's body?

"My parents decided to plant a garden," Lilly said out of the blue.

"We have a garden."

"I bet. I mean, the Grabers next door do, too. Josh Graber told me it's the norm for y'all to have gardens. Do you know him?"

"Oh, yes. Our community isn't too big, you know. We all know each other."

"He's been a good friend to me." She almost smiled. "This past winter, we became pretty close. Some people imagined we wanted to be a couple. Well, my parents did. But we didn't want to do that."

"Because he was Amish?"

"No. Not really. It was because I had no interest in having another boyfriend. And Josh, of course, was in love with Gretta."

"They are happy together," Clara agreed. "Do you miss your boyfriend?"

"No. Things between us ended badly. You know how it goes."

She really didn't. "At least you were in love once though, yes?"

"Yes."

"That is a lucky thing."

Lilly blinked. Blinked again as her eyes watered.

Immediately, Clara felt ashamed. Obviously any conversation that made Lilly think of her losses was a bad idea. "I'm sorry. Sometimes I speak before thinking, too. I was just imagining how nice it would have been to know you were loved, at least for a little while." She rolled her eyes. "Now I sound like a terribly sad sort, don't I?"

She looked up to see Lilly blinking back tears.

"I'm crying because I realize you're right. I've been going through so much pain, I forgot to think about the good things that had happened to get me to this place. Back when Alec and I were together, all he had to do was look my way and I'd be so happy. I'd forgotten that."

"Still, I am sorry to make you cry."

"Don't be." Lilly swiped a cheek with one hand. "What are you doing? Out for a walk, too?"

"Oh, no. I am on my way home from work. I'm a schoolteacher."

"That's an awesome job. Do you love it?"

"I do. I love it very much."

"I'm only waitressing at the Sugarcreek Inn. Do you ever go there to eat? I don't think I've seen you there."

"No. My mother and I are on a tight budget, I'm afraid. We don't have too many opportunities to eat out."

"Well, usually I work the lunch shift. This summer, if you ever want a piece of pie, come in. It will be my treat."

"I couldn't . . ."

"Sure you could. Gretta's there. You could visit with her."

"I suppose."

"Well, come in. It's the least I can do," Lilly said as she pulled her shoes closer and slipped them on. After quickly tying them, she stood up. "It was nice to meet you."

"I hope to see you again."

"Me too." She brushed her hair from her face. "Well, I better get going. I need to water the garden and finish cleaning up before my little brother comes home."

And before Clara could say a word to that, Lilly turned and walked away.

Clara got up far slower. After shouldering her bag, she walked in the opposite direction. Thinking about Lilly's words. How she'd said the scars made the rest of her look pretty. About her offer for free pie.

About her gratitude for the reminder her that it was a good thing to love . . . even if it didn't work out.

Suddenly, she wondered if maybe her thoughts about Tim hadn't been quite so foolish after all.

Chapter 10

All weekend, Monday, and into Tuesday, Ruby's letter burned a hole in Tim's pocket. As was his usual habit, he'd slipped it there so it would be easy to refer to when he wrote Ruby back.

But so far, he hadn't been able to open the envelope again.

Timothy felt shamed as he recalled the look Clara had given him the moment Caleb had started to announce that Ruby had sent him another letter. Tim should have been pleased that Ruby had written him again. He should have been eager to read her note. Instead, he'd been embarrassed.

Soon after, Clara had walked home with her mother and the rest of the family had gone back inside to give him some privacy. He hadn't been looking for it. With a great reluctance, he'd ripped open the flap of the envelope, nearly tearing the letter written on simple notebook paper inside. How different that was from when he received his first letters from Ruby. Just a few weeks ago, he'd gently opened the envelopes, carefully smoothed out the creases from the paper, read each sentence like it was a special gift.

Greetings, Timothy, she'd written. *Are you all right? I have not received a letter from you in four days.*

With some regret, Tim knew she'd have to wait even more days. He'd only sent off his second letter in ten days yesterday.

I miss you. When do you plan to visit your parents? Or, can you have company? Perhaps I could come see you.

One thing he knew for sure, he didn't want her to come to Sugarcreek.

Why didn't he want her there? She'd had his heart. At least, she'd thought she had. But now all his thoughts seemed to center around a far different sort of woman. Had his feelings really changed that quickly? Or was he simply infatuated with someone different? What would he want to do when he got home? How could he not want Ruby Lee then?

In spurts, he finished the note yet again, taking time between each paragraph to look out in the dark distance. The nearby lantern cast golden shadows across the page, blurring the words, bringing them in and out of focus. Tim thought the light was fitting. It was also how he felt, even now, several days later . . . confused about his feelings toward Ruby.

Like a thief in the night, he started when the door opened. Prepared to see his uncle Frank, he was surprised to see Joshua instead. He and Gretta had come over for dinner again.

"Am I interrupting?"

"Not at all," he said as he hastily stuffed the letter back into its envelope. "I would have thought you and Gretta would be on your way by now."

"Gretta decided she wanted to stay the night here. Even though it's a Tuesday night, and we'll have to get up early in the morning to open the store, I was happy to agree. It's nice to have some time with everyone that is unhurried."

Tim nodded. Not knowing what else to say, he tried to smooth the crumbled envelope a bit, then giving up, set it beside him.

Joshua watched, smiling.

"Are you amused at something?"

"Only that you are reminding me a bit of myself."

"How's that?"

"I can tell you're feeling torn."

Tim didn't appreciate the comment. He didn't want to think about how his feelings toward Ruby were changing. It made him feel guilty. "I'm afraid I don't know what you're referring to. Ruby and I are fine."

"Oh, *jah*. I imagine you are. My mistake." He shook his head. "Sorry. I guess I had just thought on Saturday night I saw something between you and . . . never mind."

"Were you thinking there was something special between Clara and me?"

"I was," Joshua replied slowly. "But, like you said, I

must have been wrong. It doesn't matter what I was thinking."

"Clara is a nice woman, but she and I are just friends."

"She is nice." Narrowing his eyes, Joshua looked him over. "It's none of my business, but the way she was looking at you looked like something else. Something more than friendship."

"We only took a walk."

Joshua held up his hands in surrender. "Again, this was my mistake. I apologize. I didn't mean to come out here to make you upset."

"You didn't upset me."

Warily, Joshua looked him over. Tim looked away, knowing what his tone sounded like. Mad and irritated. Like he was completely overreacting.

Which he was.

Joshua sat down on the porch and kicked out his legs. "Actually, I came out here to try to lend you support."

"For what?"

"Just a couple of months ago, I was wondering if Gretta and I were meant to be together. I thought that perhaps we'd grown apart."

In spite of himself, Tim's interest was sparked. "What happened?"

"Well, Gretta and I had been friends and sweethearts for a long time. Years. Maybe just like you and Ruby. But when we got new neighbors, I found myself thinking about another person. A person who wasn't even Amish."

"Did you think about courting her?"

"Not really. I liked her not because she was so different from me," he said thoughtfully. "It was because she brought out something new inside of me. She made me think that there was more to me than I'd originally thought. More to me than Gretta had ever guessed. I didn't want to give that up."

Thinking about his time spent with Clara, Tim understood his cousin's words. "How did you deal with it?"

"Not very well. I was ashamed about my feelings. Worse, I didn't immediately consider that Gretta might be thinking the same thing. When I did, I suggested we take a break."

In spite of his intentions to remain aloof, Tim was drawn in. "Did she agree to that?"

"You know what? She did." Joshua shook his head. "And at first, I wasn't very happy about that. I guess part of me wanted her to be miserable without me. When she wasn't, when she almost seemed relieved not to have to deal with me all the time, why I got a little jealous."

"Then what happened?"

"Finally, we started talking about things. About things we thought we already knew about each other. And about things that mattered to us, in our hearts. I learned that there was much more to Gretta than met the eye." He stretched, a funny smile on his face, like he was recalling each word they'd exchanged. "I guess I sound really girlish, huh?"

"Not at all. Did all this talking help?"

"It did. Before too much time passed, we grew to

truly love each other, that's what happened," Josh said with a smile. "We found love when we thought we were finding something else."

Tim didn't know if that was in the future for him and Ruby. "And are you happy about that?"

"Happy? Why, of course I am. My wedding day was the happiest of my life."

"And you've had no regrets."

"No. But . . . remember what I said. This didn't come easily. I think the Lord put obstacles in our way just so we'd think about those things before vowing to love each other for the rest of our lives. And Gretta feels the same way. We're happy."

Recalling the ease in which the two newlyweds acted together . . . and the obvious love they shared, Tim knew that to be true. "Thanks, Joshua. For sharing."

"Thanks for listening." Climbing to his feet, Josh yawned. "It's getting late and we're going to have to leave at dawn in order to prepare the store for shoppers tomorrow. I'm going to go see if Gretta's ready for bed."

He left Tim's side. So his only company was the lantern once again. But since it only illuminate his feelings of loss, Tim felt even more confused.

Because as much as he was trying to hide his feelings from everyone, the truth seemed to be shining through more brightly than ever. He was falling out of love with Ruby. Or, perhaps he'd never even been in love and he was just now seeing that. What was worse was that Ruby Lee didn't even know it.

It certainly didn't seem fair.

As he continued to reflect, he realized that there was one good solution. Perhaps Ruby should come to Sugarcreek to visit, after all. Maybe they needed some time together like Joshua and Gretta had. Maybe they needed time to talk and sort things out.

Then his feelings would come back and all would be well again. Now he knew what he had to do.

On Wednesday morning, he pulled out a sheet of notebook paper and finally wrote Ruby back. He told her he missed her.

And then he invited her to come see him.

Chapter 11

"*Guder Mariye*, Miss Slabaugh," Anson said brightly on Friday morning, almost a full week after she'd dined at his home. "It's a nice day out, *jah*?" he asked as he set his lunch pail on the bench with a clatter, hastily pushed his coat on a hook and then raced to his desk. The moment he stopped he dropped his books on the wooden top with a thump.

Clara watched it all with some misgiving. Anson was a very enthusiastic boy, that was true. But never in the two years that she'd been teaching him had he ever been so . . . exuberant. "Good morning, to you, too," she said slowly. "You seem to be in fine spirits today."

"Oh, I am."

"Is it because it's Friday?"

He blinked. "Oh, I don't know."

"I see." She turned away from him and pulled out her notes for the day's lessons. Actually, she didn't understand what was going on with him at all. But if there was one thing she'd learned during her two years it was that children's thoughts didn't always make the most sense.

And that sooner or later they'd say what was on their minds. It wasn't in their nature to hold secrets for long.

As she'd half expected, Anson started talking again. "Me and Ty tried to fish yesterday afternoon but we didn't catch nothing."

"Where did you go?"

"To the creek. There's some fish there, but not always."

Their creek fluctuated in water levels very much. "There will be more fish when the rains come, I imagine."

"Yep. That's what I told Ty. Then we'll be able to bring home dinner one night for our families."

Because he was so cute, she couldn't resist teasing him. "You're going to need a lot of fish for your family, Anson."

"Don't I know it!"

"Well, perhaps you'll get luckier next time?"

"Maybe. Cousin Tim said he thought the water was so cold, the fish didn't want to bite."

Even hearing Tim's name from her student's mouth made her pulse jump a bit. "I imagine your cousin might be right about that."

"I bet he is. Cousin Timothy is a smart man."

"Yes, he is."

"He's nice, too."

"I thought so as well." She looked at him curiously. "Anson, you are here awfully early today. Was there something you wanted to speak with me about? Perhaps you forgot to do your homework?"

His eyes widened to saucers. "Oh, no, teacher. I did my report. I wrote it out neatly before Ty and me went fishing."

"I am sorry I doubted you. And truthfully, I am very glad to see you. I like talking with you."

He brightened. "I like talking with you, too."

"Since you are here, perhaps you could help me prepare for today's lessons?"

"What? Oh, sure."

He answered agreeably enough, but something was not quite right, Clara thought. His feet were sluggish as he walked by her side to the table in the back. "Anson, we will begin studying states and capitals today. I have postcards for everyone. Please put one on each person's desk."

As she'd hoped, the new assignment brought a renewed interest. Looking at the stack of bright postcards in her hands, he looked at them in wonder. "Are these *real* postcards?"

"Of course they are. And even better, there's one postcard from every one of our fifty states."

"Even Alaska?"

She couldn't resist smiling. "Even Alaska. Hawaii, too." With a little bow, she handed them to him.

He clutched them eagerly. "How did you get so many? Have you visited all these places?"

"Of course not. I've never been farther than Columbus."

"Did you order them?"

"Oh, Anson. You are such an impatient boy. Look on the other side of the top one."

When he flipped one over, his mouth opened in surprise. "Miss Slabaugh, this person wrote you a letter from Wyoming."

"Yes, he did. From Cheyenne, I believe."

"How do you know him?

"Only a little bit. He's a pen pal to me. I have some friends who passed on my postcard to him. Other places, I simply wrote a city's chamber of commerce and they passed on my note to someone. It was exciting to see who all received my postcards."

"Wow."

"Soon, you will have a pen pal, too."

"From where?"

"From whatever state you write to. I want you to pick one of the states and place that postcard on your desk."

"I can choose?"

"Indeed you may. That's your treat for getting here so early."

Clara pretended not to notice that Anson strode over to his desk and carefully slapped the Wyoming postcard in the very center. "Pass them out as quickly as you can, Anson," she said. "I see that the rest of our class is on their way in."

With a renewed determination, he set card after card

on the desks. She was just about to greet the other students when he called out.

"Miss Slabaugh, I think my Cousin Tim fancies you."

Hope and embarrassment crashed into her. Struggling to keep those emotions to herself, she looked at the boy sternly. "That is not appropriate conversation for school, Anson."

"That is why I came early, but I was *neahfich*—nervous about telling you."

Gently, she went to his side. "You were most likely *neahfich* because Tim's business is not yours to tell."

He shook his head. "No, that's not why. I was just anxious to tell you. You should visit us again."

Hesitantly, she ventured, "Someone told me that Tim might have a sweetheart already, and that they write to each other often."

"Oh, they do, but Tim wasn't too happy about receiving Ruby's last letter."

So her mother's information had been true. "I'm sure he was. Everyone enjoys getting mail," she said brightly. "Besides, we don't know what his mood about the letter has to do with me." She neglected to point out the obvious, but tried to gently allude to it, just the same. "I promise you, a man like Timothy Graber would not be interested in a woman like me."

"But you two went walking."

"I know we did. But just because we went out for a walk doesn't mean we're anything more than friends."

"You sure?"

"*Jah*." Too torn to attempt to worry about saying anything else, she turned from Anson just as a group of eight children entered in a rush, all smiles and laughter and noise. Clara greeted each child, hugged two of the little girls who ran to her, and then with a smile, directed all questions about the postcards to Anson.

He would enjoy the attention, and their questions would prevent him from saying anything more about her and Tim. By now she was sure there never would be anything between them.

Most likely, it had been the moonlight and fireflies that had made her even imagine anything ever could be.

"You're back," Gretta and Miriam called out as soon as Lilly walked into the kitchen. "Oh, I'm so glad to see you. Things just haven't been the same since you've been gone."

"Really?"

"Oh, for sure," Miriam said. "It's been terribly quiet with nobody chirping about this and that."

"And here I thought you all were probably appreciating my absence."

"Never that," Gretta said, rushing to her side to give her a hug. "We've been so sad for your loss and have been terribly worried, too."

The lump that now seemed lodged in her throat seemed to grow to the size of a goose egg. "Thank you."

Still holding her close, Gretta said, "Are you all right?"

"I don't know," she answered honestly. "But I do know

that it was time for me to leave the house and come here. I couldn't sit in bed and be sad any longer."

"Well, of course you couldn't," Miriam said as she gave Lilly a quick hug as well. "Being busy might not cure problems, but it helps one forget about things for a time, I think. And that is a mighty *gut* thing."

"Lilly? Are you ready, dear? The dining room is filling up," Mrs. Kent called out.

Hastily grabbing an apron, Lilly waved to the two other girls. "I'm ready," she called out and rushed to the tables in her station. As a pair of women greeted her and placed their orders, Lilly realized that in this instance, work was indeed the best medicine.

"I thought you quit," a man said two hours later as she came up to take his order. Lilly stopped short. It was the sullen Amish man from before, sitting at the same table.

"I didn't," she said shortly, unafraid to match his tone. Her shift was almost over. And, though she hoped no one would have the slightest idea of how emotionally drained she was, Lilly knew she was almost at her breaking point. Her body was tired after being on her feet for four long hours. Her arms and shoulders and back were moaning about the unaccustomed strength needed to lift trays and carry them to the kitchen. The unspoken questions and whispered comments about her miscarriage hadn't floated over her, either. No, she was very aware of the talk she'd created.

But she'd done her best to smile in the face of it.

When the man still looked her over, she pointed to his menu. "Did you come here to eat or just stare at me?"

He blinked. Then scowled.

Lilly saw a firing in her future. "I'm sorry," she said, meaning it. "I'm tired and I guess I've just about met the end of my rope."

"Maybe you should rest."

"I will. My shift is almost up." She pulled out a pencil and did her best to look competent and professional. "Now, sir, what will you have?"

"It's Robert."

For the life of her, she couldn't follow his statement. "Pardon me?"

His lips tilted a tiny bit. Enough to change the expression on his face. It didn't transform it, but it certainly did create an impression of handsomeness. "I meant, Lilly, that my name is Robert."

"Oh. Well, you know I'm Lilly."

To her surprise, he smiled. Not just a miserly smile, but a full-out grin. With teeth. And with that smile, her suspicion of handsomeness flew out the window. Now he was flat-out gorgeous.

Both his looks—and her reaction to them—were startling.

Perversely, he seemed to grow more at ease the more she became skittish. "I know what I'll have now."

"Yes?"

"A slice of peanut butter pie. And a cup of coffee, too."

"Pie. Coffee."

Blue eyes warmed. "*Jah*. Lilly, I am glad you're back."

Never in her wildest dreams would she have imagined him being so forward. Snapping his menu closed, she nodded. "I'll bring it right out."

"*Danke.*"

Robert said nothing more to her when she brought his order. He simple nodded his thanks, ate about half the pie and sipped half the coffee, then left a tip and paid Mrs. Kent on his way out.

Later, when she drove home, she thought about him again, in spite of her best attempts not to. No matter how hard she tried, she couldn't completely erase the feeling that had floated over her when he'd looked her way . . . like he knew more than he was saying.

Chapter 12

"This is my postcard," Anson said proudly at dinner on Monday evening. "Each of us got one. Mine has a cowboy on the front."

Carrie craned her neck to better look at the picture. It was difficult task; Anson kept moving it out of her reach, making the postcard look as precious as gold.

Tim sipped his iced tea while Anson played a game of "keep away" with the postcard, holding it higher and higher over his plate until it looked as though Carrie would surely fall into his dinner, she was contorted so much.

Caleb frowned. "Enough, Anson. It's only a postcard. Stop making Carrie think it's something special."

"But it is," Anson fired back. "I'm going to write this man in Wyoming and he's going to write me back. I'm gonna get mail, just like Cousin Tim."

Before Tim could say anything about that, Caleb

spoke. "Tim is a lot older and has family members to write to."

"Well, I want a pen pal. And Miss Slabaugh says I'm gonna get one, too."

"This is no cause to argue," Elsa said from her spot down at the end of the table. "Now I think we should all agree to look forward to hearing what Anson's new Wyoming friend will have to say, then move on to something else."

"He's not a 'friend,'" Caleb pointed out somewhat peevishly. "He doesn't even know the person. He wouldn't know that person if he walked right up and knocked on our door."

"Enough, Caleb," Frank commanded. "I've heard all I want to about your views on this. Now, let me tell you all about the latest delivery we had at the store today."

As the conversation moved on to things about the store, Judith leaned close to Tim. "Oh, these kids. Sometimes they really do drive me crazy."

"Don't know why," Tim said with a smile.

She chuckled.

"What are you laughing about?" Caleb demanded.

"You," Judith replied. "One day you're going to need to curb your tongue."

"You shouldn't be laughing at me."

"I'm not laughing at you. I'm laughing at the noise at this table," she explained. "I can only imagine what Cousin Tim writes to his folks about."

"I thought you only wrote to your sweetheart," Anson said.

"I write to Ruby most of the time. But I like keeping in touch with my parents, too." Looking at all of them, he added, "And I can promise my letters are not full of complaints. I'm enjoying being part of a big family."

"We like having you here," Elsa said.

"The farm has never looked better," Uncle Frank added. "Never before have we had the luxury to have someone spend so much time here fixing things."

"I've enjoyed helping you," Tim said. And it was true, he had come to enjoy making his Uncle Frank's life easier.

"And we especially like your hard work," Uncle Frank added. "You've done a very good job around here."

"Things are looking bright and shiny. Almost new," Elsa added. "We are grateful."

"It's a good exchange." Realizing he should keep them informed, Tim said, "I should probably let you know that I asked Ruby Lee to come for a visit. I don't know if she'll accept, but I didn't think you'd mind, especially since you offered an invitation to her earlier."

Judith's eyes lit up. "That would be exciting if she came."

"Yes, indeed," Aunt Elsa said. "Did you recently write to her?"

"I did."

"Well, now we'll all have a reason to look forward to the mail; yes, everyone?"

Anson grinned. "*Jah.*"

"Now, then, let's all finish up and help the girls clear the table."

After reassuring Anson that he thought the postcard was a mighty fine one, indeed, Tim picked up three plates and carried them to the kitchen. There, it was Caleb who caught him in conversation. "I'm going to go out tonight," he whispered. "Will you cover for me?"

Tim stared at him. "What are you talking about?"

"I need you to pretend I'm in my room in case my parents ask if you've seen me."

"What are you going to do?"

"Nothing too exciting," he said, though his voice said far different. "Some friends are going to go into town tonight and walk around. We're going to maybe get ice cream or something."

That sounded perfectly harmless. Too harmless to need a cover. "You ought to just tell your parents that. Then you won't have to lie to them."

"I'd rather not."

When Caleb looked like he was going to turn away, Tim held him with a stern look. "There's more to this than you're telling me. I, for one, don't appreciate being lied to. What are you really going to be doing? And who are you really going to be with?"

"I'm not exactly sure what we'll be doing. Probably lots of things." His cheeks colored. "And some of the kids aren't Amish."

"And some like to do more than eat ice cream?" Tim prodded.

"I don't know. I only know what I'm planning to do." His voice turned harsh. "But if I tell Daed, he'll ask me lots of questions about it all. Questions I'm too old for."

Tim knew the opposite to be true. Caleb wasn't too old to be asked those questions at all. Actually, he was the perfect age to be questioned.

He also knew he was far older. Too old to be involved in silly high jinks. "I'm sorry, but I can't lie to your father. I'm a guest in your home."

Caleb looked crushed. "But—"

"I can't. I'm sorry."

"This house. I'm surrounded by rules and traditions and so much of what is always proper. Some days I am sure I'll never join the church."

Tim was shocked but he didn't want to show it. Keeping his voice as steady as possible, he murmured, "I hope you find some peace soon."

Caleb looked him over, with disdain and yet a hint of hope in his eyes. "Like you?"

Had he found peace? Not too long ago, he'd thought he had. But now he wasn't so sure. Now he wondered if all he'd ever really found was a lulled sense of contentment.

But no one needed to know that. "*Jah*. Like me," he said. "I hope one day you'll find peace and happiness like I have."

When Caleb walked away, his forehead a mix of lines and worry, Tim pretended he didn't notice.

The postcard project was going well. So well that Clara needed some help. She'd sent a note home two days ago, asking for a few volunteers to help the *kinner* address the cards and chart where all the cards were going on the large United States map they'd pinned up to the far wall.

Some of the mothers had sent word with their children that they could come, and had decided to make lunch for everyone, too.

So their postcard day had turned into a party. Around eleven o'clock, everyone started filing in. Sandwich fixings were laid out on a side table and drinks were placed in the large containers of ice that a few parents had brought from their homes.

After giving everyone directions on what to do, Clara busied herself with helping a few of the children at a time.

And then Tim came in.

"Hi," he said. "I heard you needed some extra help today."

"I do." Unable to help herself, she craned her neck to look behind him. "Where's Mrs. Graber?"

"Things are busy at the store. Gretta is feeling a little under the weather, so Joshua stayed home with her. Thus Frank needed Elsa's help at the store. So you've got me . . . if that's okay."

"It is, if you can spare the time."

"I can. If I couldn't I wouldn't be here."

Well, that made sense. "I hope Gretta is okay. I hope she's not too ill."

"Oh, I think she will be fine." He shrugged. "It's just the flu or something."

"Oh, sure," she said agreeably. But though she tried to be cool and complacent, once again, she was enormously aware of Tim. Today he had on blue trousers and a white shirt. His dark suspenders seemed to accentuate his broad shoulders and chest.

And his blue eyes looked as mesmerizing as ever.

"So, where will you have me?" he murmured.

She was tempted to say something nonsensical. Like she would have him wherever he wanted to be.

Then reality returned. He had a sweetheart. He'd lied about her, too. "If you could stand by the map, that would be most helpful. Then, if you could push in thumbtacks near cities that the *kinner* are sending the postcards to, I would be grateful."

"But that means I'd have to know where every state was located."

"They're labeled—" she began, then realized he was teasing her. "Do your best, please," she said instead.

When he chuckled, a few of the mothers looked at the two of them with interest.

Clara turned away before any of them started to get any ideas.

Soon, though, she had no time to think about anything other than marking off each child's assignment when finished, sending it to Tim, then stamping the postcard and helping to clear up things for the lunchtime meal.

The plates and sandwich fixings were organized and laid out and the children lined up. After they ate everyone helped clean up. With the luncheon over, Clara took everyone out for an impromptu game of kick ball, knowing no work would get done after such a fun day.

In no time at all, it was little Maggie's turn to ring the school bell and everyone left.

When the last of the children exited the door, Clara sat down with a sigh. Oh, what a day!

But the many people in the room also added to the noise and confusion. It would take quite some time to set things to rights and for the pain in her head to lessen.

"Sorry, you're not alone at last."

Clara looked up in surprise. Felt her body stiffen when she saw it was Tim. He was standing in the doorway, looking for all the world like he had nothing better to do. Slowly, he smiled.

And with that, the beat in her head pounded just a little bit louder.

Chapter 13

Tim observed that she didn't look terribly pleased about him staying. Actually, she looked uncomfortable. Uneasy.

"You decided to remain?" Clara finally asked.

"I did. Thought you might like some company and help while you cleaned up."

"It wasn't necessary."

She was still seated behind her desk. Now her hands were splayed across the wood . . . looking like she was holding on to the desk for comfort.

Or to hide her discomfort.

"I know it wasn't, but I thought it might be appreciated," he said as he crossed the room. "So, may I stay and help you? I'm afraid if you do this alone you might never get home."

She chuckled at his gentle joke. Gesturing to the chairs unstacked, to the chalkboard still messy, to the remnants of their lunch on the floor, she said, "Whyever would you think that?"

"It's just a guess."

"You are a smart man, Timothy Graber."

"I try to be." He really enjoyed her dry sense of humor. He couldn't help but smile at her expression, too. Though she looked like she was attempting very hard to act like his being there was no big deal, the way her eyes continually darted in his direction told a whole different story. "Actually, though, I am just fine. You can go on home."

Though Tim tried to remind himself that he was still waiting for Ruby's response to his invitation to visit, he couldn't deny that there was something about Clara that made him think of possibilities. Made him question where exactly his life was going.

But he couldn't tell her that. "I thought you might enjoy some company of a more quiet sort."

For a moment he thought he spied something new in her eyes. What was it? Doubt? Pleasure? Disdain? Before he could analyze further, she looked away. "I am fine. Plus, I'm sure you have other things to do."

"I don't. I don't have anywhere I'd rather be."

"Timothy, I've heard about your sweetheart," she finally said. "I'm sure she would not appreciate you being with me. Alone."

His mouth went dry. "I . . . I'm sorry I never told you about her."

"Was the letter that Caleb held from her?"

"*Jah.*"

"I see."

"No, you don't. Clara, I'm sorry I didn't tell you about her, but I didn't want you to get the wrong impression. Nothing's been decided between us . . ."

One eyebrow raised. "No?"

He could only tell the truth now. "But I should let you know that I've invited Ruby here for a visit."

She spun around toward the blackboard.

"Thank you for the offer," she said formally. "But it's time you left."

He walked closer. "Ruby knows I've been making new friends." A pang of consciousness hit him hard even as he said the words. He knew Ruby wouldn't be happy about how strong his feelings were toward Clara.

Clara spun back around and didn't look impressed.

"Clara, I stayed back because I enjoy your company and I hated the thought of you dealing with all of this . . ." His voice drifted off as she stood. "All of this—"

"Chaos?"

"Yes. Chaos. I don't want you to have to clean up the room all by yourself."

"It's my job."

"Not the best part."

"That is true. But still . . . Timothy, what do you want? You have me confused with all your secrets."

"I'm sorry."

"If we are to be friends, I would like your *eahlich-keit*."

His honesty? The request caught him off guard, mainly because he wasn't even sure if he'd been honest with himself where Ruby was concerned. "Okay. I like your company. Being with you is relaxing. Peaceful." He met her gaze. "How's that?"

With measured movements, she walked around her desk. Once again he noticed how very proper she was. Though all women wore basically the same things, on Clara everything seemed a little bit neater.

Perhaps it was her slim figure? Or the fluid way in which she moved? All he knew was that time and again, his eyes followed her.

And were unable to look away.

She gazed out the window. Tim knew it was up to him to say something next. Say anything to encourage her to talk. To encourage her to tell him what she thought about him.

But his tongue felt tied. "I mean, I think you're nice."

She blinked. And as her eyes focused, he noticed some of the light fell from them and shielded her emotions once again. "Ah."

"I mean, I don't know what I mean anymore. See, Clara, I came here against my will."

Her eyes widened. "To my schoolhouse?"

She looked so disturbed that he'd been dragged to the classroom that he almost smiled. Almost. "No. I'm speaking of Sugarcreek," he corrected gently. "See, Clara, I was happy in my own town. With the way things were. Honestly, it never occurred to me that things could be different. Or that I'd ever enjoy things being different. But now that I'm here—now that I'm becoming part of the town, part of the community, I find myself not wanting to leave. And I hardly understand how that could be."

He waited for her to nod in understanding. But instead of doing that, she merely looked worried. "Tim, I feel foolish to say this, but I've never been part of a conversation like this before. I . . . I'm afraid I don't know how to reply to your words."

He couldn't help it, he felt let down. "I see."

"Do you? I don't. I don't know how to react when you say that you like me—but you're writing to a woman at home. When you say that you want to stay here . . . but all of your obligations are back in Indiana."

When she put things that way, Tim did realize that his words all seemed to contradict each other. "I don't mean to be confusing."

"And I don't mean to brush off your words like they aren't important. They are." Her lips tilted up. "I would like to be your friend. And I would like to get to know you better."

Tim felt like pumping his fist in the air. Success! She was going to give him a chance. "I'll take that. So, may I walk you home?"

The most beautiful smile lit her face. "I suppose. As long as you promise to walk slowly," she cautioned, merriment lighting her eyes. "I'm so tired I don't think my body can handle a brisk walk."

"I'll walk as slow as you want."

"That may be far too slow for you, I'm afraid."

"Haven't you heard? The Lord doesn't give you any task He doesn't think you can handle."

She chuckled. "Part of me doubts the Lord has ever sat in a classroom with food and parents and postcards!"

"Let's clean up, then. Together we can make this place shine."

"I'll settle for a semblance of order."

Tim chuckled as he pulled open a plastic garbage sack and began to throw paper plates, cups, and napkins inside it. When he started stacking chairs so he could sweep, Clara tackled the piles of papers littering different corners of the room.

Tim was sweeping the dust and litter into the dustpan when she began wiping down the chalkboard. Then she wrote two sentences on the board for the following morning's lesson, and he gathered her things and set them neatly in her basket.

Twenty minutes later, they were done. Clara looked around in surprise. "I would have never guessed this room would have gotten set to rights so quickly. We work together well."

Tim looked at her in appreciation. Her voice had held a hint of a question. Almost as if she was daring him to disagree. But he didn't at all. "I think so, too," he murmured. "Now let's head toward home."

"I'll be happy to." Clara led the way out. After carefully locking the door, she breathed deep and exhaled. They left the covered front porch of the school and stood on the front lawn.

He smiled when he watched her tilt her face up slightly, obviously enjoying the last lingering rays of sunlight caressing her face. He so enjoyed her habit. So enjoyed that she received so much pleasure from a simple gift like the sun. Holding out his hand, he murmured, "Clara, let me carry your basket."

To his surprise, she handed it to him without hesitation. "Thank you."

Their fingers brushed each other's. For a moment, he was tempted to curve his hand around hers. To keep her hand captured under his own. Keep her close.

But of course, that wouldn't be proper. He let his fingers slide an inch to the left so her hand could go free. "I'm happy to help," he said lightly.

She simply smiled as they began the descent down the sloped hill toward the main road.

Around them, the trees rustled, reminding Tim that spring was arriving at a feverish pace. Daily, the trees were sprouting leaves, flowers poked through dark ground, and bushes filled out. Birds and deer and all other sorts of animals were having their babies. New life was beginning.

Even the days were lengthening. The sun that Clara seemed to love so much was a little higher in the sky at five o'clock than it was when he'd first arrived.

All of it made him thankful.

She looked at him for a moment before tilting her face up to the sun again, a look of pure contentment shining on it.

For a moment, he couldn't look away. She looked so happy.

He also realized he was also getting used to seeing her do it. It was a habit he was becoming familiar with.

"You do enjoy the outdoors, don't you?"

"I do. Yes. Very much. I enjoy the fresh air on my face and the sun, too."

Only half teasing, he murmured, "I have a feeling you even like winter's snow and frost."

"You would be right. Being outside is such a blessing. I like to take time to notice everything around me—to give thanks for the feel of warm rays on my cheeks."

He was tempted to tell her that he wanted to give thanks for the chance to witness that. He was tempted to ask her why she did it, though. What it meant to her.

But he didn't. They weren't that close.

Not yet. Perhaps they never would be.

A feeling of doom settled in as that reality hit him. Perhaps this would be the closest they ever got to each other. Perhaps this time was the only true private time they would have.

They walked for a bit on the side of the road. Their steps were slow and far more contemplative than the same journey he'd taken with Elsa and his cousins after the spring program.

As different as night and day, he imagined.

"I never take the feeling of the breeze on my skin for granted," she blurted, bringing him back to the present.

After a moment's pause, when a minivan sped by, she said, "I imagine you know that I had many operations for my scars."

He looked at her in surprise. Never would he have

guessed that she would bring up her scars without prompting. "*Jah.* I mean, I assumed you did. But I don't know much about what happened."

"Well, when I was six a pan caught on fire. My mother panicked and put water on the fire instead of flour or baking soda."

"So it spread?"

"It did. It jumped and scalded everything in reach."

"Including you."

"*Jah.* Even me." She frowned, but it wasn't an expression of self-pity. Instead, it leant itself more toward acceptance. Acceptance but not complete happiness. "Somehow . . . I have forgotten what happened exactly— somehow a lot of the oil sprayed on me. I was rushed to the hospital and contracted an infection."

Though she claimed speaking of the accident didn't bother her, Tim knew it must be otherwise. Every word seemed to be forced through her mouth, almost grudgingly said. But with pure determination. "It must have been a scary time. And painful."

Tim felt his cheeks heat. His words sounded so simple. So small compared to the enormity of what she'd gone through.

She blinked. "Yes. It was terribly painful. Those were dark days. I spent much of my time alone and covered in thick bandages. Inside."

"Which is why you like being outside so much."

"Exactly. That is exactly why."

They were near the creek now. The creek where they'd met and he'd been unable to look at anything but her. The creek where he'd asked her if she was married.

And she'd thought he had been teasing her.

As the hills surrounded them, and the trickling water echoed their voices, he turned to her. "But you made it through okay?"

"Oh, yes," she said without a trace of embarrassment. "I mean, I made it through." Pushing up her sleeve, she held out her right arm. The skin was different colors. Shades of bright red and white, and blotches that looked almost like bruises. In the waning sunlight, it looked painful.

Even after all this time.

"And so, you see, I look like this."

"You look all right." Tim was surprised to realize that he meant it. Now, to him, she did look just fine. The scars were part of who she was. For a moment, he was tempted to stop. Tempted to toss that basket of hers down and push up the rest of her sleeve. He was tempted to run his fingers down her arm. Just so she could feel his touch.

So she'd know that instead of being repelled by her scars, he found them very much the opposite. They made her stronger in his eyes. They made him want to protect her. To hold her. To kiss away any doubts she'd ever had about her beauty.

But of course those were fanciful thoughts.

Of course that could never happen.

Unaware of his wayward thoughts . . . she squared her shoulders and started walking again. A wry, sad smile lit her face. "Oh, Tim. We know I don't look in any way 'all right.' But I'm here in one piece. The doctors did the best they could."

"How long were you in the hospital?"

"I don't know." She shrugged. "Maybe one month? Perhaps six weeks."

"But then you came home?"

"For a time. But I wasn't done, you know. A person's skin, especially when she is small, it grows and stretches. Burned skin doesn't do those things as well. Over the years I've needed three more surgeries to try to help the damage. They took skin from other parts of my body to help."

"But you're done now?" Tim wanted to give her a hug. She was speaking so matter-of-factly, but it was also so very evident that she was keeping much of what had happened to herself.

"I suppose I'm done." She looked at him sideways. "They—I mean the doctors in Columbus—they suggested I go to a plastic surgeon to help minimize the scarring. As bad as it is on my face, and as mottled as my skin is on my arm . . . I'm afraid it's worse on my shoulder."

For a flash, he imagined pulling away her dress. Examining the skin for himself. Reassuring her that to him, she would always be lovely. Then her words hit home.

"So you'll have another surgery to repair the damage? When are you going to do that?"

"Not ever."

Confused, he stopped and looked directly at her. "But you just said the doctors recommended it."

"We can't afford it."

"Not ever?" His mind raced. He'd heard of charitable institutions that helped people who needed treatments. Perhaps if they wrote to one of them, explained her situation, told everyone about how she lived so bravely, but yearned for more . . .

"It's almost too late now," she murmured. "And, well, I suppose my mother was right. It is unnecessary."

"To refuse you help seems harsh."

"Perhaps. But I saw her point. Already my surgeries cost the community a lot of money."

Tim could only imagine. Once his mother had been put in the hospital with pneumonia. That one week stay had been terribly expensive. But then he recalled another bit of information. "But I thought your father had insurance?"

"Oh, yes. He did, thank the Lord. I was lucky, indeed. Yes, but even so, it was thousands of dollars. Then he passed away and money became very tight. My mother was worried that the expense of the surgery for something like vanity wasn't a good idea."

"Vanity? Clara, I don't want to sound mean, but there's a big difference between helping your skin look healed and a fancy lady's need for a perfect nose or something." As soon as he said the words, he regretted them. "I'm sorry. All of this is none of my business."

"There's no need to apologize. I don't mind speaking

about the surgeries as much as other people do. They're part of who I am."

"I think you should go to the doctor now, just to see. If you want."

"I used to think about it," she murmured. "Sometimes I've sat and wondered what things would be like if that accident had never happened. Now, though, I think my scars let me see the world a little bit clearer than most others see it. I know people can be harsh. I know that bad things can't always be wished away. It helps to teach the children that, too."

It was in his nature to want to fix things. "Maybe one day you can still get the surgery."

"I don't think so. I'm almost at peace with it."

Tim felt humbled. He'd heard her use of "almost" and knew she was being completely honest with him. She knew what she looked like, and she wished things were different.

But she was doing her best.

"I think you're pretty great."

"Don't think that, Timothy. All of us are scarred by life. By things that happen. Mine just happen to be on the outside. Bold enough for anyone to see."

"But the way you deal with things. You are such a giving person."

"Some would say the same of you. Here you are, living with your aunt and uncle and helping around their farm. All because they asked."

"It wasn't that easy, I'm afraid. I didn't want to come here at first," he said again. He didn't know why he cared, but he wanted her to see all of his faults. To know that he, too, wasn't near perfect.

"That's okay. Things are more meaningful when they're more difficult, *jah?*"

"Yes." Tim saw her house in the distance. "What will you do now?"

"I'm going to work in my garden. And you?"

"I'll do some chores. It was nice to walk with you, Clara. Thank you."

"And thank you, Tim. Goodbye."

When she walked away, he felt like part of his heart went with her.

Even though they were only friends and could never be sweethearts.

Chapter 14

Lilly was kneeling in the middle of her mother's new garden, trying to figure out which were weeds and which were cucumber plants when Ty and Anson came rushing through the hedge that separated their land from the Grabers'.

As they raced in front of her—almost stepping on something she knew was a tomato plant—she called out to them. "Hey, you two, settle down."

Both boys stopped. "Lilly? What are you doing?"

"Trying to garden. What are you two running in such a hurry for?"

"We get to have a sleepover tonight!" Ty replied. "Mrs. Graber said I could spend the night."

"We're going to sleep in the barn," Anson added with a cheeky grin. "It's going to be scary."

Just to tease, Lilly frowned. "Are you sure you want to do that? You might not be able to sleep . . ."

"Oh, we're gonna get scared in a good way," Ty explained. "So I need my sleeping bag."

Lilly looked from one boy to the other and tried to imagine what her mother would say. "Boys, are you sure it's okay? You've gotten your signals crossed with our parents before." As she thought of the many times they'd "accidentally" come home late from each other's homes or "forgot" to tell both parents that they were going fishing, she figured a little clarification wouldn't hurt.

Ty impatiently kicked a clump of dirt. "Yes."

She was just about to tell her brother to watch where he was kicking when Anson stepped in front of her. "It really is okay this time, Lilly. My *mamm* said since it's Friday night, sleeping out in the barn won't hurt anything. Plus she said she heard the rains are going to start coming. If we don't camp out now, we won't get to for some time."

She couldn't help but smile at that. Every moment seemed to be laced with special anticipation with these two. "I suppose not. Well, good luck finding a sleeping bag, Ty. I haven't seen one in forever."

"That's because I put it in my room."

"Oh. Of course. Well, have fun," she said as she scooted around to the next row of vegetables and flicked away a grasshopper that had landed on something that looked important.

When it chirped and darted off, she jumped a bit herself. So far, gardening was so not for her.

Anson looked intrigued by her antics. Leaning closer, he said, "What are you doing?"

"Trying to figure out which green things are weeds and which ones are not. Of course, they all look the same to me."

Anson looked at her homemade sign, then reached down and pulled up a sprig of green. "This ain't a green bean. It's a dandelion. You growing those, too?"

Lilly wasn't sure if he was joking or not. Taking the plant from him, she shook her head. "No. Hey, how did you know this wasn't a green bean seedling?"

"I don't know." He shrugged. "I just do."

When they scampered off into the house, Lilly leaned back on her knees and sighed. The weed in her hand looked green. So did the other little hundred shoots springing from the rows and rows in front of her. "This is hopeless," she said with a moan.

"Maybe not," Caleb Graber said as he walked out of the bushes. When she looked at him in surprise, he chuckled. "Mamm sent me over to tell you that she really did give them permission to sleep in the barn. You know how Anson and Ty get with their plans. They aren't above fibbing a bit to get their way."

She stood up. "I just grilled them myself."

When he stopped in front of her, he whistled low. "Gardening today?"

"That's still to be determined. At the moment, all that's happening is I'm getting freaked out by bugs and pulling all the wrong stuff. At this rate, we're going to have a wonderful garden of dandelions. Caleb, do you know the difference between what's supposed to be here and what isn't?"

"I suppose I do." Rolling up his sleeves, he crouched down. "I'll help you, Lilly Allen." Squinting his eyes, he quickly pulled eight or ten weeds and tossed them in her green plastic wheelbarrow. "This here is clover, Lilly. And this is a dandelion thistle." He touched two of the leaves. "See the difference between them and your beans?"

Finally, she did. With renewed vigor, she yanked and pulled a half dozen more. "Am I doing this right?"

"*Jah.*" His green eyes—eyes the color of the fresh-pulled clover in her hands—twinkled a bit. They reminded her a lot of Josh's eyes, and how much she'd been drawn to Josh when they'd first moved in. She imagined there was a group of girls in his community who dreamed of being Caleb's sweetheart one day. She knew she'd be hoping for his attentions if she was a few years younger.

As if feeling her regard, he shrugged. "It's not hard, once you know what to look for."

"I'll try to remember that," she said dryly.

He looked toward the garage. "Charlie here?"

"Sorry. He's still gone. He's visiting some friends and getting registered for the fall semester at Bowling Green. He won't be back until Sunday night."

Some of the light dimmed in his eyes. "Oh. Well, thanks anyway."

"Did you need to go somewhere? I'd be happy to drive you to town. It's the least I could do after you've pulled so many weeds."

For a moment she thought he would accept, then he

shook his head. "I better not. My parents wouldn't like that."

Wouldn't like that? What was going on? "Caleb, are you okay?"

"I am. Just feeling restless." When she knelt down to pull another weed, he pushed her hand aside and pulled up a completely different plant. "That one there is a strawberry plant, Lilly. Keep that in the ground, *jah*?"

"I'll try."

Rolling his eyes, he nudged her aside and finished clearing weeds from the row of strawberries.

As he did so, she balanced in a squat and watched him. "I remember being restless and a lot of other things . . . especially since they weren't all that long ago. I think everyone at fifteen and sixteen is restless."

"My family doesna think so."

She couldn't help but notice he sounded bitter. "Trouble at home?"

"Not really. Just some differences in opinions. I'm in my *rumspringa*, so I'm allowed more freedom . . . but though my parents say I have it, I don't. Not really."

"Talking about things helps. Do you have a girlfriend? Sometimes having someone special in your life can help you sort out things."

"No."

Recalling Joshua's talk about Sunday-night singings, a time when many of the teenagers got together to hang out, she said, "When's the next singing?"

"I don't go to those."

"Why not?"

He stilled. "I have my reasons."

"Which are? I'm not trying to judge you," she said quickly. "I'm just curious."

Caleb pulled another two weeds, tossed them in the barrow, then stood up and brushed dirt off his pants. After a moment, he said, "I'm not interested in all things Amish right now. I feel trapped. I want to see new people. I want to experience things."

"And I bet those feelings aren't going over so well at home."

"You would be right."

"Be careful what you wish for. I got restless and then did some things I wish I hadn't. Now I've had enough experiences for ten or twelve people."

But instead of grinning right back at her, his gaze hardened. "At least you have done something."

Lilly knew it was no use to explain that she would have given a lot not to have gone through so much. Even now, she was still finding even the easiest tasks monumental.

"Thanks for your help with the weeds, Caleb."

"Anytime. Tell the boys to find my *mamm* when they leave here." He turned and slipped through the hedge again.

Lilly pulled a few more weeds, then couldn't help comparing his attitude with the man she'd waited on at the Sugarcreek Inn. Both had stared at her like she should automatically know what they wanted.

Who knew? Maybe she did.

Maybe she should have told them that she knew what they yearned for all too well—something new and fresh and different.

And, of course, peace.

With a sigh, she stood up and brushed the dirt from her knees. Overhead, clouds were rolling in. A change was in the air, just like Mrs. Graber had warned the little boys about.

But what was really hard was that she was in no hurry for any more changes at all.

Frankly, she thought she'd been through enough.

On Thursday afternoon, Tim stood by his horse and buggy at the train station and double-checked the time with the information in Ruby's last letter.

Anson noticed. "How much longer?"

"The clock and letter say ten minutes."

"Then I guess we're gonna have to wait a while longer."

Tim chuckled. It had probably been a sign of weakness to drag Anson with him, but he'd wanted the company, and he'd wanted a buffer between him and Ruby when she first arrived.

Though his aunt and uncle had looked at him curiously when he'd asked if he could bring Anson along to the train station, they'd agreed readily enough.

Anson, being Anson, had been eager to leave school a little bit early and eye the trains.

"Miss Slabaugh said sometimes mail rides on the

trains. Do you think maybe my postcard will be in one of the mail sacks?"

"I don't know."

"When do you think I'll hear from my pen pal? It's been a week."

"I don't know that answer either."

"James thinks he's going to hear first because he wrote to a fella in Indiana, but I don't know about that."

"I'd say it's anyone's guess."

Anson nodded. "We're not supposed to bet, but I bet James a fishing lure that I'll hear first."

"Probably wasn't a smart decision. You're parents will not be pleased to hear you're making bets like that. Especially not in school."

"I couldn't help it. James always acts like he knows everything. Sometimes I get tired of it."

"I hear what you're saying, but two wrongs don't make a right, you know. You should learn to ignore his boastful ways. That would be a better way to go. There're people who want to be right everywhere, and that's the truth."

"I suppose." Anson rocked on his heels, shifted the straw hat on his head as a pair of *Englischers* smiled his way, then looked right and left down the train tracks. "I hope she comes soon. I'm getting tired of waiting."

"I hope so, too."

As people congregated around them and a couple nearby hugged and kissed, Anson glanced his way again. "So, are you going to kiss Ruby hello?"

Tim looked at Anson in surprise. "Why in the world would you ask such a thing?"

"Because I'm curious. Everyone around here is kissing. They're kissing a lot."

"They're English."

"Amish kiss, too," Anson retorted. "I know that."

Tim was beginning to regret bringing the boy along. "I know that, too."

Warming to the topic, his little cousin continued. "Once, I saw my brother Joshua kiss Gretta when they thought no one saw them." He wrinkled his nose. "It lasted forever."

"They are married. And, you shouldn't have been spying on them."

"I couldn't help it. They were in the hall outside the kitchen. What else was I supposed to do?"

"Turn around."

Anson rolled his eyes. "There was nowhere else for me to go. Anyway, they stopped as soon as I walked over to them and said I didn't think they should kiss so much."

Tim could only imagine what that scene had been like. "Anson. That was rude."

"So was kissin' in the hallway!" He looked at Tim sideways. "But later, after Joshua told me I shoulda been minding my own business, he said there was nothing wrong with kissing."

"There's not. As long as there are genuine, loving feelings involved."

"Oh, I think Joshua felt loving all right." Before Tim could chastise him again Anson pulled his jacket. "So, will you kiss Ruby? Do you have genuine, loving feelings for her?"

This had to be why the good Lord had made him an only child. There was no way he could have dealt with such intrusive questions time and again, day after day.

Especially since he didn't know what his feelings were for Ruby any longer. Did he still feel loving toward her? A knot settled in his stomach as he worried about the answer.

"Are ya?" Anson nagged.

"No. Now stop asking me so many questions."

"But all I'm asking is—"

The train whistle blew just in time.

"Quiet, now. I need to look for Ruby." Tim wasn't sure how much Anson heard over the roar of the train whistle and the steady pulse of the powerful engines.

Time seemed to stop as the massive structure pulled to a stop next to the platform. Anson giggled as another whistle blew, a door opened, and a conductor called out, "Depart quickly. This train will leave in ten minutes."

Around them on the cement platform more people joined them, awaiting the disembarking passengers. Other men in uniforms and baggage carts pushed their way to the front.

Anson reached for his arm and held on tight as a man on a cell phone almost knocked into him.

Tim craned his neck to try to see Ruby. Through the tiny windows, he saw several people standing near the train doors, impatiently waiting for them to open. None of them looked like her, though.

And then with a metallic whoosh, doors on several of the cars slid open and passengers started piling out.

When he'd arrived by train, both the train and the station had been far less crowded. Today, there seemed to be at least twice as many people shuffling around, each as impatient as the next to escape the station.

Still holding his arm tightly, Anson hopped a bit, attempting to see over the heads of the men in front of him. "Can you see anything, Tim? Do you see Ruby?"

"Not yet."

"What if she didn't come? What would we do then?"

"She came. We just need to be patient."

Anson sighed. When he started hopping again, Tim moved them to the left where the crowd had thinned.

However, nowhere did he see an Amish woman.

Though less than ten minutes had passed, already the station was emptying and the train's engines were growling impatiently to continue.

A horn blared, and someone called out, "Five minutes! All aboard to Cleveland!"

Yet more passengers rushed from the ticket area and filled the platform. Anson stepped even closer to Tim, his eyes wide as a Middle Eastern couple trotted by, the woman's head covered in a beautiful flowing scarf.

"Maybe we missed her," Anson said. "Maybe we should go walk around."

Tim didn't want to admit it, but he was afraid his young cousin was right. Most everyone around them had been paired up and they were now leaving the area. "If we don't see her soon, we'll do just that," he promised.

And then the waves of passengers broke, and standing

right next to a metal bench with black graffiti sprayed across the top was Ruby.

"I see Ruby," he said with a smile.

Anson looked right and left, then when he too caught sight of Ruby in her violet dress, black cape, and white *kapp*, he grinned. "I see her, too! She's pretty, Tim."

"*Jah*, she is," he agreed as they walked forward. "Ruby Lee? Here we are."

She turned, her frightened expression immediately relaxing into relief. "Tim? Oh, Tim I'm so glad to see you! I didn't know what I was going to do if you didn't show up."

"We've been over there," Anson explained. "Standing by light post number five." Tilting his hat back, he smiled. "I'm Anson."

"How do you do? Tim has mentioned you in his letters. It's nice to meet you. I'm Ruby Lee." Her eyes flickered toward his. Tim read confusion there, but he wasn't sure of the source. Was she wondering why he'd not seen her the moment she'd gotten off the train, or was she wondering why he'd brought Anson along?

"Let's go get your bag," he said simply. "Baggage claim is in through these double doors."

"There's no need for that." She pointed to the compact black rolling suitcase parked next to her feet. "It's all here."

"It's not very big," Anson said. "How long are you stayin'?"

Tim glared at Anson. "You shouldn't ask things like that."

She chuckled. "I don't mind. Anson, I'm not staying too long, and my suitcase is small because I don't need much. Plus, I figured if I needed something, your sister Judith could let me borrow it."

"Oh."

Tim took her bag and led them to the buggy. "Are you hungry?"

"Not so much."

"I am," Anson said. "I thought maybe we could go eat at the Sugarcreek Inn on the way home."

Tim chuckled. Only Anson could wheedle so well. "You thought about pie, did you?"

"There's mighty good pie there."

"Do you mind?" Tim asked Ruby. "Having a little break before we head back home might be a nice treat."

Her brows rose. "*Back home?* You mean to your aunt and uncle's home, yes? Your home is in Indiana."

For a moment his mouth went dry. He had spoken like Sugarcreek was where he belonged. When had that happened?

But instead of dwelling on that, he murmured, "Anson is right, the pie is mighty good."

She reached out to him, her eyes gentling as her hand curved around his forearm. "That would be fine. I like pie, too. I like anything you want to do."

Ah. There was the Ruby he had remembered.

Her sweetness ran through him, taking him by surprise. How had he forgotten how generous she was? How sweet and giving?

It had been the right thing to do, to invite her to visit. "Let's go, then," he murmured. "Let's go eat and I will show you Sugarcreek. My temporary home."

Anson grinned. "You're going to love it here in Sugarcreek, Ohio," he said. "Everyone does."

Chapter 15

"I see Tim is sitting over in the corner with his sweetheart," Gretta said to Lilly as soon as she entered the kitchen. "They look very cozy together. Did you speak with them? What is she like?"

Lilly stared at her in confusion. "Tim?"

"*Jah*. Tim. He's got dark hair and lovely brown eyes, too."

Lilly hid a smile as she followed Gretta's gaze out the picture window that divided the kitchen and dining room. "Oh, him. He's the man with Anson, right?"

"*Jah*. He's Tim Graber, Joshua's cousin. He's here visiting for spring planting. Now his sweetheart Ruby has come, too. It's created quite a stir at my in-law's house, I tell you. They're here all the way from Indiana."

That was one of the phrases that never failed to make Lilly smile. The way Gretta talked, one would think Indiana was across the Pacific Ocean. "I haven't said too much to them yet. Mrs. Kent seated them."

Gretta's shoulders slumped. "Oh."

"But I'll go get more information, if you'd like."

"Go do that soon," Miriam said, joining them at the window. "We want to know what this Indiana girl is like."

"I'm sure she's nice," Gretta said primly.

Lilly heard something in Gretta's voice that said otherwise, though. "Do you not want to like her?"

"No . . . I do. It's just that I'd hoped he would fancy someone else. Someone here in Sugarcreek."

"Then he could stay."

"Yes." Gretta eyed Lilly again. "When are you going to go take their order?"

"Right this minute."

"And get some information, too!" Miriam ordered with a laugh.

Before they could boss her around any more, Lilly left the kitchen again.

As she filled two water glasses for some other customers, she couldn't believe how light and easy she felt.

Laughing with Gretta and Miriam had been just what she'd needed. Their antics made her feel young again. Young and silly and happy. She was so lucky to have such a good job, and to fit in with the two girls in such a way that she'd never have expected.

In fact, she was becoming so close to her Amish friends that she wasn't even missing her English ones.

A few months ago, she would have never imagined that happening.

Of course, a few months ago, everything in her life had felt upside down.

Now she only had a big gap in her heart.

Eager to push those painful feelings aside, she walked up to the three customers of interest. "Hi, there, Anson. Looks like you've got some company today."

"I sure do. This is my cousin Tim and Ruby."

"I'm Lilly Allen—"

"Lilly's my neighbor," Tim supplied.

Ruby's eyes narrowed. "For a little while, yes?"

"Of course."

When all three looked back at her, she noticed a bit of tension between the couple. Anson, of course, just looked hungry. "Are all of you ready to order?"

"I am! I'll have peanut butter pie."

"Good choice. Gretta made one this morning. Tim and Ruby? What would you like?"

"Blackberry pie for me," Tim said.

"I'll just have some water."

Anson frowned. "You're not eating?"

"I'm not hungry. I try not to eat between meals."

"Would you like coffee? It's fresh," Lilly asked. Anything to move the conversation along.

"*Jah*," Tim said. "Ruby?"

"Coffee would be fine."

"All right." Then, feeling as if Gretta and Miriam were staring holes in her back, she tried to get a bit more information. "Are you liking Sugarcreek so far?"

"It is just fine," Ruby replied, her voice stiff. She directed a cool glare Lilly's way. Obviously, she was ready for Lilly to go away.

"I'll be right back with your coffee," Lilly murmured, turning away and practically racing back to the kitchen.

"Well? What is she like?" Gretta asked as soon as Lilly strode through the door.

"I don't know. She seems kind of quiet."

"Really? What did she order?"

"Water. And then, reluctantly, coffee. Tim wants a slice of blackberry and Anson wants peanut butter."

Gretta smiled. "That Anson, he could eat a whole peanut butter pie all by himself, I think. I'll slice him a piece."

"And I'm already taking care of the blackberry," Miriam said. "Though I have to say I don't trust anyone who doesn't come here for dessert."

"Lots of girls like to watch their figures, you know," Lilly said. "There's nothing wrong with that."

"I suppose," Miriam answered with a frown. "But it doesn't seem normal."

"Well, go bring these out and chat some more," Gretta urged. "I want to know what they're planning to do."

"You should just come out with me," Lilly said.

"Oh, I couldn't. It would be too pushy."

"You've got me being pushy!"

"You're not about to be part of her family," Gretta said. "Joshua told me he wouldn't be surprised if they became engaged this coming week."

"Wow. All right. I'll deliver this and see what else I can find out. But I feel ridiculous."

Miriam just shooed her out the door with a grin.

With the plates and the cups of coffee on her tray, she

wandered back over. "Here's some pie. And two coffees, too."

Ruby took her mug with hardly a smile. *"Danke."*

"You'll have to let me know what you think of the pie, Tim."

Anson shoveled a bite into his own mouth. "Mine is good."

"I'm glad." She was just trying to think of something else to chat about when Ruby looked her over, then started speaking in Pennsylvania Dutch to Tim.

Embarrassed, Lilly turned back to the kitchen once again.

"Well?" Gretta asked eagerly.

"I've nothing new to report. And don't ask me to go see her again! Now she thinks I'm a pest, for sure."

"Hmm."

"I suppose she seems pleasant enough." Lilly looked at Gretta curiously as she finished slicing the pies and wiping down the edge of a plate with a clean paper towel. "Who had you been thinking of for him, anyway?"

Gretta turned to wrap up the pies. "Oh, no one special."

Lilly looked at Miriam who simply smiled. "Come on. There's definitely something else going on. What is it?"

"Tell, her, Gretta," Miriam urged.

A little sense of foreboding began to creep through her. Surely Gretta didn't have her in mind? Was that what this was about?

"It's someone who lives here in Sugarcreek."

Oh, what was she going to say? "Yes?"

"And this girl is a nice person. Really nice."

"Name?"

"She's speaking of Clara Slabaugh," Miriam said impatiently. "Do you know her? She's the schoolteacher. She's, um, scarred."

"I know who she is," Lilly replied, so relieved Gretta hadn't been thinking of her. "I've met Clara."

"I'm surprised to hear that," Gretta said. "She hardly goes anywhere."

"Clara and I met walking near the creek the other day." Remembering the meaningful conversation they'd shared, she added, "I really liked her. We sat down and talked together for quite a while."

"Really? I'm surprised. She usually doesn't say much to *Englischers*. And she usually doesn't say much to anyone for very long."

"Unless it's Tim. They went walking together the other night. It seemed like they'd got along real well, too." Gretta peered back out at the threesome. "Oh, I was hoping they were a pair."

"I don't know, Gretta. I think Tim and this girl are a pair already." Lilly looked through the window again. The three of them seemed to be having a pleasant time.

Miriam nodded. "Yes. By the looks of things, I think he's already taken."

"Perhaps you are right," Gretta frowned. "But still, I think it's a shame that Tim and Clara won't ever be together. They seemed so perfect for each other."

"Girls, you're here to work, not peer out the window like peeping Toms," Mrs. Kent called out.

"Sorry," Lilly called out. Quickly, she rushed back into the dining room and picked up the coffeepot. Then she slowed down, refilling coffee for some, refilling iced tea glasses for others.

When she arrived at the Grabers' table, she smiled Anson's way. "Your pie's all gone! That was fast."

Looking glumly at his plate, Anson mumbled, "It was too good. It ended too fast."

"I'm sorry for that. Would you like another piece? I could go get you one, if you'd like. Any flavor. My treat."

Anson stared at her with wide eyes. "You'd do that, Lilly?"

"Of course. I mean, if it's okay with you all."

"Can I get more pie?" Anson asked Tim.

Just as Tim nodded, Ruby shook her head. "I'm sorry, but I'd rather you didn't. I've been traveling all day and would like to get to your aunt and uncle's house. Besides, they may not like to hear that you've eaten so much."

"They wouldn't have to know."

"Of course they would," Ruby said briskly. "I'd tell them."

As Anson looked crushed, Tim hurriedly said, "Lilly, if you could hand me the check, then."

"I'll be right back," she said. For a moment, Lilly considered sticking a piece of pie in a plastic holder for Anson to take with him, but she ultimately decided against that. She might be friends with the ten-year-old, but it wasn't her place to step into their business.

When they eventually left, and the restaurant thinned

a little bit, she sat down at one of the tables and wrapped knives, spoons, and forks in white napkins, restocking for the next day.

Gretta came out to join her with a cup of fresh, hot coffee. "I still can't believe she was in such a rush to get to home," she said. "Poor Anson."

"It's nothing, I suppose. Though I was tempted to give him some pie to go."

"It's just as well you didn't. He would have shown Carrie and then there would have been hurt feelings all around."

"She didn't look like she trusted me at all," Lilly said. "Do you think it's because I'm English?"

"My guess is it's because you're pretty." With an embarrassed smile, Gretta said, "That's why I didn't trust you months ago."

"I wonder how long she's going to be here?"

"It's just a guess . . . but I have a feeling that Joshua's family is going to say a little too long," Gretta murmured.

When the door opened with a chime, her eyes turned merry again. "It's your cranky customer again."

Lilly wondered what he was going to be like today. Happy? Sullen?

Well, there was only one way to find out. Picking up a menu, she crossed the dining room and greeted him. "Hello, Robert. How are you today?"

"Fine, *Danke.*"

"Any place special you'd like to sit?"

"By the window is fine."

"Coffee again?"

"*Jah*. And a slice of buttermilk pie, if you have it."

"We do. Miriam made it fresh this morning."

He didn't smile, but of course, she didn't expect him to.

Moments later, when she placed everything in front of him, he looked her over. "Are you feeling better?"

"What?"

To her amazement, his cheeks reddened. "You seem to be working a lot now. And, well, I heard that you are almost back to working full-time. I was just wondering if you were feeling better."

"I am. Thank you."

He said nothing, simply nodded. But after she'd served his pie and the rest of the restaurant emptied, she felt his eyes continually rest on her.

She was almost tempted to stare at him, too.

Chapter 16

"She's here," Clara's mother said on Sunday morning when they were packing the buggy to go to church. "Timothy's sweetheart Ruby arrived yesterday."

"Oh. Well, I hope she enjoys her stay," she murmured as casually as she could manage.

"Several people saw Tim and Ruby at the Sugarcreek Inn. I heard he looked very smitten."

Clara fought to keep her expression neutral. "That is *gut*. She traveled a long way to see him."

Her mother narrowed her eyes as she grabbed her cape from the hook by the door and fastened the hook and eye closure. "Perhaps they will declare themselves while she is here. That would be exciting."

"Yes." Clara knew her mother was saying those things just to get her feelings in knots.

"If your paths cross, make sure you don't say too much to him after church. We don't want her to feel jealous."

"Muddah, I will be fine. Stop acting like I'm a child."

"I just don't want you to embarrass yourself."

"I won't. Let's go."

Silence filled the buggy as they left the driveway and began the trip to the Millers' home, the place for church that week. After they'd only ridden half a mile, small drops of rain began peppering the windshield.

Daisy, their buggy horse, shook her head a bit as she continued on.

"It's supposed to rain all day," her mother said gloomily.

As if on cue, the drops became bigger. "I think you're right."

"We need the rain, though. Did you notice the peppers and the zucchinis? They're not near as big as they usually are by April."

"Yes, the rain will help them."

Forty-five minutes later, they pulled into the Millers' yard. Clara yanked on Daisy's reins, then raised the brake so her mother could get out in front of their barn. After her mother alighted, she directed Daisy over to an area where the rest of the buggies were parked. Once settled, she got out as well and made sure Daisy was securely tied to the hitching post.

By now the rain was falling harder. The sudden storm was creating an ocean of mud around the Millers' farm. Red dirt and clay mixed in with the gravel to create an oozing mess. Clara shook her head in irritation. Now she would have quite a chore that afternoon, cleaning up her boots, Daisy's hooves and legs, and the buggy's wheels.

As the raindrops continued to fall, she picked up her pace, keeping her eyes to the ground in an effort to dodge the puddles.

"Clara, hold on," Gretta called out. "I've got an umbrella. Come here and get underneath it with me."

"Gladly!"

Once they were under the umbrella, Gretta hooked Clara's arm and started chatting. "I'm so glad to see you. I've been worried about you."

"Why?"

"Once Ruby arrived . . . well, I wondered how you'd take it."

"I haven't seen them together. But it's okay. We're simply friends, you know."

"I know. But still . . ." Her voice drifted off as they reached the covered area in front of the barn's main entrance. After shaking her umbrella, Gretta set it along the wall with the dozen others, then faced Clara again. "I guess we better not talk about Tim anymore."

"There's no need to talk of him at all. Really," Clara said, "Tim means nothing to me."

Gretta narrowed her eyes. "I see."

Clara looked away, realizing that her adamant protests did just the opposite of what she'd intended. Now it seemed like Tim meant a whole lot more to her than ever.

Which was probably the truth.

The barn's vast interior was a fine place to gather. Though, as usual, it was terribly noisy. Scattered about were groups of adults and their children, anxiously catching up on two weeks' worth of news and gossip.

After Gretta walked to her husband's side, Clara walked to some of her students who'd been waving her over. They all hugged her like she was a long lost-friend. One of her first-graders had lost a tooth. Another's cat had a litter of kittens.

As she always did, Clara found herself caught up in their excitement. "Perhaps your mother could bring the kittens at the end of school one day," she offered. "I'd love to see them."

Just as two of the little girls clapped with glee, Anson tapped her on the shoulder. "Teacher, look who I brought to meet you. Ruby Lee."

She barely had time to school her features into polite interest before Ruby was holding out her hand and greeting her.

"Hello," she said in response. "I'm glad to know you."

"*Danke.*" Ruby Lee nodded politely. "I understand you are the schoolteacher."

"I am."

"Anson here says you know his family well."

As Anson looked up at her and grinned, Clara looked at him fondly. "That is true. I went to school with Joshua and Judith, and now I teach Anson, Carrie, and Maggie."

"But Tim's talked of you, too. I'm not quite sure how your paths have crossed as much as they have."

"He's come to my classroom to help some."

Ruby's eyes narrowed, then obviously not seeing any

need to be jealous, her face transformed into a more genuine smile. "Tim has always been *bamhatsich*—kind. That's really nice that he's become your friend."

Ruby had a way of talking that made it sound as if Tim had been feeling sorry for her. Pitying her. Clara was taken aback. "Yes. He is a nice person."

"My community asked me to consider teaching, but I told them I couldn't possibly do that. Not with a wedding to plan."

"You're gettin' married? When?"

Clara was appalled. "Anson, that was rude."

"Oh, I don't mind you asking me about that, Anson," Ruby murmured as a gleam of warmth appeared in her eyes. "Nothing's set yet, but of course Tim and I will be saying our vows soon."

"I didn't realize you two were so close to being married," Clara murmured.

Ruby looked at Clara. "Tim's so shy, I don't think he wanted to tell everyone. But it will happen."

"Congratulations."

"*Danke.*" Ruby looked around with a frown. "Services are about to begin. I best go take my seat near Judith."

Clara stood motionless for a moment, watching her walk away. After a good, long moment, Anson tapped her arm again. "Yes?"

"Lean down," he instructed. When she did, he whispered, "I don't think she's telling the truth."

Ruby Lee definitely seemed more sure of things than Tim. But of course, it wasn't her place to judge. "Let's not worry about that. It's none of our business."

"But, teacher—"

"Let's go sit down, Anson, before we cause a scene."

She looked around. Her mother was already sitting in the first row. Clara had no desire to sit so far up front. With a smile, she scooted next to Miriam and her mother and tried to relax. It was important to listen to God's word and count her blessings.

But it was difficult to do. No matter how hard she tried, all she could think about was Ruby's knowing looks . . . and the news that Tim was most definitely taken.

Gossip being what it was, several other girls were looking her way. Some were even whispering about Ruby.

Clara had no desire to join in the discussions. In fact she was so rattled by Ruby's words that she hoped she wouldn't have to converse with anyone anytime soon.

As she sat with the other women, Clara hoped the day's church service would be the longest one ever.

Chapter 17

There was an uproar in her classroom. *"Kinner!"* Clara called out, clapping her hands for emphasis. *"Kinner*, it is time to take your seats and be quiet."

Like molasses, each student grudgingly went to his or her desk. One by one, they sat. But that was where their obedience ended. No spirals were getting pulled out. Neither were pencils.

She cleared her throat and did her best to look intimidating. *"Shoolahs*, it is time to start our day, yes? Get your desks organized."

After a moment, they complied, but not before staring at each other. Some of the students were grinning, too.

Clara looked from one to the other with a growing sense of concern. Something was going on. Something mighty strange, indeed.

Perhaps it was the rain outside? Maybe it was making

them especially squirrelly. Well, that couldn't be helped. "Let's begin our day." She pointed to the calendar on the back wall. "Now, who would like to tell us today's date and weather?"

But instead of raising their hands, the children only stared at her with expectant eyes. Waiting and watching.

But waiting for what? She had no earthly idea.

Clara looked from one child to the other. What was going on?

Anson finally solved the mystery. "Miss Slabaugh, aren't ya going to ask James if any postcards came to his mailbox on Saturday?"

Clara relaxed. Ah. They were excited about their postcard project. "How many did we receive in the mail on Saturday, James?"

"Four."

"Four? Well, isn't that something. Please bring them up. And, children, let's all gather around our United States map, shall we?"

Far more quickly, the children moved to the other side of the classroom and sat.

Silently, they watched James as he pulled the cards out of a folder and walked to her side. When he handed them to her, his expressive face raged with emotion. She read embarrassment and a bit of excitement there.

A slight sense of foreboding tickled her stomach. What did he know that she didn't?

Her hands curved around the cards. She looked at the first, from Minnesota. That photo showed children playing in the snow. New Hampshire's photo was lovely, with its depiction of the mountains.

South Carolina had a beautiful picture of the beach on the front.

She flipped again. Then almost dropped all the cards into her lap.

There, staring right back at her, were three dancing girls, standing on top of a brightly written *"Nevada."*

Dancing girls! Doing her best to look calm and collected, she eyed them more closely. They wore outfits of red and gold sewn from a sparkly material. Their stomachs were bare, as was much of the rest of their bodies. High heels made their legs look long and lean. Bright red feathers in their pinned-up hair were outlandish and fierce. By all accounts, she should be scandalized.

But it was their expressions that drew her eye. Yes, their faces were painted, but there was a joy in their eyes that made Clara's heart contract a bit.

Privately, she thought she'd never seen more beautiful women.

Nervous laughter drifted through the room as her scholars waited for her to make a comment. All twenty-four pairs of eyes watched her every expression. Never before had she felt so exposed.

Clara scanned the group. James, in particular, looked full of mirth. Yes, he was very much enjoying this bit of embarrassment.

Obviously, they all were expecting her to be shocked and dismayed by the sight of such women.

She was.

But other emotions flew through her as well. Envy and jealousy were also there. Those two painful emotions that she'd ruthlessly pushed away since she was six and had become forever scarred. In spite of her acceptance with her looks, after all this time . . . she still wished she looked different.

Wished she looked different to others as well.

Slowly, she set the postcards down and walked in front of her desk. "*Danke*, James, for collecting these cards for me. It looks like we'll have four new places to mark on our United States map."

Several little girls gasped. Anson's eyes widened. James's eyes narrowed.

But it was little Kathryn who blurted out what had to be in everyone's mind. "But Teacher! Wait! Aren't you gonna say something? Those women had no clothes on!"

Well, she supposed that it would have been too much to hope for a quick and easy end to their discussion about the postcards for the day. Schooling her features as best she could, Clara looked at the scantily clad women up and down. "Hmm. I'm afraid you're mistaken, Kathryn. They do have on clothes."

"But not much." Little Kathryn looked at the other children for support. "Not enough."

Two boys in the back snickered.

Clara sighed. "Well, I suppose we better discuss this, then. James, has everyone already seen the picture?"

Uneasiness flickered in his brown eyes. "Maybe."

"Oh, just tell her the truth, James." Anson rolled his

eyes. "Teacher, he showed it to everyone when they walked in the door today. Even the little ones."

"Ah. I see." She pinned New Hampshire's postcard on the map to gain some time. What should she do?

The kids were definitely waiting for a reaction from her. What did everyone expect of her?

Shock. Anger. Embarrassment. Most likely, their parents were waiting for that as well. Maybe a few would be angry with her. Here, by widening their horizons, she'd brought the children in contact with everything their community tried to protect them from.

Yes, if she tore up that postcard and talked about the evils of dressing with next to no clothes on and painting a face, most likely everyone would be relieved. It was her duty to be a Christian woman. It was her duty to reinforce the rules that their church and their community believed in.

And for every day before, she'd done that.

But as she felt that postcard in her hand, she knew that in this instance, it was something she couldn't do. Even more importantly, she felt that the Lord was giving her an opportunity too . . . to share what lay inside her heart.

"James, what was it about the postcard that you found so appalling?"

After a moment's pause, he chuckled. "The way they look, of course! Those there are terrible women."

Holding up the card, she scanned the photo again, and then turned it so it faced the class. "I'm not so sure these women here would care for that description."

"But—"

"Let's face the truth, James. Do we know they are terrible? Without value?"

"No, but—"

She widened her eyes. "I, for one, don't know them at all."

"You're not supposed to know them!" one of her girls in the front row called out. "Miss Slabaugh, don'tcha see? They're *fancy* women."

Several nodded. "We should throw that postcard away, Miss Slabaugh," Anson said. "We shouldn't be lookin' at pictures like that."

"Is that what your mother said?"

A faint blush colored his cheeks. "No. I mean, she doesn't know about it."

"Ah. Well, when I look at this, I wonder what these women's lives must be like. Very different from ours, yes?"

Hesitantly, a few nodded.

"Let's read the back. Whoever sent the card wrote us a letter. Maybe this will give us some clues about them."

When a few *kinner* leaned forward, she paused. "Or, have you all already read the postcard, too? James, when you showed everyone the photograph, did you take the time to read them the note, too?"

Sheepishly, James shook his head.

"Ah. Well, let's read it now, shall we?

" 'Thank you for writing to our state. Your letter was passed to me from a member of our tourism bureau.

Since I truly love to travel our great country, I asked to write back to you. There are many things to love about Nevada. We have deserts that stretch farther than your eyes can see. We have the Hoover Dam, a marvel of modern machinery. We have the glitter of big cities, where many people come to visit, to experience new things. Perhaps I should have sent you a photo of one of those things.

"However, I thought this particular postcard might capture my home the best. These showgirls are bright and lively, and I've always thought they had a mischievous glint in their eyes. That, to me, suits Nevada, and my city, Las Vegas, to a T. Las Vegas is bright and lively and different . . . and not for everyone. But, perhaps . . . much could be said about other places, too?

"In any case, best of luck on your project. Sincerely, Melody Brock.' "

A roomful of students stared at her in surprise. Mentally, she gave thanks to the pen pal who had taken the time to write. She had given them a golden opportunity to discuss the dangers of judging a book by its cover!

"Ah." Clara cleared her throat. "Well, I have to say that I enjoyed this woman's note. Just like our Sugarcreek, Las Vegas isn't for everyone. But it does sound interesting to me. I wouldn't mind getting to learn more about a place filled with so many things that are bright and shiny and new."

Anson winced. "But the girls—"

"We don't know them. Maybe they aren't nice women. But maybe they are. I sure don't want to judge them based on what they're wearing." She winked. "Besides, something tells me that they don't wear these fancy costumes all day."

"But—"

"Anson, they are not Amish. That, I know. They have different values. But we can't hold it against them. That wouldn't be very Christian, now, would it?" Choosing her next words carefully, she continued: "Don't you all ever wish the *Englischers* who see us in our buggies or in our shops would care to get to know us better? Some outsiders think we are none too smart."

"I'm smart!"

"*Jah*, that is true, Kathleen. You are smart, indeed. All of you are. And you are smart enough to know that it's not right to judge a person by only outward looks. Sometimes when you do that, you miss out on a lot."

Stunned silence met her. She hoped she'd given them a lot to think about. Oh, her heart was sure thinking about other things, too. How she wished that some of the men in her community would one day overlook her scars and see the rest of her.

That the people who were blessed with pretty skin and lovely limbs wouldn't take them for granted.

But that was all too close to home. Handing the rest of the postcards to one of her eldest students, she said, "Let's read the rest of our mail and pin them up on our map. Then, I think, we had best work on spelling."

James frowned. "My *mamm* won't like you putting up those dancing girls on our wall."

It was too late to second-guess herself. Especially since she'd just presented a mini-lesson about not listening to other people's thoughts about what was good and bad. "Then I guess she won't. But it's time to move on now. Now, who would like to read the postcard from South Carolina?"

As ten hands went up, Clara breathed a sigh of relief. Perhaps this impromptu lesson didn't create much of a disturbance, after all.

Later that day, when she was alone in the classroom, Clara looked at the postcards again. The colorful collection drew her eyes time and again during the day.

She so enjoyed looking at pictures of the mountains and beaches. The photo of the sand dunes in Indiana had been a big surprise.

But her eyes kept sweeping back to the trio of women in red. Now that she was alone, she stared at them.

Instead of pretending not to notice all the skin that was showing, she compared it to her own. She admired their flawless shoulders. The way their right arms were finely muscled and covered in smooth skin.

With the way their cheeks were perfect and lovely.

Quietly, she organized her desk and then went around the room and picked up a few stray pieces of trash.

She fully expected to have a visit from an irate parent very soon. The community had most definitely not hired her to pin up photos of dancing girls on the schoolhouse walls.

And when the children went home and talked about how she hadn't painted the women with scarlet words, why some would not appreciate that at all.

Yes, she was surely about to be in a heap of trouble. But in spite of all that, she had no regrets.

Except, perhaps, the feelings of envy that had flashed over her when she'd first gazed at the trio of beautiful women. Just for a brief moment, she'd wondered what it would feel like to be beautiful . . . both inside and out.

That, of course, wasn't right. No one should ever be that vain. So full of pride or envy.

When she looked at the clock, she'd realized that an hour had already passed. So quickly! For the first time ever, she left her book bag on top of her chair. Already she knew she wasn't going to work that evening.

Only taking her lunch basket and her key, she carefully locked the door and started home. A faint breeze fluttered her dress. The dark clouds overhead warned that rain was on its way.

However, she didn't care. No, right at that moment, she felt free and pleased with herself and just a little bit daring.

She knew from experience that there would be plenty of time for regrets later.

Chapter 18

"I heard about the showgirls," Tim said one week later when their paths crossed in the baked-goods section of the Graber Country Store. His lips twitched. "It must have been some postcard."

"It was," Clara replied as calmly as she could, though her insides were churning. Now that some time had passed, she was imagining the worst about her reputation as a teacher.

To her surprise, so far no one from the community had paid her a visit. But she didn't doubt her decision to pin up that card was a topic of discussion around more than a few of her students' dinner tables.

Though none of the children had come right out and said their parents had been shocked, a few looked distinctly uncomfortable anytime they looked toward the postcard wall. The easiest thing would have been to take the offending card down or flip it over and pretend that it had never arrived—but Clara found she wasn't eager to do that.

No longer did she want to pretend that stifling stereo-types and unfair judgments were good when they were not. It was a step forward in her path to become more confident. She needed to believe in herself, and in her abilities as much as possible. For too long, she'd been standing in the shadows, hoping for others' approval. Those habits were proving to be dangerous.

Now as she stood across from the one man who seemed to see her as a whole person, she willed herself to continue to act as confident as possible.

Pretending interest in a plate of peanut butter cook-ies, she murmured, "I suppose Anson had a lot to say?" She could only imagine how her terribly chatty student had conveyed the discussion to his family over a family dinner.

"Oh, I'd say he did. We now know so much about those dancing girls, if one showed up in Sugarcreek, I imagine we could call her by name."

"I'm sorry." Foreboding flitted through her. "Are you shocked?"

"Not at all."

"I must say I'm surprised about that."

A hint of mischief laced his gaze. "You shouldn't be. Most folks aren't all that prudish, you know. I, for one, am glad you talked about the dangers of judging people by their looks. Anson and Carrie and Caleb were truly impacted by your lesson. I'm most impressed."

Though several people walked by, obviously curious about their discussion, for once Clara didn't mind being the center of attention. Her mind was intent on his words . . . and his feelings about her. "I had hoped most parents wouldn't be mad, but I did expect one or two of them to pay me a visit. Discussing showgirls from Las Vegas is not part of the usual curriculum."

With a sideways glance, Tim turned toward her. "Actually, you might be surprised about the focus of the conversation at our house."

"And what was that?"

"We talked about your feelings, Clara," he said softly. Shifting his weight, he looked her over, as if he was searching for an injury. "No one wants you to be hurt by the unkindness of others. Especially not me."

Why did he say such a thing? Clara knew he was in the store with his sweetheart, Ruby.

Was it just in his nature to be so kind? Or did he have deeper feelings toward her?

"I'm not hurt," she sputtered. "I haven't been for some time." The moment the words were out of her mouth, she wished she could take them right back. Since when had she decided to be so honest?

"I am glad for that."

Her heart skipped a beat. There was something about his warm gaze, the way he always looked at all of her, saw all of her, that made her feel good. Inside and out.

But he was not her man. He was never going to be anything more than her friend. Resolutely, she forced herself to remember that. Taking care to keep her voice light, she murmured, "I have to admit I could have used your support while school was in session. For a time I was hoping to be anywhere else. Twenty-four pairs of young eyes gazing at dancing girls was a circumstance I don't care to repeat."

He chuckled. "I don't think you needed anyone else there at all. You did just fine."

"Only time will tell." She dared to smile . . . and he returned the favor. His warm attention made her want to stand up a little bit straighter. To be more than she ever thought she could be.

Someone coughed in the aisle behind them. Bringing a fresh burst of awareness through her. Of what they must look like.

Oh, but they were cozy, standing close together like gossiping housewives. Taking their time to talk . . . forgetting the other pressing concerns of the day.

But perhaps her apprehension was unfounded.

Around them, other shoppers picked up items and placed them into the Grabers' signature woven baskets. No one seemed to pay them much mind.

No one except for Tim's Ruby. She was standing in a dark green dress across the store—out of speaking distance, but not out of sight. No, she was almost directly across from them, chatting with Judith. Clara blanched when she met the beautiful girl's hazel eyes. Ruby was eyeing her coolly.

And while Judith was chatting to several customers and pointing to a few buildings across the street, Ruby seemed to have eyes for only one thing—Tim. It was terribly obvious that Ruby didn't care for her man to be speaking with Clara.

It was a new sensation for anyone to be looking at

her in that way. As if she was in competition for a beau.

It should be obvious to one and all that Ruby had nothing to worry about with Clara.

Tim turned his head when he saw who had claimed her attention. His lips thinned. "Ah. It looks like Ruby is finished with her shopping list."

Clara couldn't help but notice that he sounded aggrieved. That his tone was less than loverlike. But none of that mattered; not really, anyway. She and Tim had become friends of a sort . . . and she would only embarrass herself further in the community if she neglected to remember that. Pasting a smile on her face, she said, "And how is she liking Sugarcreek?"

"I think she is liking it fine. She is an easygoing type of person."

In Clara's opinion, the looks Ruby was shooting her way didn't seem terribly easygoing. In fact, they verged on irritated. But that was not something she was going to mention. "That is a *gut* quality, don't you think?"

"Perhaps."

Clara was just wondering about his vague response when he turned. His lips curved into a smile when Ruby moved away from the store's counter and approached. "Clara here was just wondering how you were enjoying Sugarcreek," he said.

"I like it," Ruby said simply. "I'm enjoying getting to know Tim's cousins, too. I'm sure he will miss them when we leave."

We leave? Had things changed? It had been her understanding that Ruby was only staying for a short time while Tim would stay far longer. At least until the summer. "Are you two leaving soon?"

Tim shook his head. "No."

"That's not what we talked about last night, Tim," Ruby corrected. Looking almost triumphant, she said, "I'm afraid I filled Tim's ears with so many stories about home that he became homesick. His place is in Indiana. It's where he belongs, of course. He needs to be near his parents and the people who know him best."

"I can imagine that would be the case," Clara said quickly. "For me, it would be hard to leave Sugarcreek. It has everything I have ever thought I wanted." As soon as she said the words, she glanced at Tim, then shyly looked away. Hopefully, he hadn't read her mind. Hopefully, he had no idea that until he had arrived, she'd given up hoping for a husband.

But now she knew that wasn't the case. Now she knew that there was one man who could make her feel like a woman. Like a person who was more than a scarred schoolteacher.

No matter what happened, she'd always be grateful to him for that.

Sympathetically, Ruby looked her over. "You have a lot to be thankful for then, *jah*?"

"Why is that?"

"Well, it is a blessing that leaving Sugarcreek will never be something to worry about. I mean, you have no reason to leave, do you?"

Ruby's words were true. And they'd been guilelessly said. And filled with sweetness.

So why did it feel like there was a certain edge to her words? Against her best efforts to think otherwise, Clara felt hurt. Gritting her teeth, she forced out a pleasant response. "You are correct. I doubt I will ever have a reason to leave."

Tim's lips pursed. "We had better get going. I promised Ruby here I'd take her to some of the shops around town."

Moments later, they left the store. Clara knew she should leave, too. After all, she had been in the store for almost an hour. But unlike Tim and Ruby, she had nowhere special to go to.

The realization filled her with despair. How could it be that she could have lived all her life in one place, yet have no wide circle of friends?

Feeling her eyes prick with unshed tears, she hurried to the counter. It would be best for for her to scurry out of the shop to the sanctity of the fields around her home. Then, outside with nature, she'd feel accepted once again.

"Oh, that girl," Judith said when Clara set her basket on the counter. "She is absolutely the wrong person for Tim."

Gretta joined them. "Oh, I'm so glad to hear you say that," she whispered. "Ruby Lee and her clinging ways bother me."

Clara looked from one girl to the other. "Neither of you think they are a good match?"

Gretta frowned as the three of them watched, beyond the store window, Tim clasp Ruby's elbow as they joined a crowd of boisterous young men clambering down the sidewalk beside them. "Of course not."

Her friend's comment made her spirits lift. But she was too afraid to share her real emotions. Tim was Gretta's family. "They seem . . . happy together."

"Happy? Do you think so?" Judith continued to gaze out the window. "They might be, but I'm not so sure. There's something between them that doesn't ring completely true."

"She is a lovely person," Clara said. "I mean, she's pretty."

"She is," Gretta agreed, "but I don't think a person's looks matter all that much."

Clara knew different. People might say looks didn't matter, but they did. And because of that, and because she was so fond of Timothy, she did her best to stay positive. "I hope they do find peace together," she said just as Mr. Graber approached. "Everyone needs a partner in life."

Gretta held out her hand. "Clara—"

"Ah, Clara," Mr. Graber interrupted with a pleased smile. "Do you have a moment? I wanted to ask you about Monday's lesson."

Judith giggled.

Suddenly, all thoughts of love and friendship dissipated into dreams as a feeling of fierce dread washed over her. "Yes, sir?"

"Do you have a moment to spare now?"

"Of course." She steeled herself to hear his displeasure. Perhaps she deserved it. And this was not a surprise. She had known that there would be consequences.

Leaning on the counter, Mr. Graber said, "I'm curious as to why you didn't hide the postcard."

"At first I thought I might. But then I realized all had already seen the postcard. I decided it would be a worse thing to pretend it didn't happen. Sometimes, difficult things need to be talked about." When his eyes widened, she hastened to explain herself. "That said, I really am sorry if your children were upset—"

Laughter interrupted her apology. "Not at all! I was merely going to ask if those dancing ladies were as flashy as Anson said they were. Are they really wearing feathers in their hair? Red feathers?"

"They are, indeed. Their outfits are like nothing I could have ever imagined."

Across from her, the other girls giggled.

But Mr. Graber patted her arm. "Good for you for reminding them that they shouldn't judge by what's on the outside. That is an important lesson in life, *jah*? All of us need to remember from time to time that the Lord has made us all different for a reason."

"Yes, I agree. Our world would be a terribly boring place if we all were the same."

"Or looked the same. Or thought the same." Pure kindness laced his words. "You are a fine teacher, Miss Slabaugh. I thank you for that."

Clara was stunned. "I . . . I thank you for the compliment."

By this time, Judith had finished ringing up her order. "Here you go, Clara. Twenty-seven dollars, please."

"Oh, yes, here."

As soon as she paid, Clara hurried out to the sidewalk—her mind spinning all the while. Seeing Tim and Ruby had been difficult, but then Judith and Gretta's words had made her feel better about herself.

Then, of course, had come Mr. Graber's compliment. Clara knew she should concentrate on his words the most. After all, being a schoolteacher was what she was most proud of. But the other parts of her . . . the feminine, girlish parts, could only seem to focus on Tim.

Giving up the struggle, she prayed to the One who could help her the most.

Father, give me direction. Am I supposed to only think of being a schoolteacher? Is it wrong to want a friendship with Tim? To covet him? To wish that I had a chance of happiness by his side?

Or, dear Father, have you already given me guidance and I've been too blind to see?

She pondered that one for a moment. Now that would be a difficult thing to realize. That she'd been so wrapped up in her own desires that she hadn't been leaving herself open to the Lord.

Just as she reached her buggy, Clara looked at the sky. Once again, the clouds were darkening. Yet another storm looked to be heading their direction. Clara didn't know if that was a sign of the things to come, or simply a message that she best stop fussing and pick up her pace. All she knew was that she was about to be soaked to the skin.

Chapter 19

Overhead, the clouds were gathering and the wind picked up. As Tim drove his uncle's buggy down the hilly side roads, past a small pond and a thicket of woods, he wondered if they'd make it home before the clouds broke and the rain came. Clicking the reins a bit, he pushed Jim to pick up the pace.

"Tim, perhaps you could slow or stop for a bit," Ruby murmured, interrupting his thoughts. "I think we should talk."

"Now? The rain is coming."

"We won't melt. Plus, at least here we'll get a bit of privacy. We won't get any time alone at your aunt and uncle's house."

She was right. There was no chance for private conversation around all of his cousins. Gently, he slowed the horse and turned right into an empty lot. When Jim was nosing at the tender spring grass, Timothy looked her way. "Is this all right?"

His question had come out a little sharper than he'd intended.

"It's fine. Well, as fine as things could be, I suppose."

"What do you mean by that?"

She crossed her arms across the black apron on her chest. "First of all, you were being mighty friendly with that schoolteacher."

He was tempted to tell her that she had been far less than friendly toward Clara. Though, of course, if he were honest, he knew there was not one single thing she had said that was rude. It was the tone that had overtaken her. "We were merely being neighborly. Is there anything else you wanted to discuss?"

She turned her body so that her knees touched his thigh. "Us, of course."

"Yes?"

"I want to know when you are intending to come back home to Indiana." Before he could reply she tapped her foot. "Next week? Next month?"

"You know I can't come back so soon."

"Whyever not?"

Torn between frustration and confusion—he really had thought she'd understood the time frame—he said, "I've told you, I canna leave until my uncle Frank says he no longer needs me. I promised I'd stay through spring and summer at the very least."

"That is too long, Timothy."

"It can't be helped. I can't go back on my promise."

"But what about us? What about our promises to each other?"

"Ruby, the only promises we made to each other involved this separation. We said we were going to give each other some space."

"I said those things before you were gone forever. Now I want you back." Reaching for his hand, her expression softened. "I've been missing you."

Her touch wasn't soothing. Instead, it felt clingy and possessive. "I've missed you, too."

"Then don't you think you should come back now? Come back with me when I go? We could tell everyone that we didn't want to be apart any longer."

"No."

She blinked. He knew she was at a loss for words. He knew she wasn't happy with what he was saying. But it couldn't be helped. Sometimes it didn't matter what a person wanted. All that mattered was what a person could do.

He would have thought she knew this. He would have thought that she would have tried to see his point of view. "You knew I was going to live here. It's not a surprise. Besides, we even mentioned we'd try to open our eyes to other people. And other relationships." Ironically, that had mainly been for her benefit, since she was two years younger than he.

She jerked her hand away. "Is that what you've been doing, Timothy? Seeing other people?"

"No."

Hazel eyes flashed. "I think differently."

Warning bells went off in his head just as the clouds broke and pelted the roof of the buggy. Jim neighed a bit and stomped his right hoof as lightning cracked over their heads. "Who do you think I would be seeing?"

"That teacher, of course."

"Clara?"

"Of course that's who I mean." With a sigh, she scooted a bit to her right, giving them space. Giving her the ability to glare at him.

"Clara and I are friends. Nothing more."

"It seems like there is much more going on. You and she went walking the night before I came."

Tim didn't care for the way she was making the most innocent visits seem like things to be ashamed of. "And what do you think is wrong with that?"

"Everything. You and I have an understanding. You need to stop having anything to do with her or else you're going to have to let me go. There's other men in our town, too, you know."

"I see." Tim almost welcomed the ultimatum. He didn't care to be lectured. He didn't care to be forced to do things he wasn't ready to do.

And he certainly didn't care to have his relationship with Clara analyzed. Especially when he had a suspicion that there was much truth to Ruby's words. Ever since he'd first met Clara, he'd felt a strong connection to her. He hadn't been able to ignore it anymore than he'd been able to ignore the rain falling from the sky.

Now, as that rain was coming down even harder, soaking the roads, he felt almost peaceful. A decision had been made. "I think it would be best if you left."

"So you can be with her?" she snapped.

Instead of matching her tone, he shook his head wearily. "I don't know. But I do know we should stop writing to each other. I do know that we each need to move on."

"I can't believe you're treating me this way."

Feeling helpless, he reached out for her hand. "I don't want to hurt you, Ruby. But I don't want to hurt you one day in the future, either. And it's become obvious we won't suit."

"Once you get home, everything will be like it used to."

"I don't think so. Maybe I've changed. Maybe I've changed too much. But we can't go back to how things used to be."

Tears pooled in her eyes. "This isn't what I thought was going to happen."

"I know. And I'm sorry." Quietly he added, "But you know that all our arguing can't be good."

"And you don't think we'll get better?"

He shook his head sadly. "No. I don't want to fight with you, Ruby. And I don't like making you sad. But I'm not going to change my mind . . . or my heart."

For more than a few seconds, she stared at him, then she finally nodded. "All right. If we can find out the train schedule, I'll make plans to go back as soon as possible."

Two tears ran down her cheeks. He felt terrible. The last thing he'd ever want to do was make her cry. But her tears were not enough to take back everything he'd just said. "If you would like, I can ask Caleb or Anson to take us to their neighbors, the Allens. They're English.

We can call the station from their house . . . or use the Internet."

"Very well." And with that, she faced the front of the buggy, obviously waiting for him to take her back to the house.

He complied. Jim clopped along the road and the rain poured around him, and Tim knew things between him and Ruby were over.

The moment he stopped, she hopped out of the buggy and hurried into the house—just as if the rain would make her melt after all.

Feeling like a failure, he watched her go. Surely there had been a better way to break things off. A way to honestly discuss what was lacking in their relationship. He wished he'd had the knowledge to handle things better.

Slowly, he got out of the buggy and walked Jim into the barn. Rain splattered on his hat and the already muddy ground sloshed under his boots. Next to him, the horse neighed his irritation with the weather, with the mud on his hooves. Tim had a feeling Jim was complaining about the whole wet, muddy, miserable situation they were in.

Patting the soggy horse on the rump, he smiled grimly. "I feel the same way, horse. I feel exactly the same way."

The moment Clara walked in the door, she immediately sensed something different in the air. The rooms were darker than normal. None of the candles that her mother liked to burn were flickering. "Mother?" she called out nervously. "Mamm, are you here?"

"I'm in here. In my bedroom."

Clara rushed in, thinking all the while that things were mighty irregular. Though her mother was prone to relaxing on the couch, never did she stay in bed all day.

That is, unless she was terribly ill. "Are you sick?" she asked, then stood in silence when she saw how pale her mother was. "What happened?"

"I don't know," she said helplessly. "I woke up feeling out of sorts, then things seemed to get worse. My head and my stomach hurt. I've gotten a sore throat, too."

"But you never said anything when I stopped in to tell you goodbye this morning."

"I had thought I'd get better, but instead I feel worse. Today was a bad day. I feel so dizzy, all I want to do is sleep."

Clara worried her bottom lip. For years, her mother had suffered from declining health. The doctors who had treated her never seemed to find anything specific wrong. Because of that diagnosis, she'd gotten into the habit of imagining that very little was actually wrong with her mother . . . beyond a constant state of depression.

This seemed different, though. "Mamm, if you feel dizzy and sleepy, then you should try to rest." After helping her mother smooth the sheets around her, Clara put the kettle on. But by the time the water had boiled, her mother was fast asleep.

Still reeling from the conversation she'd had with Tim and Ruby, Clara was too restless to begin preparations for supper.

Feeling at odds, she picked up the checkbook and few bills that her mother had obviously been trying to pay sometime that day.

Though she'd always done her best to bring home a paycheck, the finances were the one area of their life where her mother had always been in charge.

Clara had always appreciated that. But now, she thought it was perhaps time to take on that responsibility as well.

Sipping the chamomile, she opened the ledger and pulled out a pen.

First she paid the mortgage, then a few other minor expenses. After entering the totals, she became curious as to how the bills compared to the years before. She flipped through the book, eyeing her mother's neat handwriting and skimming over assorted entries.

Something felt a little off. Just as Clara was trying to figure out just what was wrong, she spied a plain brown envelope peeking out of her mother's things. The flap was open, and inside was another savings book.

One she'd never seen before.

Clara pulled out a pencil, and attacked the numbers again. Flipped to their saving account, just to make sure of things.

But what she read caused her eyes to widen. No, this couldn't be right. She flipped back through more pages. Found a bank statement and carefully unfolded it.

And felt her heart sink.

Her father had left them very well off, financially. They were very far from being the poor pair of women Clara had always imagined they'd been.

No, that wasn't putting it correctly. They were far from the poor pair of women her mother had always told her they were. For the last five years, her mother had lied to her. Lied to her about everything.

Her father had left her money. There also had been funds set aside in case she'd needed another operation. She could have been hiring someone to help with the cleaning once or twice a week, when things at school were especially hectic.

She could have felt more secure about nearly everything. Like she had options.

When she could have been free to pursue her dreams . . . free to think about a life without people staring at her . . . she'd been confined by lies.

Her mind raced. Minutes ticked by. And then there was only one thing to do, she realized as she slowly closed the ledger and put everything away.

It was time to begin anew.

Chapter 20

"Ruby, I can take you to the train station, if you would like," Lilly offered after clicking on a number of screens on her computer and showing Ruby and Tim when the next trains to Indiana were going to leave. "It's a pretty long ways from here."

"Thank you," she said coolly. "I would be most grateful."

Warily, Lilly glanced toward Tim, but there was no help there. His face looked carefully blank. She cleared her throat as she moved her mouse around and clicked on another screen. "So, it says here that there are seats available on the train leaving tonight, as well as the one leaving tomorrow morning at ten A.M. Which time do you prefer?"

Ruby stepped in front of Tim to get a better look. "Do we have time to make this evening's train?"

Careful to keep her face expressionless—because,

really, Tim Graber looked like he was about to lose his temper at any moment—Lilly said slowly, "It leaves in two and a half hours. We'd need to leave in about an hour for you to make it. That seems too soon."

"I don't think so at all. Lilly, please book that train. I don't have much to get ready at all."

Tim scowled. "Ruby, I wish you would be more reasonable. There is no reason for you to get on this train and travel all night."

"I am being reasonable. I'd prefer to leave as soon as possible, I think."

"Your family would never forgive me if I let you travel alone at night."

"Luckily for you, it's not your choice, is it?"

Lilly was tempted to slink out of the room. She hated the idea of getting in the middle of a couple's argument. Though, she supposed she had no choice. Both Ruby and Tim seemed to be wrapped up in their own world, and at the moment, it was a pretty ugly one.

Not that they seemed to care, but if Lilly had to go drive to the train station in an hour, she was going to need some time to get organized, too. "What do we do? We need to decide."

"She'll go tomorrow."

Warily, Lilly looked to Ruby. She looked mad and extremely irritated, but after a few increasingly long seconds . . . she nodded. "That will be fine."

"Can you book her a ticket?" Tim asked.

"I can." With a few more clicks, she was able to write in Ruby's name, enter her destination, and with a credit card, she booked the ticket. Tim had already offered to reimburse her with cash. "Ruby, you're all set."

"Thank you for doing that."

"You're welcome," Lilly said as Ruby walked out of her kitchen and through the back door without a backward glance. "Wow," she murmured to herself. That girl was mad!

As they both watched Ruby trot down the Allens' driveway then dart through the hedge, Tim sighed. "I'm sorry you had to witness our fight. Ruby is upset with me—though I guess you noticed that."

"I had an idea things weren't all roses," Lilly said. Talk about an understatement!

Still looking out the window, Tim grimaced. "I suppose I could have handled this better, but I'm not really sure how I could have."

Since she was practically involved, anyway, Lilly looked him over. His face looked set in stone, his shoulders tight. Obviously he was expending an enormous amount of energy in order to keep all his feelings to himself.

And though they didn't know each other well, and his business certainly wasn't hers . . . she spoke. "I broke up with my boyfriend a while back. No matter how good the reason is, breakups are hard."

"I'm not really even sure what happened."

Lilly had seen Ruby's face. That girl had been mad enough to hold a grudge for years. There was no going back from that! "Trust me, you two are done."

For a moment, he looked taken aback, then he slowly

smiled. "I imagine you are right." He glanced toward her kitchen door. "It all just seemed to happen so quickly. All I told Ruby was that I needed to stay here at least until fall."

"That's it?"

"Well, there's a little bit more." He scratched his chin. "I said that I liked being friends with Clara."

She knew who Clara was, of course. The gal had risen in her estimation ever since Anson had come over and spent a whole evening recounting the Las Vegas postcard, and her warnings against judging people by their face value. "I don't really know her—I've only met her once by the creek—but I think she's pretty great."

"You do?"

Lilly shrugged. "She's impressive. At least to me. She's got a good job, she's not afraid to say what's on her mind—and I think she's pretty. Tim, it's not my business, but maybe all this was meant to be."

"Being here and meeting Clara and pushing Ruby away?"

"Yes."

"I've been thinking the same thing," he said quietly. "But how do I say those things to her? I asked Ruby to visit and now . . ."

"You'll find a way. And maybe it won't be all that hard," she said gently. "I'm no expert on love, but I am discovering that sometimes the best thing to do is to ignore what everyone else thinks and concentrate on what you want."

"I imagine you might be right."

196 • *Shelley Shepard Gray*

Lilly smiled his way as he said goodbye and slowly walked out her kitchen door. Boy, was she glad she wasn't a Graber tonight. She had a feeling that house was going to be filled with ugly tension.

And someone was going to finally lose their temper. She wondered who would blow first.

"Would you bring me some water?" Clara's mom called out. "I'm terribly thirsty."

In a daze, Clara obediently picked up the container she kept in the refrigerator and poured a glass. Only when water splattered along the counter did she realize her hands were shaking.

Being lied to for years had something to do with that, she supposed.

Trying again, she filled the glass, then mopped up the spill on the counter with a dishcloth. And tried to get her bearings.

"Clara? Did you hear me? Are you coming?"

"I did," she replied, feeling as if each word had to be pried from her lips. "I'll be right there."

She couldn't help but let her gaze stray back to the ledger again. The source of truth. Or the hiding place for all those lies.

Resentment fueled her feet as she carried the glass into her mother's room. Where she lay reclining on the bed. Almost looking worse. Almost.

"Ah. I was beginning to think you'd forgotten about me," she said as she reached for the glass. After taking one careful sip, she set it on the bedside table and eyed Clara. "What have you been doing since you got home?"

"I've been keeping busy," she replied. "I decided to help you pay some bills."

Nothing but a vague interest filled her mother's gaze. "That wasn't necessary, Clara. Paying bills is the least I can do for our household. When I feel better tomorrow I'll get to them."

Clara agreed. It was the absolute least she could do. Resentment and anger, fueled by hurt and righteousness, rose within her. Though a tiny voice inside warned her to mind her tongue, Clara found she was tired of listening. Tired of trying to be good. As good as everyone wanted her to be.

"I'm glad I did take the time to look over things." With a slow, meaningful look she added, "I was even able to examine our savings account."

"Ah." Her mother shifted, looking a little uncomfortable.

Clara reached behind her mother and adjusted one of her pillows. "Both of the accounts."

"Both?"

"Mamm, why did you never tell me about the money you had from Daed?"

Her mother's face turned as white as the pillow behind her. "There was no need . . ."

"There was every need. You led me to believe he'd left you—*left us*—with nothing. That wasn't the truth."

Worry flickered in her mother's gray eyes. "It was none of your concern."

"I'm afraid it was." Tired of speaking in circles, Clara folded her arms over her chest and glared. "You've lied to me about that money. You made me think I had no choice in life. That I had no prospects beyond teaching school and living here with you."

"It is a daughter's duty to care for her mother."

"Without ever finding a love of my own? I think not." She shook her head with impatience. "I could have had that surgery."

"It would have been wrong."

"For whom?"

"For you. It would have only been for vanity's sake, and that is a sin, Clara."

"I say you're wrong."

Sitting up a bit, her mother's eyes flashed. "What?"

"I said that you are wrong. I say that surgery wasn't a bad thing. You were wrong to not let me have it."

"You have no idea how many surgeries I sat through, worrying about you. I couldn't do another one."

Her mother's pain was nothing compared to what Clara had to go through. But now that she'd finally spoken what was in her heart, her anger started to dissipate. "I feel sorry for you. I feel sorry that you insisted on keeping me here. I'm going to leave."

"Where in the world would you go, Clara?"

"I'll find a place. I need some time to be on my own. I'm going to take the last year's salary and start my own bank account."

"But how will I manage?"

"I don't know. I guess you'll either have to do more for yourself . . . or accept more help."

"This way you're speaking, this tone . . . the things you are speaking of, they are all bad. Daughter, you are shaming me."

The words stung. What she was doing stung. So much of her being was screaming for her to turn right back around and apologize. To pretend that she'd never seen their bank account. To pretend her own mother had never taken advantage of her.

But for better or worse, she couldn't. It was too late.

And the only thing left to do was to find a new place to live.

Because it was time to start living.

Chapter 21

Clara was in a daze when she left the house. With methodical movements that could only come from years of experience, she got the buggy and Daisy ready to go, and gently motioned her toward town.

The rain had started again. Little drops hit her windshield in angry slaps, mirroring her mood. "It's all right, Daisy," she murmured as they made their way onto the main road and headed toward town. "It's all right. We'll just get through this as best as we can."

Her determination, along with God's grace, had gotten her through many a tough time. She supposed that was how she was able to do her best in front of her students day after day. She knew it was how she'd been able to accept the confines of her mother's needs and expectations.

But Clara knew herself well enough to realize that that determination and single-mindedness had also become a flaw. It was like she'd had a horse's blinders on. She'd become so intent on only focusing on what she thought she had to do, she'd forgotten to look around to see if perhaps there was something else in her future.

As the rain continued to pour and the *Englischer*'s cars continued to slowly drive around her, their curious faces peering at her as they passed, Clara finally gave up the solid control in her life. Little by little, she loosened the strings of her consciousness and allowed someone else in her life. Into her thoughts.

The only being who could truly make a difference. The only one who could make things clearer than the muddy worries she currently had. Her real father. "Father?" she murmured. "What is it you want of me? I'm not so sure anymore. I've held my burdens and tried not to let them weigh me down. I've done my best to accept my responsibilities and to accept the way things are. But now . . . well, but now I'm wondering if maybe they were merely trials that you'd like me to overcome."

The sign signaling the entrance to downtown loomed ahead. She still wasn't sure why she was going to town, or who she intended to see.

All she knew was that she felt as if she was being pushed forward. Guided by powers other than herself.

And after all this time, she was very grateful for that. "Lord, have I failed you? Or did I need to go through these trials, just like Job in order to truly be as one with you?"

No sense of peace wrapped around her. She hadn't really expected it. But she did feel something new. A feeling of courage and hope that had been held at bay for far too long.

And she let those feelings guide her as she parked the buggy under the long overhang outside the Grabers' store.

"We're going to get so wet, we'll be able to wring out our clothes," Gretta called out as she scurried across the parking lot. "I had to run to the post office and got caught in the storm."

"This rain is terrible," Clara agreed as she got out of the buggy. "All the water is making it difficult to get around. Some of the side streets are flooding."

"I heard that the creek is rising, too."

They walked briskly into the store, which was unusually quiet for a Friday afternoon. Joshua was standing at the counter. His eyes lit up when he saw Gretta. "I'm glad you're back," he murmured, kissing her lightly on the cheek.

Clara turned away, lest she get caught staring. Joshua's and Gretta's love for each other was a tangible thing. They both looked so happy to be with each other, seemed to only have eyes for each other, that it seemed almost a shame to be in the same room with them.

"Are you looking for anything special, Clara?" Joshua asked moments later.

"Yes, though I don't know if you can help me with it."

"What is that?"

Caleb appeared out of one of the back storage rooms. As he walked closer, she looked at all of them. "I . . . I need a new place to stay."

Gretta frowned. "Did something happen?"

"It's a long story, but the fact of the matter is that I find I need to live on my own for a bit."

She'd hoped that would be enough said, but instead, Gretta gave her a knowing smile. "Did something happen with you and your mother?"

"*Jah*, but there's other reasons, too," she said quickly. "I hope you don't think this is bad, but it's time I went out on my own."

"Mrs. Miller would probably let you stay in the apartment over her garage," Caleb said. "I heard she was looking for some extra money, but didn't want to rent it to someone sowing their oats." His lips twitched. "Somehow I don't think she'd have to worry about that with you."

"No, she wouldn't. I'll go visit with her now."

"Would you like some company? I could go with you," Gretta offered.

"I'll go with her, if you don't mind, Joshua," Caleb said. "I know Mrs. Miller well."

Joshua nodded. "That's fine."

Gretta reached out a hand. "I hope everything works out."

"I hope so, too."

Caleb walked her down the street. Though each was under the safety of an oversized umbrella, Clara knew the bottom of her dress was going to be wet enough to wring out.

After a short walk of three blocks, they came to a beautiful old white farmhouse on the corner. Everything about it was as neat as a pin.

As was Mrs. Miller. Clara knew the woman, of course, but had never spent much time in her company. They'd never had much in common. Mrs. Miller's children were a good seven or eight years older than Clara, and while Clara's mother was almost completely inactive, Mrs. Miller was the complete opposite. She was constantly organizing quilting bees or charity auctions or helping to baby sit *boppli* in the community.

She smiled broadly when she saw Caleb.

"Aren't you a sight for sore eyes on such a rainy day! Come in, come in!"

"You know Clara Slabaugh, yes?"

"Oh, yes." She looked at her, a bit puzzled. "It's kind of you to pay me a visit."

"It's more than that," Clara said. "Caleb mentioned you might be interested in renting out your apartment over the garage?"

She nodded slowly. "I might. Do you know of someone who needs a room?"

"Me."

"You? But, don't you—"

"She needs a change, Mrs. Miller," Caleb said confidently. "She'd be a perfect tenant, too." Smiling, he said, "No wild parties."

"No, I imagine not." She looked at Clara up and down, then nodded. "Come sit down. We'll have some *kaffi* and talk."

Clara looked at Caleb with worry. "Can you spare the time?"

"Sure. The storms are keeping everyone at home . . .

and well, sometimes it feels like Joshua and Gretta wouldn't mind some time alone," Caleb replied.

Mrs. Miller chuckled. "They are in *lieb*, of course. That's how newlyweds should be. Sit down, you two. We'll sip *kaffi* and have a little snack. I made raspberry bars! You'll each have to try them. They are delicious."

Raspberry bars did sound delicious. So did an understanding ear. With a feeling of hope, Clara took the offered chair. "*Danke*," she murmured. "*Kaffi* and a treat will be most welcome."

Chapter 22

"Anson, it's nice to see you. Would you like some lunch?" Lilly heard her mother say as she entered the kitchen.

"I already ate."

"Well, then, what do you and Ty plan to do today?"

He sighed. "Nothin' much. It's raining again, you know."

"All it ever does is rain," Ty added, his voice thick with irritation. "I can't believe that we finally get a week off of school, but we can't do nothing because the rain is so bad."

Lilly poured herself a glass of juice as her mother did her best to come up with suggestions for the two boys. None of them sounded very exciting, even to her. "Mom, I don't know if putting together a puzzle is exactly what they want to do."

"I don't see how it matters, they can't play outside."

"Why don't you two build a fort in your room?" Lilly

suggested. "Charlie and I used to do that all the time. Go grab some sheets and stuff out of the linen closet and make a hideout. When it's terrific, I'll bring you grilled cheese sandwiches."

Little hoots of excitement erupted from them as they high-fived each other then ran upstairs.

Lilly smiled, feeling pleased with herself. "Now we can have at least thirty minutes of peace and quiet."

Her mom squeezed her shoulder as she reached inside a cupboard and pulled out a pan. "You, my dear, are a blessing. Do you work today?"

"I was supposed to, but Mrs. Kent called me earlier and asked if I minded taking the day off. The weather's so miserable, not too many people are wanting to go out to eat. I told her I was perfectly fine with that."

"All right. So, you're settling back in at the restaurant?"

"I think so."

"Feeling okay?"

"Good enough." It was on the tip of her tongue to talk to her mom about all the new friendships she'd made. How she was feeling like a real part of the community, getting to know her customers, becoming true friends with Miriam and Gretta.

Opening up the fridge, her mother pulled out a soda. She sipped from it with a look of relief before sitting down across from her. "Mom, are you okay?"

"I think so. My stomach's a little queasy, that's all. I must have eaten something that didn't agree with me."

"You went to sleep really early last night, too."

"That's no surprise. Your little brother is wearing me out. I wish he'd sleep past six A.M. at least once a week."

Lilly laughed. "He sure does like to be busy, that's the truth."

"That was a good idea about the fort."

"Thanks. Like I said, Charlie and I used to build those all the time."

A few hours later, after Lilly had gone up to read in her room, her mother peeked her head in. "Have you seen the boys?"

Lilly put her book down. "Aren't they in the living room?"

"No, they got bored with that. Then said they were going to play in the garage for a while, so I pulled the car out. When I checked on them, they were playing four-square. But now they're gone."

"I'll help you look."

"Okay. But, this is strange, Lilly. It's not like them to wander off."

"Sure it is," she retorted. "They're little boys. And Anson and Ty, together, get antsy. I'll go check Ty's room and the basement. Maybe they're just playing hide-and-seek."

Her mother looked doubtful. "Maybe. I'll check the garage again and the rest of the house."

But after another fifteen minutes, there was still no sign of the boys anywhere. "I just don't understand where they could be."

"Maybe we should check to see if Ty's raincoat is here?"

Her mom snapped her fingers. "Good idea."

Lilly followed her mom to the mudroom where they kept all the boots and extra shoes. "Anson's boots are gone. So are Ty's rain boots."

"Maybe they decided to go walk in the rain?"

"It's pouring out."

"I know . . . but you know how silly they can get." Her mom took a deep breath and tried to smile. "I bet you're right. I don't know why I'm worrying so much. I'll just go take a peek outside and call for them."

"I'll do it, Mom. Don't worry. I bet as soon as I call them in for popcorn and hot chocolate, they'll appear in a flash."

But even after calling for Ty and Anson for a good ten minutes, Lilly didn't hear or see a single sign of them.

If anything, the storms escalated during the next thirty minutes. When Lilly came in, her mom looked on the verge of tears. "I'm going to kill those boys!" she said. "Right after I hug them."

"You know what, Mom? I bet they went to Anson's house. They probably didn't even think to let you know. I'll walk over and see. And I'll take my cell phone and call you right away."

"That's a great idea."

Since thunder and lightning had started, Lilly decided to take the car. Mrs. Graber opened the door as soon as she parked in their gravel driveway. "Lilly? Is everything okay?"

She rushed over. "I hope so. Any chance those boys ran over here?"

"Boys?" A line appeared between her brows. "You mean Anson and Ty?"

The slow sinking feeling that had been playing on her emotions grabbed hold of her and held on tight. "Yes. Have you seen them?"

"No."

Briefly Lilly filled Mrs. Graber in on their search.

Stepping back, she waved Lilly inside. As soon as she closed the front door, Maggie and Toby ran over. Mrs. Graber smiled a bit, but only looked distracted. Then Tim joined them.

"What's going on?" he said.

"I came here looking for Ty and Anson."

"But they went to your house to play."

Briefly, Lilly relayed how they'd been making forts, then were in the garage, and then nowhere to be found. "I've been calling outside for them, and my mom has searched every place in the house. So . . . they haven't shown up."

Mrs. Graber shook her head. *"Nee."*

"I better call my mom and let her know. We were both really hoping to see Anson and Ty here."

"Lilly, any luck?" she asked as soon as she answered.

"No. Mom, what do you think we should do?"

"Put Elsa on the phone, would you?"

"She wants to talk to you," Lilly said, handing the phone to Mrs. Graber.

Lilly traded nervous glances with Tim as Mrs. Graber and her mother started naming off places where the boys could have run off to. Then her mother gave a gasp that Lilly and Tim could actually hear through the receiver.

Beside her, Mrs. Graber swallowed hard and closed her eyes.

"What's wrong?" Lilly asked.

Slowly Mrs. Graber looked Lilly's way. "Your mother has just noticed that the fishing poles are gone."

"That probably doesn't mean anything, do you think?" Tim strode to the window. "After all, it's pouring. Surely you don't think they would have gone to the river?"

Lilly fought back a sob. "I'm afraid you don't know those boys. Bad ideas always seem like good ones when they're together."

Mrs. Graber squared her shoulders. "We are going to need some help. Lilly, could you take Tim to the store and bring back Josh? Frank is in Walnut Creek this afternoon. He went with an *Englischer* to discuss carrying some special items for the fall. Gretta will have to mind the store. Then a pair of you will need to go down to the creek. I can't leave Toby and Maggie."

"I'll take Tim to the store right now," Lilly said.

Tim grabbed his coat. "I'm ready."

"Be careful!" Mrs. Graber called out.

"We will," Lilly replied. "And I promise, if we hear any news, my mom will come running over."

Five minutes later, Lilly was directing her car onto the main road toward town, Tim by her side.

Chapter 23

Clara and Caleb had just returned from Mrs. Miller's home and were telling Joshua and Gretta about the apartment when Lilly and Tim came flying into the Grabers' store.

"Tim!" Clara sputtered, then immediately felt her cheeks heat. He spared her a gentle smile for a second before turning to Joshua. "We need you and Caleb," Tim said without preamble. "Now."

Caleb stepped forward as Joshua looked from Tim to Lilly and back to Tim again. "What has happened?" he asked. "What's wrong?"

"Anson and Ty went missing," Tim replied.

"At first we thought they were at each other's houses, but they weren't," Lilly added, her expression grim. "It was my mom who finally noticed that their fishing poles were gone. We think they went to the creek."

Clara's stomach knotted. Just the other day, she'd noticed how swollen and powerful the usually lazy creek had become. The constant rains had transformed the creek into a tiny, violent river.

"I'm afraid everyone's fearing the worst," Tim said. "We need to find them."

Gretta looked frantic. "Maybe you two are wrong. That creek is flooding. With all the rain we've been having, it's a fair dangerous place to be around. Why, everyone knows that. Surely you all don't think the boys would do something so silly . . . do you?"

"I'm afraid so," Lilly said. "Lately, they've been really pushing boundaries and going off without telling anyone. I'm afraid they're down there . . . somewhere."

Gretta shook her head. "But the currents—"

Caleb stepped in. "Nine- and ten-year-olds don't *think*, Gretta. Not about danger. Not about things that could go wrong." Almost sheepishly he added, "I can tell you that from experience."

"Elsa wants you both to come home to help search," Tim said, forcing Joshua and Caleb back on track. "We need you right now."

The tension in the store escalated unbearably. Clara noticed a new resolve in Joshua's eyes as he grabbed his hat and strode toward the door. "Then let's go."

"Wait! I want to come too," Gretta said.

Joshua shook his head. "I'd rather you stayed here. Someone needs to stay and mind the store." When tears filled her eyes, he looked at her in concern. "Will you be all right by yourself?"

Though Clara wanted to join in the search, too, she

understood the logic of Joshua's words. "I could stay with her," Clara volunteered. "We would be fine together."

Gretta shrugged off Joshua's hand. "I'm not afraid of being here, I'm afraid of what you will find. And afraid of how I'll live with myself if I don't do everything I can to help in the search. I want to come." Looking at them all, Gretta squared her shoulders. "Can't we simply close the store?"

"It can be done, you know," Caleb volunteered. "There's no law in our family that says the store must be open six days a week."

They all looked at each other. Clara felt both part of the group and out of the loop. But her concern for Anson, one of her favorite students, overruled everything. "I'd like to try to help, too." Though her voice quavered, she added, "If something is wrong, you'll need as many people out looking as possible."

Tim walked to her side. "We can't fear the worst. Nothing good will come of that."

Clara knew his words were true, but among them all, there was a very real sense of urgency. "Let's decide and quickly."

"Clara's right. We need to leave immediately," Lilly said. "My mom and I already spent too much time searching the house."

With a tender look at his wife, Joshua nodded. "At a time like this, we should only be thinking of one thing . . . family. That's what's most important. If we find the boys soon, I'll come back here. How many can you fit in your car, Lilly?"

She smiled. "Everyone. Come on."

Lilly popped up two more seats in the rear of her SUV. Clara slipped into one of them, right next to Tim. Likely, the seats were made for children, not adults. It was a close fit. Their sides brushing each other was impossible to ignore. "You okay?" he murmured.

When Clara looked into his eyes, she noticed that he, too, was completely aware of how close they were sitting. The heat from their bodies melded together. For a moment, she imagined one day being so close to Tim on purpose. Hugging him. Wrapped in his arms in a powerful embrace.

She shook her head to clear it. "I'm just fine," she said. "I'm so glad to be included, why, I'd have sat on the floor in here."

He smiled at her quip. "I'm glad you came, Clara. I'm glad you're here."

Though there were other concerns, she couldn't help ask about one that was important to her heart. "Is your visitor still here?"

"Ruby? Oh, no. She's gone. We decided to, um, take a break from each other."

There was no time to discuss that, but Clara pocketed the information away with a tiny burst of happiness. Perhaps when things settled down . . . when they found the boys safe and sound, she and Tim could talk about things between them once again.

After everyone buckled up, Lilly turned on her headlights and windshield wipers, then pulled out of the parking lot. Gretta had taped up a hastily printed note saying they would be closed for the day, due to a family emergency.

As soon as she entered the highway, Clara watched as Lilly turned to Joshua, who was sitting in the passenger seat. "In the outside pocket of my purse is my cell phone. Could you give my mom a call? Maybe she has some news."

"Sure." After Joshua opened the flip phone, he got the number from Lilly, punched it in, and waited.

Anxious to hear the latest, everyone in the truck fell silent when he spoke into the receiver. Though Clara was all the way in the back, even she could clearly make out his words.

"Yes, Barbara, we're all here. Have you heard anything?"

They all paused with bated breath until Joshua looked Lilly's way and shook his head. After a few more moments, when he was to saying nothing more than a terse yes or no, he clicked off.

"What did she say?" Lilly asked.

"She called your dad, Lilly. He's on his way home now. She also wanted to know if there was a faster way to get to the creek than the parts behind all our houses." He turned around in his seat. "Does anyone know about that?" he asked the group.

"I wouldn't know the land like you," Lilly said. "Do you know, Josh?"

Josh shook his head. "Not that I can recall. Clara? Caleb?"

"There's not," Caleb said quickly. "If there had been

a way, I would have known about it. Sometimes kids go there to drink or fool around."

"I walk on the road home from school," Clara volunteered. "I'm afraid that creek only is big near our properties. Out of all our houses, I'm guessing the Allens' has the most direct path. We should park there and then walk."

Joshua nodded. "That's what Barbara suggested. So that is what we'll have to do."

"I'm just going to have to get there as soon as I can." Lilly's hands clenched the steering wheel.

A rumble of thunder punctuated her words, reminding all of them of what they were up against—one of the biggest rainstorms in months. The driving rain was treacherous and the impending nightfall was worrisome, too.

When Lilly slammed on her brakes, barely stopping in time at a red light, they all hung on in alarm.

"Be careful, Lilly," Gretta warned. "Don't let your emotions grip you too hard."

"I'll do my best," Lilly stated. "But I can't help it. Ty's out there. And Anson, too. We have to find them. Before . . ."

But even from her place in the back, Clara knew that Lilly's nerves were at a breaking point.

She couldn't find fault with that, though. Clara felt like tears were on the way for her, too.

She thought of how upset she'd been with her mother. How intent she'd been on starting a new life, thinking that an apartment of her own would solve her problems. Clara shook her head in dismay.

What was happening with these boys was a terrible reminder of just what was important in life. Not secrets and pride. It was love of family and being there for each other in thick and thin that mattered.

As the rest of the group talked quietly, planning strategies and attempting to think of other places the boys could have gone, Tim looked at her. "Are you okay?"

"I don't know."

"Why were you at the store?"

"It's a long story. But it has something to do with my mother."

Instead of looking surprised, a slow smile lit his face. "You've had enough, hmm?"

Glad he understood immediately, she nodded. "You could say that. Now my problems and worries all seem so silly, though. I shouldn't have cared so much about myself. I shouldn't have concentrated so much on what I want. On how I think I should be treated. That's a flaw, I think."

"Don't ever act like your feelings don't matter," he murmured. "They count."

His caring tone felt like a welcoming hug. "You always know what to say. How is that? Has that always been the case?"

"No. Usually most people have found me to be too quiet. Ruby always wished I'd share more feelings. But I had a difficult time with that. I never had the words."

"I would never know that you had a difficult time. You seemed to always know the right thing to say to me."

"That's because you're special to me," he murmured.

When she looked at him in surprise, he carefully reached for her right hand and smiled.

She smiled, too, but inside, she was quaking terribly. He was holding her *right* hand. The ugly one.

The hand that most people tried so hard to never look at . . . the hand most people took great pains never to touch. For years, parts of the skin had been numb, as her body had been trying to adjust itself to the healing process and the nerves became stronger.

But at the moment, her right hand felt like the best part of her, cradled in his hand. She felt his strong, callused skin. Felt his warmth and strength.

In fact, she was so completely aware of him, it felt as if the nerves in her hand were the most powerful of all.

They abruptly broke apart when Lilly pulled into her driveway and her mom ran out under the cover of an umbrella. "Come inside."

Lilly shook her head. "We don't have time, Mom. We've wasted too much already."

"Please, come into the garage at least. You need to be prepared for the weather or we'll be worrying about all of you, too."

Reluctantly, they filed out of the SUV and trotted into the garage.

Clara noticed Mrs. Allen's face was ravaged by worry. It looked like it was taking everything she had to even speak with them.

"There's been no news?" Josh asked quietly.

"No." Barb sniffed. "They still haven't returned. I'm scared to death."

Joshua asked, "What about the police? I would have thought they'd be here already."

"They're sending over two officers, but they've asked us to do as much as we can, too. There's been a number of stranded motorists and some power outages, as well as a terrible wreck on the exit ramp of the freeway, with four cars involved.

"The policeman I talked to said we'd most likely have better luck looking in their spots than a group of people who didn't know them," Barbara added. "Plus, he said sometimes scared children won't come to a stranger."

"That makes sense," Josh said. "Let's split into groups. Caleb, you and I will make a team."

"I'll take Clara," said Tim. "We'll search the area near her house."

"There are a few fishing holes toward my home that I think I told Anson about one time." Clara added, shaking her head in frustration. "I'm afraid I once told him they were the best fishing spots."

"This isn't your fault," Lilly said. "None of us could have guessed that the boys would go to the creek when it was so high. Gretta, how about you and I walk a bit in the opposite way?"

"And I'll keep everyone informed as best I can." Barbara reached into a pocket and pulled out a worn tissue. "Please check in within the hour."

"We can do that," Tim said. "Do you have any rain-coats or even plastic garbage sacks?"

"I got some from Elsa," Mrs. Allen said, pointing to the stack of coverings waiting to be donned.

After slipping her feet into an old pair of Elsa's galoshes, Clara pulled a rain slicker over her head and followed Tim, who wore his own boots, his black hat, and a large green trash sack with a hole cut out of the top.

"Please hurry. And please look everywhere," Barb said. "Even . . . even in the water," she sputtered. "Just in case—"

"We will," Josh said. "We will look everywhere until we find them. No matter what."

In front of everyone, Tim reached for her hand. Clara slipped hers in his. And then they were off toward the creek.

They were walking too fast for conversation.

But not so fast that they couldn't do the one thing each of them knew was most important. To pray.

Chapter 24

"Anson! Anson? Ty!" Clara called out. "Ty? Ty Allen? Can you hear me?"

She held her breath, straining her ears to listen for even the smallest sound.

But still, no one answered her calls.

Two hours had passed since they'd begun the search. After the first hour, the downpour had miraculously lessened to a light sprinkle.

In the distance, there was a break in the clouds. A wan ray of sunshine had appeared, seeming to direct them, just like the star in the sky had once guided the wise man so many years ago.

"Ty! Anson!" Tim yelled beside her, his deep voice seeming to shake every tree branch surrounding them and splattering them with water. Startled, a sparrow alighted, squawking in protest at their disturbance.

But still, no boys answered their call.

"I'm beginning to lose hope," Clara confided.

"Don't. We need to stay positive. We will find them."

She appreciated his sentiments, but if she'd learned anything, it was that sometimes life didn't always turned out the way people wanted it to.

And in that case, it was better to be prepared. "But if we don't find them. Or if we find them and they're—"

Tim reached out to her and squeezed her shoulder. "Don't say it," he commanded. "We will find those boys and they will be all right. Think positive, Clara. Please." His voice turned deeper, huskier. "Don't give up. Promise me you won't give up."

There was such a plaintive note in his voice, Clara had no choice but to give him what he asked for. "I promise. I promise I won't lose hope."

"Thank you." With a ragged sigh, he pointed to his right. "Let's move on. I don't think we've tried this direction yet, do you?"

To the right were thick bushes and a myriad of ash trees covered from trunk to limb with thistle-covered vines. On the ground lay a thick blanket of brown leaves and dots of ripe green grass shooting through a few gaps. Had they been there before?

She honestly didn't know. It was all starting to look the same. But she couldn't find any of their footprints, so perhaps that meant they hadn't searched there yet.

Still fighting the dull sense of foreboding inside of her, she shook her head. "I don't think we have, Tim. Let's go."

The soggy ground slurped underfoot as Tim reached

for her hand and they veered right. The clouds above shifted again. Seconds later, the light sprinkles had turned to thick raindrops. She blinked them away as they kissed her skin.

Their coverings had not offered much protection under the pouring rain. Underneath the raincoat, Clara's dress was soaked. The wet leather of her boots rubbed blisters onto her heels.

But still they continued. "How much longer until we check in with the others?" she asked as they walked down a trail.

He pushed up his sleeve. "Twenty minutes." The moment the rain had lessened, he'd pulled the trash bag off his shoulders and had stuffed it in his backpack, claiming the plastic had been too hot and confining. Now, as the rain fell harder, he pulled back out the plastic bag and slipped it over his shoulders.

An hour ago, they'd all gathered along the river's edge and checked in with each other. Lilly had yelled for all of them to meet near the widest section of the creek, where she gathered the reports.

That hadn't taken long, because no one had had any news.

Lilly had called home and told her mom to report their latest news to the police. Then, no one wanting to just sit and wait, they all made arrangements to meet in another hour, this time at the banks of the creek, where the Graber and Slabaugh land met.

Through it all, Clara clung to Tim. He was her support. She dared not say anything to any of the families, but she dearly loved that Anson. He was special to her . . . one of her favorite students, though she knew she wasn't supposed to have favorites. Now, as they stumbled back down their muddy tracks and gazed once again along the shores, Clara peeled her eyes and forced herself to keep her promise to Tim.

Pushed herself to have hope. To remember that it was God who was in charge. And that there was a reason all this had happened. And that He was watching over Ty and Anson far better than any of them could.

Thank you, Lord, she prayed. *Thank you for guiding us. For being with us. For watching over Ty and Anson when we cannot.*

Over and over Clara prayed her simple prayer. As she opened her heart to Him, she felt a little better. It was as if a haze had been lifted from her eyes, and she could see her surroundings more clearly. In a new light—not weighed down by glum thoughts and negativity.

With her fresh perspective, she kept scanning the area. Right and left. Looking for the boys.

Looking for anything that would lead her and Tim to them.

And then her heart jumped. "Tim! Tim, there's a thicket of bushes over to the left, right by that patch of purple wildflowers. Do you see it?"

"I do. What about it?"

"I think there's something different about it." She moved closer. "I think there's something stuck to the branches. Do you see it? Does it look like something shiny is peeking out?"

He squinted. "I don't see anything, let's go look."

Clara smiled at him, grateful that he'd taken her sighting seriously.

Carefully, they approached the spot, both scanning the area intently.

The bushes were prickly. In no time, Tim's makeshift raincoat was ripped and torn. But he hardly seemed to notice as he lifted branches. "I think there is something here," he said.

She leaned closer. So excited to have good news.

But what they uncovered only heightened her worries. There, knotted and caught among the branches, was fishing line. Tied to one end was a red fishing lure— the fishing lure Anson had brought to school one day to show her.

"This is theirs," she said, her voice sounding unnaturally high pitched. "They were here."

He lightly touched the knots and crimps in the plastic line. "They must have tried to get out of the rain and gotten the line caught. This is amazing, Clara. Now we have an idea about where they were. Good job."

"It's not that good. We haven't found them."

"Keep positive, remember?"

Resolutely, she nodded. "I remember."

His steady gaze never left hers. "We should call out to the others and let them know what we found. Would you like to do it? Or shall I?"

She was touched that he'd even offered. But that was the kind of man he was. Giving. Considerate. "I've got a good strong voice. I'll do it."

He squeezed her hand. "Good job."

Facing the others, raising her face into the storm, she yelled. "Hello? Hello, this is Clara! Everyone, we found fishing wire! We think the boys were here."

Twenty seconds later, a voice floated out of the distance. "Location?"

"Near my house. Near the Slabaugh house! And about two hundred feet from the wide gap of the creek."

"Stay there!" the voice demanded. "We're on our way."

As they heard the faint flurry of voices race to join them, Clara turned to Tim. "We will find those boys," she stated. "And they will be okay."

"That's right. God's looking out for them. He's holding them until we can get there."

Buoyed by his statement, she smiled, then called out again. "Ty? Anson? Can you hear me?"

Tim joined, yelling the boys' names every few seconds. But no one replied.

Until her mother did. "Clara? Clara Slabaugh? What in the world are you doing, walking outside in the rain?"

"Ty? Ty? Anson!"

Lilly knew her voice was getting hoarse from yelling so much. Together, she and Gretta had made wide circles around her house, and then did the same thing with the Grabers' home. Now they were heading back toward her house for a quick break. Gretta needed to use the bathroom and Lilly wanted to check on her mom. The last time they'd talked, her mom sounded scared to death.

When her phone rang, Lilly answered her mother's call eagerly, then felt the world spin around her as she processed the news. "That was Kasey, our policeman friend. He said that Clara and Tim found some fishing wire."

Gretta frowned. "But nothing else?"

"He didn't say, but I don't think so."

A tear fell from Gretta's eyes and mixed in with the pouring rain. "I'm worried, Lilly. That boy has no fear. He could have jumped in that creek on a dare."

"I'm worried, too. Ty and Anson do stupid things together. They hardly ever think about things like consequences."

"Or worry about making other people worry," Gretta added grimly.

"Or keep us informed. I can't tell you the number of times they've gone to each other's houses without telling our moms where they're running off to."

"At least they'll be together."

"I hope so." Lilly was prevented from saying anything else because a line of four cars pulled into the driveway. "Hello? Hi. What are all of you doing here?" she asked when all the doors started opening and people began piling out.

"Mrs. Kent!" Gretta said. "Mamm! Miriam! What are all you doing here?"

"Where else would we be?" Mrs. Kent said. "As soon as we heard that Anson and Ty were missing, and that people feared they were near the creek, we put a Closed sign on the door and started gathering up everyone we knew."

The front door opened. As she stood in the threshold, her mother stared. Even from where she was, Lilly could see that her eyes were red-rimmed and swollen.

"What's going on?" she asked, looked at Lilly worriedly. "Is something wrong? Do you have bad news?"

"No, Mrs. Allen. We came here to help," Mrs. Kent said as she led the procession inside. "We brought casseroles and thermoses of coffee."

"I packed two boxes of cookies that we had for sale today," Miriam added.

A group of men stood under the front porch. Some were bearded, others clean-shaven. All looked united in their efforts. "We have more rain gear and some walkie-talkies," one said. "I went to a few friends' houses who couldn't get away and got what supplies I could. We're going to go pass them out, and go see what else you need."

As others talked about what they brought, Lilly stared at them all in shock. Everyone had literally dropped everything in their lives in order to lend a hand. Even in the middle of a thunderstorm.

Even Robert had come.

Awareness gripped her as she watched him visit with a few other men. His arms were crossed as he leaned against the wall. Compared to the others, he seemed a little taller, a little more muscled.

A little more attractive, with his neatly trimmed brown beard and blue eyes. Her pulse jumped when she watched him grin at someone's quip. His teeth were brightly white and lit up his face.

Then he looked her way. Those blue eyes caught hers and held on. She couldn't look away.

They hardly knew each other, but he'd come to her house to help. Certainly it was only because of Anson and Ty . . . but part of Lilly felt a connection to him. She knew that he'd also come for her. Knew that she meant something to him . . . even if he wasn't sure quite what. Honestly, she wasn't sure what he meant to her either. But she was certainly glad he was there.

Thank you, she mouthed to him. Not sure if he could read her lips. Not sure if he was actually staring at her.

But just as Mr. Yoder called the group together, Robert looked her way again. *You're welcome*, he mouthed.

As soon as Mr. Yoder divided them into search teams and tersely called out instructions, Robert left with his designated group.

Lilly closed her eyes and prayed for his safety.

"Lilly, Gretta, come out of the rain for a bit," her mother called out, interrupting her reverie. "You can help us make baskets of Styrofoam cups and thermoses. We can deliver them to groups as they get closer."

"But, Mom, we should go back out there, searching. Ty is out there."

"I know that."

"Then you know I can't just stay here. Doing nothing."

Her mother winced at the words. Instantly, Lilly ached to take them back. Her mother hadn't been merely doing nothing. And it was more important than ever that someone was at the house, keeping it as an information base.

"I'm sorry," she blurted. "I didn't mean it like that." Warring emotions churned inside her. She wanted to find Ty, but she didn't want to make her mother cry either.

"We all know what you meant, Lilly." After wiping her face and arms down with a towel, Gretta nodded calmly. "I think this task is a good one. We've been walking in circles without any luck. At least preparing these baskets will feel like I am doing something useful."

There was something to be said about that, Lilly knew. As her mother showed the assembled ladies the kitchen, and where they could deposit purses and rain gear and coats, Mrs. Kent began organizing them all.

Gretta's mother came over and gave her daughter a hug. "Are you okay?"

"I'm fine. Just worried."

"You must take care of yourself. *Jah?*"

"I'm fine, Mamm," she said, though Lilly could have sworn her cheeks blushed a bit. Curious, Lilly looked her way. Gretta kept her head down, but a secret glow seemed to emanate from her.

Over the next half hour, they bagged cookies and granola bars and slipped them into baskets with a thermos of hot coffee and cups.

Nervous chatter echoed off the walls as everyone tried their best to sound positive. To ask about each other's jobs and children. Almost like any other day.

Then the phone rang and all went silent.

Her mom ran to the phone and picked it up. "Hello?" she asked anxiously.

Lilly leaned closer.

Her mom gripped the phone and licked her bottom lip. "Are you sure?"

Her mom sounded so forlorn, so upset, Lilly's heart started to pound. Had they found the boys? With a nervous expression, Gretta turned to her and gripped her hand.

"What . . . what can I . . ." She closed her eyes. "Yes. I see. Thank you. Yes, I'll wait." With a shaking hand, she hung up.

Lilly gripped her arm. "Mom, who was that? What happened?"

In a daze, her mom looked up. "That was the sheriff. They . . . they think they've found Ty's raincoat," she said, before breaking into sobs. "They've called in the canine unit from Berlin. They're going to see if the dogs can help, though it's doubtful because of the rain and the creek."

Her tears ran faster as she looked at Lilly. "I'm so afraid. What . . . what if we've lost him? My baby? Our baby. What are we going to do?"

"Mom you can't think like that. You can't talk like that," Lilly said, feeling stronger than ever before. "We have not lost Ty or Anson. We will find those boys. We will. We have to."

"And we will keep praying," Gretta's mother gently added. "No matter what happens . . . no matter what God has in store for us, we will keep praying."

Gretta hugged her mother tight. "That is *gut* advice, Mamm. Yes, that is what we will continue to do."

Lilly looked at her friend—the girl who had once felt like her enemy—and noticed that she was ghostly pale. Instinctively, she knew Gretta was most likely thinking about losing her little sister Beth.

How sometimes even the most horrible things did actually happen.

"Don't give up," she whispered. "Please, keep praying and don't give up."

Gretta nodded, turned quickly, then sank to the floor in a dead faint.

With a stifled gasp, Gretta's mother ran to her side. As Lilly watched Gretta's mother revive her, she wondered just how much more any of them could take.

Chapter 25

"Clara? Is that you?" her mother called out again through the mist, just minutes after everyone had convened about the fishing wire and then parted to search for more evidence.

"Yes, Mamm," she answered, giving Tim a wry smile as she did so. Only her mother could show up in the middle of a crisis and sound so aggrieved.

Only her mother could make her emotions feel even more off balance.

Another dozen steps brought her mother into view. She was standing a few feet in front of the Slabaugh front porch, glaring at them like a mother hen. "I've been calling and calling for you, daughter. Didn't you hear me?"

By her side, Tim looked at her in sympathy, then cupped her elbow as they slowly made their way up the slippery hill to her home. "We'll get through this," he murmured. "It will be all right."

"*Danke,*" she murmured. When Tim spoke to her that way, when he touched her, Clara felt that his words were true. That everything really was going to be all right.

As soon as they reached the crest of the hill, it was only a short walk to reach her mother under the shelter of their front porch. "Two boys are missing, you know."

"I know, but you should be worried about your own health, too. You should go inside and change clothes. Why you're going to catch your death of cold!"

It was on the tip of Clara's tongue to berate her mother for being so thickheaded. Once again, she was thinking about herself and her needs—not the greater concerns surrounding them.

However, this time, Clara didn't speak of it. Arguing with her mother at a time like this wouldn't make a difference. It wouldn't change her mother's ways.

And in the end, it wouldn't make things better for Anson and Ty. So she pushed a question her mother's way instead. "What are you doing out of bed, Mamm? You've been terribly ill."

"I, too, wanted to help in some way. I wanted to offer our home in case it was needed."

Clara was stunned. Had she really heard that right? "Our home? Th-Th . . . that was kind of you," she stammered.

Almost tentatively, her mother smiled. "It was the least I could do, *jah?*" Before either of them could reply, her mother looked them over and frowned. "Oh, but you two are soaked to the skin. Come inside for a bit and warm up."

"We can't. We are part of the search party. Tim and I only came here to check on you."

"Well, would you at least like some hot tea in a thermos?"

Tim answered. "I would be most grateful for it, Mrs. Slabaugh. Our hot coffee is long gone. We'll stay out here so we don't dirty your floors."

After looking from one of them to the other, her mother finally nodded. "All right. I'll be right back."

As soon as she turned back to the kitchen, Tim reached for Clara's hand.

Clara's instinct was to pull away—she didn't want to risk having her mother see their linked hands—but he held steady, his palm warm and comforting against her own. "I'm staying by your side," he said. "We're going to get through this together."

She knew he was referring to more than just the search for the boys. He was talking about everything. About a future. His belief in her felt like receiving the greatest gift on the darkest day. "Even if you aren't sure what has happened between me and my mother? Even if we don't know what's happening with the boys?"

His lips curved slightly. "Even all those things. Clara, I don't need to know everything. All that matters is that you need me."

Reaching out, she linked her fingers with his other hand. How could something so wonderful be happening in the midst of so much worry and pain? "*Danke*," she murmured.

"No, thank you, too. It's times like this when we truly need all our friends. Yes?"

"*Jah.*" It was truly an incredible thing how her emotions could flare up excitedly, and then plummet in disappointment with each exchange between them. All the time they'd been searching, Clara had noticed a definite change in their actions toward each other. Now they touched more often. Held hands. He said he was glad she was by his side.

But when he said things like that, about how he was glad for the goodness of friends, she wondered if perhaps she'd made too much of those things.

All too soon, her mother returned with a thermos. For a moment, she stopped, obviously startled by the sight of Tim and Clara holding hands. Then she started forward again.

Clara broke away and took the container of hot tea from her. "This will taste good," she murmured.

She was just about to follow Tim when a tentative touch on her shoulder stopped her. "Clara, please forgive me for lying to you about the money. I had my reasons, but they were selfish ones."

The words tore at Clara's insides. She wanted to forgive her mother, and understand her point of view, but now wasn't the time. Her emotions were too raw.

Besides, there was something more vital to concentrate on than hurt feelings. "The boys are missing. Their safety is what's most important. I can't even think about this now."

"But we'll talk later?"

"Yes. Later. When all of this is over. Now, Mamm, we must go."

A crestfallen look shadowed her expression. "I understand." Just as she turned to go, her mother directed a steely-eyed look at Tim. "She is in your care now. Please take care of my Clara."

Clara watched her mother retreat back into the house. She couldn't help but stare at the front door, feeling totally confused.

Tim obviously noticed. "Let her be, Clara," he murmured, gently curving an arm around her shoulders. "What you said was exactly right. There will be ample time for discussion and reflection later."

As they looked into the distance, the horizon hazy from the steady stream of water pouring down, she steeled her resolve. "Well, then, let's go, shall we?"

"Where to? Back to the water's edge, or closer to the woods?"

They had no time to reflect on that before more voices rang out in the distance. "Clara? Tim!"

Without hesitating another moment, they ran from the shelter and back into the elements. The pelting raindrops kept their pace fast. The excited voices kept their hope alive.

When they reached the others, Clara smiled a greeting, then listened intently to the sheriff's latest instructions.

"We've found one of the boy's boots—and a raincoat."

"Whose?" Joshua asked.

"Most likely, Anson's, but it doesn't really matter. We also found two sets of tracks. It looks like they're still together."

"Praise God," one of the ladies in the group said.

"This means that the search is narrowed, but I have to be honest and tell you all that it also means that I'm even more worried." The sheriff looked at each one of them hard. "Time is of the essence. If they've lost a boot, it's because they weren't able to keep it on, or put it back on."

"They could have been swept in the current," Tim murmured.

For a moment, Caleb and Joshua shook their heads in protest, then seeing the sheriff's grim expression, stood stiffly.

"I'm going to move everyone around a bit," the officer said next. "Sometimes viewing an area with fresh eyes helps. So, please listen to where I'm directing you to go."

Tim turned to her. "I bet you could go back to your mother's if you'd like. Or even back to the Allens'. You've been out here for hours. Would you like to go in and keep dry for a bit?" Tim asked gently. "We've now been out here almost three hours."

"Never. As long as the boys are out here, I will be, too. I won't go in until we discover what happened."

Reaching for her hand again, he squeezed gently. "All right."

When a police officer told them to hunt around one of the skinny paths that led into the woods, Clara and Tim accepted gratefully. Any thing was better than standing still.

But as the minutes passed, and they spied nothing except for more debris on the banks of the creek, their burning optimism began to pass.

What if everyone's worst fears came true? What would they do? How would they survive such a loss?

In the distance, the sheriff blew a sharp whistle. It was the signal that yet another hour had passed. And they were losing their race with time.

"Ty? Anson!" Clara called out. "Anson, Ty, can you hear me?"

"Ty! Anson!" Tim blended his voice with Clara's, hoping their combined sound might finally spur a response.

He was becoming bone weary. His throat was sore and his skin now felt like it would never warm up. Beside him, Clara seemed to be shivering uncontrollably. Unable to stop himself, he pulled her into a hug. She needed his warmth, and perhaps she needed his support, as well.

Tim knew he desperately needed Clara's help. He was quickly losing hope and had begun to imagine the worst. Unbidden, his mind was playing tricks on him, imagining the boys' funerals. Imagining the pain they'd all go through as each member of the community tried to come to grips with the fact that they'd lost two of their own.

"Anson? Ty?" he called again.

At first, only the faint snap of twigs sounded as they both strained their ears for any reply. For anything.

But then they heard the faintest of voices. "Tim? Tim is that you?"

Pure joy lit Clara's features as Tim struggled to reply. "Yes! Oh, yes, it's me. I mean, it's Tim. Miss Slabaugh is here, too! Anson, we're so happy to hear your voice. Where are you?"

One second passed. Two. "I'm not sure."

"Keep talking, Anson," Tim encouraged. "Keep talking. Miss Slabaugh and I will come to you."

"She's out looking, too?"

"Everyone's out looking for you," Clara yelled through happy tears. "Child, where are you?"

"In some bushes."

Tim was so relieved, he almost chuckled. Squeezing Clara's hand, he said, "Prepare yourself, I'm going to call out our news!"

"Yell all you want. This is wonderful-*gut* news. The best!"

As loud as he could, he cried, "We hear Anson!! We're in the woods near Clara Slabaugh's house!!"

The woods fairly shook with cheers. Then Clara turned to where she heard the boy. "Anson? Anson say something so I can find you, child."

"Miss Slabaugh? Are you mad?"

"Of course not." As a matter of fact, tears were falling down her cheeks, she was so happy. "Anson, I'm the happiest I can ever remember being. Hearing your voice is a wonderful thing. Please let us find you. Keep talking now."

"I'm so tired!"

His voice was tired and faint. Reedy. It broke her heart. But she didn't dare offer him sympathy. Not until she found him. Not until she knew he was going to be all right. Summoning up her best teacher's voice, she called out again—this time her voice was tough and stern. "Now, don't you even start complaining, Anson Graber. Not when all of us have been walking in circles in the rain. Now you follow directions and keep talking," she ordered. "And I know you can, Anson, so don't tell me that you cannot. You've *never* been too tired to talk."

For a moment, no reply came. Warily she looked toward Tim. Perhaps she'd been too harsh? Then, they heard a thin, cracked voice again. "Ty's hurt."

"Tell me all about it," she coaxed, straining to follow his voice as they stumbled through the brush. "Tell me where he's hurt."

"I think it's his arm, but I'm not sure. It might be his leg. He got hurt bad. We fell into the creek and got carried away by the current. Then Ty and me hugged a tree that got stuck. But then no one found us."

Beside her, Tim darted ahead, scanning the area frantically. When Anson's voice faded again, Tim motioned for Clara to push the boy into speaking again.

"You're fading, Anson! Speak up, now."

"But Miss Slabaugh—"

"Don't you *Miss Slabaugh* me, Anson Graber. And speak up, please. How many times have I told you to speak clearly? Now, you will raise your voice and tell me about Ty."

"All . . . all right."

"Anson?" It was difficult, but she put every ounce of iron she could in her tone. "You will talk to me right now. What has happened to Ty Allen?"

His voice came out stronger. "After . . . after we waited forever, we pushed each other out and crawled here."

Tim rushed forward, looking through the brush. Clara followed on his heels. "And then, child?"

"Um . . . Ty called for help and I did, too. But no one heard us."

"But now we're talking, yes? How's Ty now?"

"He's not doing much of anything now. He's sittin' still and his eyes are closed. Miss Slabaugh, I'm scared."

"I know."

She climbed over a very large log. And then, like the most beautiful birthday present in the world, there they were.

Snuggled like two puppies.

"Oh, Anson! Praise God, we've found you! Hello!"

Tim grinned as he knelt down and helped pull the boy up. When Anson's eyes lit on Clara's, she reached for him.

"Oh, Anson, you are surely a sight for sore eyes."

"You did find me," he said in wonder.

As Tim reached for Ty, she wrapped her arms around the chilled, scared, wonderful, wonderful boy. "I told you, Anson, I'd find you. And I never lie about things like that."

His weak smile lit up her heart.

Ty was unconscious and limp in Tim's arms. "Tim?"

"His heart is beating," he murmured as he pulled off his coat and folded it around the boy.

In the distance, they heard the others approach. Just as Tim had promised, Jesus had been watching out for them. Holding Anson and Ty close until help could arrive.

"Thank you," she whispered. "Thank you, oh, so very much."

And as the sheriff and Joshua and Caleb broke through the brush and ran toward them, Clara was reminded that with God's help, anything truly was possible.

She hugged Anson close and relished the moment.

Chapter 26

"Here's to the best friends a man could ever ask for," Uncle Frank said to the crowd gathered at his home for an impromptu celebration. "I have to tell you all, I know the Lord was with us today. He gave us the eyes and ears and abilities to search for the boys. I am grateful for his grace and for all of your friendships."

"We are blessed today," the bishop said. "Blessed to have each other, English and Amish. This day is one we will all look upon and remember with gladness always."

Tears threatened to prick Tim's eyes as he looked around the home. So much had happened since he'd arrived. And so much had happened over the course of the afternoon—it was difficult to completely take in.

Soon after he'd called out to everyone, the paramedics and police came. Minutes later, other search parties joined them. They had taken care to give each other support as the boys' vitals were taken and the paramedics knelt around Ty.

Little by little, the group moved back as a discussion ensued about Ty's condition. While Anson looked to be suffering from hypothermia, Ty was unconscious. A cut above his hairline confirmed everyone's fears—the boy had a concussion and a broken arm. His parents and Lilly were now by his side at the hospital.

They'd allowed Anson to come home, as long as he'd promised to rest and Elsa made plans to visit their doctor the next day. So, though things were still worrisome, they were much better. Far better than they'd dared hope for all those hours earlier.

Men around Tim shook hands. Women clasped shoulders and hugged Elsa and the other women folk. Clara and Gretta had attempted to wash dishes, but they'd been pushed out of the kitchen by Mrs. Kent and Miriam, who said that Clara and Gretta had done enough for the day.

The girls had stepped aside with grace, though Tim could tell they, too, were uncomfortable with all the fuss being made over them.

Tim was uncomfortable, too. The sheriff had called him and Clara heroes, though Tim knew they were nothing of the sort. All they had done was their best, and that was no different than anyone else who'd been involved for the day. Everyone had hoped and prayed, had gotten soaked to the skin while they'd yelled for the boys and searched through the woods and along the shoreline.

Tim also knew he and Clara had not searched alone. The whole time, he'd felt the Lord with them. Tim knew it had been He who had led them on the path. It had been the Lord's guidance, and their hopes that had led to a very *gut* outcome.

Joshua, now in fresh clothes and his hair still damp from the shower, crossed the room and took a seat beside him. "I hope I never have another day like this," he murmured as he slumped back against the couch. "I don't remember ever having been so scared."

"I feel the same way. I have to admit I wasn't always sure we would have something to celebrate." He held out his hands and felt a slight tremor that refused to go away. "I think my hands are still shaking."

Without a word, Josh held up his hands next to Tim's. His, too, still looked unsteady.

Caleb looked their way. "You two all right?"

"We're fine," Joshua said.

"Then why do you have your hands out in front of you?"

"No reason," Tim replied. "Like your brother said, we're just fine right now."

Later, after Joshua fetched Gretta and took her home, Clara moved to sit next to him. "I'm going to leave in a few minutes, too. I just wanted to tell you goodbye."

He was sorry to see her go. "Do you have to leave so soon?"

"I think so. It's been a long day." With a weary shake of her head, she looked at him and smiled. "A terribly long day."

"Are you all right?" he asked. "We never talked about what happened with you and your mom. We could do that now, if you want."

Clara looked to where her mother was sitting. Tim's eyes followed. To him, the older lady's posture held none of the salt and vinegar that it usually did. Instead, she looked years older and more fragile than ever. "Your *mamm* looks exhausted."

"I imagine she is."

"From the search . . . or from what has been going on between the two of you?"

"That, I cannot answer. Maybe a bit of both." With a shrug, Clara said, "Earlier today, I found out that she's been less than truthful about our money situation. It stunned me, and made me upset."

Treading carefully, he said, "Is it worse than you thought?"

"No, it's far better." Such pain filled her gaze that his stomach clenched. "I'm afraid she's been keeping a whole savings account from me since my father passed away. She's told me for years that my father left us practically nothing. I've been struggling with it. Wondering how my father could have never saved anything. It just seemed so out of character for him."

"And now you realize that he had been thinking of you both. That it wasn't what he'd done at all."

"I feel guilty for even thinking the things I did. But I've felt so trapped by my responsibilities. I've felt so much pressure to work at the school and to do extra sewing projects to help pay for our costs." Her voice lowered. "I even resented them both for it."

"Why would she do something like that?"

"I can only guess it's so I'd never leave."

Tim could only relate her circumstances to what his parents had done. To tell him that they loved him enough to share him with the rest of the family. To let him go. "Her actions don't sound very loving, do they?"

"No. But today's events remind me that I need to stop thinking about my hurts and reach out to her. But it is going to be hard."

"I imagine it will be. Perhaps she has her reasons. It sounds like she's a woman in pain."

"Perhaps." She stood up. "I'm sorry to burden you will all of this. I didn't mean to. I simply came over to tell you good night."

He stood up as well. "I'm glad you did. And, I . . . I want to tell you that I'm very glad we were together today. Side by side. I think we made a wonderful-*gut* team."

She smiled at that. "I do, too. Our teamwork was even more special because we had such a welcome outcome."

He reached for her hand.

Whether by impulse or desire, she took it.

He curved his fingers around hers and squeezed gently. "I want you to know that I meant what I said about me and Ruby. The two of us are done."

"I see."

Did she? She still looked so doubtful. "Ruby and me,

we were like a pair of old shoes. Once, a time ago, we fit just fine. Now, not so much." Looking at their linked fingers, he murmured, "Clara, you might not believe me, but I've grown to care for you."

"As a friend?"

"As much more than that." At the moment, he felt as exposed as he had felt just hours before, when they'd been at the mercy of the storms and the wind. What would she say to that?

Would she even believe him? Maybe she thought he was a fickle sort of person. Leaving Ruby and now turning toward her.

"At times . . . I've felt the same way," she said shyly.

For the first time in what felt like ages, his heart felt hope. After all this time, had he finally found his life's partner?

He hoped so. Yet, Clara didn't look completely at ease. Most likely, it was because there were so many unanswered questions between them. But perhaps that was all right? Perhaps that was enough for now?

"Your words make me very happy. But, I . . . I better go. It's been a long day," said Clara.

"I know it has. We'll both feel better after a good night's sleep. Can I pay a call on you tomorrow? To see how you are doing and to perhaps talk some more?"

"If that's what you want."

"It is. I know what I want now, Clara."

Her eyes widened before turning toward the front door.

The moment she left the room, he leaned against the

back of the couch and breathed deep. Tension left his shoulders and back as he exhaled and reflected on everything that had happened. Together, they'd found the boys.

And they had also trusted each other to share their feelings. Finally, Tim felt as if he was back on the right path.

"Are you ready to talk about things now, Clara?" her mother asked as they slowly made their way home in the buggy.

She wasn't. She was emotionally drained and still turning over Tim's words in her mind. But if her mother was ready to explain, she needed to be ready to listen. "We can talk."

"Do you remember everything that had been going on when your father died?"

"My sisters had just married."

"They'd just married and had chosen to move a distance away. I felt that they'd done it to spite me."

"Mother, their husbands had jobs to keep."

"Yes, but we would both be lying if we didn't mention that they were relieved to be away from me."

"They love you, they just needed space."

"I felt abandoned, just the same. Not long after, your father passed away."

"And you felt abandoned by him, too?"

"I did."

Clara felt that those were selfish feelings. Instead of saying that, she kept her mouth closed.

"I'm sure you remember me being depressed for months."

"I had a difficult time, too, Mamm."

"I know. But, things are different for you."

"How?"

"You've already been through so much. You're a strong woman, Clara. In many ways, I think you're the strongest person in the family."

Clara had never imagined her mother would characterize her in that way. "You think so?"

"Oh, yes. I thought you were so strong, I wanted to lean on you, too. And so I did. At first I didn't mean to become so dependent, but I knew we didn't have the best of relationships. I was afraid if I didn't try to hold on to you, you'd leave."

"You didn't have to lie to me."

"Now I see that. When I first learned of your father's savings, I wasn't so sure. I was afraid if I let you have your surgery, let you move away, gave you options, you'd leave, and then I'd be completely alone."

Anger fumed in Clara. Anger laced with pity. In some ways, the woman sitting beside her seemed like a stranger. How could her own flesh and blood betray her so much?

But another part of her did understand what her mother was saying. She'd been afraid and lonely and without options.

And sometimes when a person is without options, they do unexpected, crazy things.

"I'm not sure what you want me to say, Mamm, other than I forgive you."

"Do you? Do you, really?"

"I hope so. I want to."

And as they slowly rode home, Clara was amazed to realize that she'd spoken the truth. She truly did want to forgive her mother and not hold on to negative, destructive feelings.

And because of that, she knew everything between them was going to be all right.

But as she thought of a future with Timothy, she wasn't so sure. She hadn't thought about the fact that his home was in Indiana, while hers was in Sugarcreek.

How could she leave her mother? Just as importantly, how could she ever ask him to leave his home?

Chapter 27

Tim stopped by her house early the next morning. Amazingly, the sky held no traces of the terrible storm. The air felt crisp and clean. Clara thought it was too bad that the glorious day didn't match her mood.

"You're here early today."

"I couldn't wait any longer to talk to you. About us."

"Oh." Clara closed the door behind her and Tim looked at her quizzically. They walked to a small flower bed where roses would soon be blooming.

"What is wrong?"

"Tim, this is all happening so fast," she ventured. "There's much between us that's unresolved."

"What needs to be resolved? We had a real connection yesterday, Clara. Never in my life had I reached out to someone like I did to you. It was special. I know you felt it, too. And it's been that way from the moment I met you."

"I feel it, but liking someone's company doesn't always mean they should marry."

"What bothering you?"

"All right. For instance, where do you intend to live? I thought you were only in Sugarcreek for a short time."

That brought him up short. "That is true. Indiana is my home."

"I see. So, you would want us to live there."

"Of course. But don't worry, Clara. You'll enjoy it, and they'll enjoy you, too. There are nice people there. And my parents, they're going to love you. They're the best."

Oh, but his exuberance was convincing. But he was also forgetting that she had many responsibilities here in Sugarcreek. "I'm not so sure I would want to start over in Indiana," she said slowly.

"It might be a little difficult for you at first, but in no time, you would be fine. I mean, we have no other option, right? I'm a farmer. I farm my parents' land. They are ready for it to be mine as well."

His words made sense. But moving so far away from Sugarcreek wasn't an option that she felt ready to take. "I have my job here. I'm the schoolteacher."

"You'd want to stop teaching, anyway, when you have *kinner* of your own."

Despite their frank discussion, Clara felt her cheeks heat. "Perhaps."

He flushed, too. "I mean, one day."

Reaching out to him, she gently squeezed his arm. "There's more to consider than just my job. My mother is here in Sugarcreek, too."

"I thought you were ready for a break from her."

A bit of humor lit her dark eyes. "I am ready to stop living with her, that is true. But I'm not ready to remove myself from her life. Not when she needs me."

"I know she's your mother and you love her, but everyone grows up and moves on, don'tcha think? Especially girls. Yes? Isn't that what your two older sisters did?"

"Yes, but just because they did doesn't mean that I can." Clara tried to keep her voice slow and even, but deep down she knew her insides were breaking. More than anything, she wanted to reach for a future with Tim.

But she also knew that the future would never be bright if she ignored other people's needs in order to get what she wanted.

His look of confusion and disappointment hurt. Slowly, she added, "Right now, I'm all my mother has. And she's in poor health. I can't move so far away. What will she do?"

"Maybe she'll have to move in with one of your sisters."

She shrugged. Those were options—but they'd involve both her sisters' and mother's acceptance. Clara just wasn't sure if any of them would agree to that plan.

Tim covered her hand with his. "I don't have the option of asking another sibling to look after my parents. I'm an only child, Clara. If I leave my parents alone, they'll have no one."

She knew that. And understood the implications. "So neither of us can move."

"Would you consider talking to your sisters?"

"I'll try." After years of accepting what she was given, Clara knew it would be hard to push for what she wanted.

"Please try. Clara, don't you see what I'm saying? Don't you hear me? I've fallen in love with you."

I've fallen in love with you.

Clara stared at him, stunned. How many times had she imagined hearing those words? How many times had she ruthlessly squashed those expectations as well? Before Tim had come, she'd given up so many dreams. Now he was laying those hopes before her. All she had to do was reach out and clutch hold of them.

But could she? As she looked into his eyes, she knew the answer . . . as much as it pained her. Not yet.

"Tim," she began softly, "I promise, you are not alone in your feelings. But I cannot let only these fresh feelings of love guide my future. I love other things, too."

Tim looked at her face. Her beautiful full, petal pink cheek, and the hard lines of scars on the right. To him, she was beautiful. To him, she was perfect just the way she was.

He didn't want to change her.

And because of that, he wasn't sure what to do.

Perhaps the tolls of the last few days had finally gotten to him. Perhaps he cared too much, or not enough. But suddenly, Tim knew he was completely, emotionally exhausted. His emotions felt too strong, too fresh, and all of him felt too vulnerable. "Perhaps it would be best if we didn't talk anymore about this right now."

"Tim, there's nothing left to say. We have responsibilities to others. We wouldn't be the people we thought we were if we abandoned them."

She might have made sense. But at the moment, he didn't care. Standing up, he wrapped her in his arms and held her close. "Goodbye, Clara."

She leaned closed to him for a moment, then stepped away. "Goodbye to you, Tim. And thank you for being by my side yesterday."

As he walked back home, Tim knew what he needed. When he saw his uncle, he asked if he could return to Indiana early.

"What's this about?" his uncle asked. "Does it have to do with the search yesterday?"

"No. It's more to do with Clara and me. There's some things I need to sort through. And I feel the need to see my parents again."

"But I thought you were going to stay until fall?"

"I know I promised it. And I intend to keep my promise. Would you mind if I just went home for the weekend? I would feel better staying if I knew they were doing okay without me."

"Yes. Yes, of course, that would be a *gut* idea. We'll book you a ticket right away."

He reached for his wallet. "I'm afraid my funds are a little short. After I get some money out of my savings, I can pay you back . . ."

Onkel Frank pushed his hand away. "Don't even consider that. I'll pay for your ticket, Timothy. It's the least I can do."

It was too much to accept. "That's not necessary."

"I think it is. You found my son, Tim."

"We all did our best. Besides, it was Clara—"

"Oh, I'm grateful for Clara. I'm grateful to everyone who dropped everything and lent us a helping hand. But you are my nephew and I love you like one of my own. I'm happy to help you now. In any case, you've been putting in lots of hours around here. I think you've earned yourself a round-trip ticket to Indiana, at the very least."

"*Danke*. I'm going to go pack my bag."

"You are *willkum*, Tim. But don't forget to give up your problems and worries to the One who is most important in our lives. Putting your faith in the Lord will ensure everything will work out the way it is meant to be." He paused.

Tim was sure he had more to say, but was holding back. "Yes, Onkel?"

"It's nothing. You go on and get ready."

Four hours later, he was on the train. Unfortunately, everything he was going back to paled next to the things he was leaving. The boisterous, noisy, loud cousins. The warm Sugarcreek community.

And a certain shy woman who had more heart and bravery in her soul than any one he'd ever met.

He wished it helped, knowing that someone like her loved him.

Unfortunately, the idea didn't help one bit. He knew he was facing a decision that would change the rest of his life.

Chapter 28

"Tim, what a surprise it was to hear that you were waiting at the station," his father said by way of greeting. "You were not supposed to come back for at least another month."

"I know," he said as he stepped forward. "Coming home was a sudden decision."

Before Tim could say another word, his father engulfed him in a bear hug. "Now don't look so glum, son. I didn't say I wasn't happy to see you! I am, of course. I just am curious as to why you hopped on a train."

After grabbing his suitcase from the baggage cart nearby, Tim answered. "I was anxious to see you and Mamm. I wanted to make sure you two were doing all right."

His father's eyes narrowed. "I see."

Further discussion was impossible until they left the crowded terminal and slowly made their way to the parking area. After walking past several rows of parked cars, a line of buggies and horses stood near a fence and some shade trees.

Though the buggy was black and most looked alike, Tim led the way to their own. There was something about their buggy that he'd know anywhere. It was that familiar.

His father took hold of the reins and then they were on their way. "Care to tell me again what brings you home, son? This time the truth would be nice."

Tim hedged. He was in no hurry to launch into a long discussion about his love life. Not while they were driving. Not when he knew he was going to have to repeat it again to his mother. "Perhaps we should wait until the three of us are together."

"We could. But I think not." The buggy moved along the road. The traffic was light, so light that at times it seemed as if there was no one else around but the two of them. "Let's start with Ruby. You might be surprised to hear that we heard quite a story about your time with her."

"That visit was a difficult one."

His father spared him a sideways glance. "She made it sound like it was a bit worse than that."

"What did she say?"

"Timothy, enough. Talk, son."

"You see . . . it is like this. My feelings for Ruby have changed. You even warned me that that would be the case, Father."

"I remember." Buddy, their horse, approached the stop sign with care, and stood complacently when Tim's father applied the brake for a moment before moving through the intersection. When they sped up to a good pace again, his father eyed him. "There is nothing wrong with following your heart, Tim. It was right for you two to do some thinking."

"It's a relief to hear you say that."

"So, I can understand why Ruby was upset. But still, you have not told me why you are here. It's obviously not because you were in a hurry to make amends."

No, that was definitely not why he had rushed back. He'd left Sugarcreek because he'd needed his parents' help and strength. He needed advice from the two people who knew him best.

Further introspection drew him to realize that he'd been acting like a spoiled child. When Clara hadn't been immediately agreeable to his plans, he'd taken off instead of acting like a man. Instead of working with Clara to see how they could make things better. His actions shamed him.

But not the feelings in his heart.

"The fact is, I've fallen in love."

His father's hands tightened on the reins. Buddy neighed a bit in protest. "Sorry, horse." Then he turned to Tim and frowned. "You're in love already? Again?"

He was smarter now. Instead of throwing out words, he thought about them, putting his heart and mind into his voice. "This thing I had with Ruby, it wasn't love. More likely it was habit. She's a good woman, and I know she will make someone a wonderful-*gut* frau, but she's not for me."

"She thought she was."

"I never told her. I never made her a promise. But, if one looked at my actions, I have to admit that they did seem like they were filled with promises."

"You wrote to each other often."

"We did. At first I was lonely for my life here. And, the truth is, I wanted to love her. I liked my life here. I liked the future I'd imagined."

"It was comfortable, yes?"

"Yes." Though it was the truth, it was still hard to admit. Part of Tim couldn't believe he was even thinking about throwing it all away for a future that was unknown.

"But this other woman, you care for her now?"

"Yes. My feelings for her are far more complex. She gives me peace when I'm by her side. I feel that anything is possible when I'm with her."

"And?"

"And she has a lot of heart. She is . . . unique, Daed." Briefly, he described Clara's childhood trauma to his father. Without any exaggeration—or omissions. He talked about how the scars affected her, and how the flaws made him admire all that much more.

As he talked, his father guided Buddy down the country roads. Every so often, cars zipped by. Every once in a while, another buggy approached going the opposite way. They'd wave hello. And still Tim would talk about Clara.

Little by little, Tim watched the tightness lessen around his dad's thick, work-hardened shoulders and a more thoughtful look appeared in his grayish blue eyes. "She sounds special, Timothy."

"She is," Tim agreed, relaxing a bit, too. "When I look at her, I see everything."

"Now that is something, *jah?* Sometimes seeing 'everything' is a difficult thing to do. It is so much easier to look at only what we want to see."

"That isn't how it is with Clara."

"I hope to meet her soon."

His father's comment surprised him. Tim had thought he would have been upset about his sudden change of heart. He thought he'd receive a lecture about the dangers of falling in love too quickly. But instead of peppering him with questions, his father sat in silence for a bit.

Tim did the same. Buddy was making good time. They'd be home soon. Because he father had suddenly clammed up, he looked at the area and noticed the changes. Along the roadside, trees had filled out. Lilac bushes were blooming, filling the roadside with a delicate scent.

Their neighbors had tulips and daffodils blooming all over their yard.

And then, up around the bend came their farm, the white buildings standing stark and brilliant against the green fields.

Before he knew it, they'd pulled in.

And because they were about to see his mother, Tim turned to his *daed*. "Are you disappointed in me?"

"Not at all."

"But you haven't been asking me questions, or asked

me about my plans for the future with her. You haven't asked me much at all."

"Timothy. Your plans for the future are with Clara, yes?"

"Yes."

"Then she is the one who you should be discussing all this with. Not me. Not your mother."

"But I need advice. I ran home because it's always been the three of us, together. I'm sorry to do it, but I'm afraid I'm going to leave you. I want to live in Sugarcreek, where Clara is happiest. But I can't do this without your blessing."

To his shock, his father chuckled. "Oh, Timothy. Yes, for all of your life, it has been three of us. But it hasn't always been like that for your mother and me. We felt sure that one day you would go off on your own. It's the way of the world, yes?"

"So you think I'm making the right decision? To live with Clara in Sugarcreek?"

"I cannot answer that. That is something you must work out with your Clara. Not your mother and me."

"But you're my parents. And the farm—" He stopped himself, unable to say it. Leaving them felt like a betrayal. After all, who would take care of the farm if he wasn't there? Who would take care of them if he wasn't there?

"The farm is only land, son."

"But it's our home." Tim couldn't understand why he wasn't listening. "It's your home." Plus, they needed him.

"Home, Timothy is where your family is. And if you've found your mate, it is where she and you will be happy.

Together. Now, go on inside and hug your mother while I put up buggy. And let her fuss over you, too."

"Yes, Daed."

"Tim, from the moment the neighbor told me you were at the train station, she's been bustling about, cooking up a storm. Even if you just ate, pretend you're hungry."

In something of a daze, Tim nodded. Hopping out of the buggy, he shouldered his bag and walked into the farmhouse that his mother had been born in.

As his father had described, she was fussing in the kitchen. A pie was on the counter, biscuits were near the oven, and the delicious aroma of cinnamon and apples permeated the air. Her back was to him chopping carrots. "Mamm?"

"Oh, Tim! You are home! I'm so happy." With hardly a backward glance, she put down the knife and hugged him tight.

Though he'd only been gone a few weeks, his mother looked a little older to him. Or maybe it was he who had gotten older. He hugged her back, and kissed her cheek. "I'm happy to see you, too."

She looked him up and down. "You are a sight for sore eyes, you are."

"As are you."

Arms still around him, she leaned back a bit. "You look a bit thinner. You feel thinner, too. Have you been not taking care of yourself? Do they not feed you in Ohio?"

"You know Elsa. She's a wonderful-*gut* cook. They fed me well."

"Maybe. But, perhaps all her cooking was not the same

as mine, hum?" Bustling across the room, she started giving orders as she always did. "Well, wash up and sit down. I'll pour you some iced tea and fix you a plate. While you are eating, you can tell me the cause for this surprise visit."

Tim knew better than to ignore his mother's wishes. As she turned to the bread box and started slicing home-made bread, he walked to the sink. "Well, there's a girl. Named Clara. Clara Slabaugh. She's the schoolteacher. Everyone likes her."

"Including you, I see." His mother smiled as she piled on too much turkey, cheese, and lettuce onto the pieces of bread. "Already, she sounds wonderful-*gut*."

"She is that, Mamm. She is wonderful-*gut*. And more."

He sipped on his tea as she loaded a pile of potato salad and some pickled beets on his plate. When she placed the heaping plate of food in front of him, he groaned. "Mamm. This is too much."

"It's not all that much. Eat, now. Eat and start telling me all about your time with Frank and Elsa. And how you met this Clara."

"I can't do all that and eat at the same time."

"I'll give you five minutes to eat quietly then."

He knew she wasn't joking. After giving thanks, he dug into the sandwich.

Moments later, right on time, she sat down and smiled. "I went and got your father, so he could hear all about this Clara, too. Now you may begin. Start from the beginning. How did you two meet?"

Tim didn't even dare tell his mother that he'd said

a word about Clara on the ride home with his father. One quick glance at his dad said that there would be trouble to pay if he mentioned it. "We met near a creek. A creek that recently flooded and almost took Cousin Anson and his best friend Ty with it."

Over the next hour, he ate and talked and then talked some more. Being with his patient, quiet parents was a soothing balm over his frayed nerves.

As they asked questions, he filled them in on Clara and Frank and Aunt Elsa, and the rest of the family.

"Why don't you come out with me when I go back?"

His mother's eyes widened. "You just got here and you are already ready to return?"

"Maybe."

His father looked at his *mamm* and laughed. "Timothy Graber, I think we should return to Sugarcreek with you and pay Frank and Elsa and all the folks there a visit. If this woman has you so tied up in knots, she must be a terribly fine person indeed."

Pure relief filled him as he realized that once again, his parents were as supportive as he could ever wish for them to be. "Clara is a fine woman. She is one of the best people I know."

His mother reached out her hand to Tim, then gently squeezed it. "Then that is all I need to know, Tim. I do believe you have chosen well."

He knew he had. Now he just hoped he and Clara would be able to overcome all their obstacles and step forward into their future together.

He, for one, was ready. And he couldn't wait to begin.

Chapter 29

All her life, Clara had believed in the power of prayer. Prayer had gotten her through many a difficult time and provided much comfort during some of her darkest hours. She'd prayed for the doctors and nurses before each of her surgeries, and prayed for healing after them.

She'd prayed for patience with her mother, and for joy in her life.

And the Lord, so abundant in his gifts, graced her with many wonderful things in return. She had healed. Her mind worked well, and she'd never lost the use of her right hand, even though at first that had been a concern.

She'd also been given the opportunity to teach. From the moment she'd started at the school, she'd felt that working with children had been her calling. Their accepting attitude of her was a blessing she relished.

Most recently, she'd prayed for the safety of Anson and Ty Allen. The fact that both boys could now be outside playing near the creek again was almost a miracle. At the very least it was evidence to the astounding power of prayer.

And things with her mother, while not good, were not as bad as she'd believed them to be.

Yes, she was a blessed woman. She had much to be happy about. It didn't seem right to ask for more than she was given. To ask the Lord to help her find a solution with Tim. It seemed like she was asking for too much.

So that was why she'd decided it was time to move on. She was going to go ahead and move to Mrs. Miller's garage apartment and at least gain her independence. She needed to do something for herself, no matter what else the future brought.

Her mother hadn't been too happy with Clara's decision, but she had gone along with it.

"I don't understand why Timothy left," her mother murmured as she sat at the kitchen table and watched Clara pack up a few dishes. "I thought you two had found something special together."

"We did. I mean, I think we did," Clara said as she pulled down a bowl and wrapped it in newspaper.

"Then what happened?"

"I'm not sure. There were a lot of obstacles," Clara said evasively. "Maybe there were too many."

"I hope not." As she sipped her coffee, she looked at Clara over the rim. Everything about her posture showed that she was anxiously waiting for Clara to share more information.

Clara turned back to the open cabinet and pulled out a plate. "He is supposed to be coming back soon."

"And will that solve some of the problems?"

"I don't know."

"Clara, I want to listen and try to help you, too."

Turning back to her mother, Clara realized she was telling the truth. Perhaps things between them really were getting better. "One of the difficulties is that Tim's home is in Indiana," she ventured slowly. "Mine is here in Sugarcreek. Neither of us wants to move."

"He is an only child, yes?"

"He is. He wants to farm their land. He loves farming. And getting a prime piece of land is a difficult thing. I don't blame him for wanting that."

"And you? What do you want?"

"To be more independent." As she thought of her postcard lessons, of the recitals she'd organized, of the hugs and pure enjoyment she received from the *kinner*, Clara said, "Also, I don't want to stop teaching. I'm not ready to say goodbye to my students."

"I understand."

"You do?"

"Of course, Clara. I've noticed how your eyes light up when you see your students. I know you wouldn't want to leave them."

"I don't want to move far away from you either," Clara admitted.

Surprise and more than a little bit of wariness flashed over her mother's expression. Slowly she set her mug of coffee down. "After everything we said to each other, after everything that has happened . . . you still think that?"

Crossing the room, Clara took a seat by her mother. "Mamm, I love you. And you've taken care of me through so much. I owe you everything."

"Oh, no you don't. Please don't ever think that," she whispered, her voice stricken.

"Why not? Mamm, I know all my bandages and surgeries weren't easy."

"No it wasn't. But I didn't mind. After all, it was my fault."

Clara blinked "What?"

"I shouldn't have been frying anything that day. Or at the very least, I should have had the pan farther back on the stove." She bent her head and clenched her fists in her lap. "I should have been more watchful in the kitchen."

Clara was stunned. She'd had no idea her mother had ever even imagined such a thing. "Mamm, it was an accident."

"It was, but I didn't handle it well."

"What could you have done?"

"Not panicked. Not thrown water on the fire." Obviously agitated, she stood up and crossed the room. "I can't tell you how many times I've replayed that scene in my mind. Wished and prayed that I had responded to everything better." Turning to Clara again, her voice cracked. "I failed you, and I'm sorry."

"You did not. Mamm, you did the best you could. I've never blamed you."

"I didn't do enough. I should have kept my head and thrown flour." Closing her eyes in shame, she said, "It's my fault you are like this. I can never make it up to you. Never."

Shaking, Clara joined her mother and clasped her forearms. "Mamm, please don't say those things. It's over. It's been over for quite some time."

"I don't think it will ever be."

"It was an accident," she said again. "I promise, I've never blamed you."

"That is because you are such a sweet girl. But others haven't been as kind. Others have assured me that a better mother wouldn't have let such a thing happen to their beautiful daughter."

"Tim thinks I'm pretty now," she blurted. As the words floated between them, Clara stared at her mother. "I don't know why I said that."

Her mother smiled. "Perhaps because his words made you happy?"

Clara couldn't meet her gaze. Yes, Tim's words had made her happy, but they also brought forth a wave of guilt.

"But you've always told me vanity is a sin."

"It is when vanity overtakes the rest of your life. Vanity is a sin when it becomes the only thing one worries about. But I don't believe that being pleased to hear that the man you love finds you lovely is a bad thing. When he shares something so meaningful, it's something to be treasured."

Clara felt like she was talking to a total stranger.

She couldn't ever recall her mother discussing love and courtship with her. Digging deep into her memory, she couldn't even remember overhearing such a conversation take place with her sisters.

But what stood out the most in her mind was her mother's refusal to allow her to have that last surgery. "If you really think all these things, why did you refuse to let me have that last operation with the plastic surgeon? He would have made me better."

"He couldn't promise anything," she murmured.

"Yes, but . . ."

"He had you seeing his work through your wishes instead of the truth. Your father and I knew that surgeon was never going to make you become the woman you had wanted to be. We felt it was better to not let you get your hopes up."

"You never said that."

"Clara, I don't know if you will ever understand what it was like to sit in the hospital waiting room and watch what happened to you. Each one of those operations left you weak. For days—sometimes weeks—you'd cry from the pain of the skin grafts. And each time, the surgeons would promise miracles. That their hands would make you into the girl you once were. But they never did. I was afraid it would be the same."

Clara had few memories of the days after each surgery. Her sister Ruth had once told her that she'd been given lots and lots of pain medication, and that her mother would cry whenever the medicine was too slow to take effect.

Now, as an adult, after worrying for just a few hours about Anson's safety, Clara was starting to have a better idea of what her parents had gone through. But even knowing all that . . . she couldn't help but feel that things could have been handled differently. "I should have had the choice about that last surgery, Mamm."

"I know. My reasons weren't good ones. But my intentions were. You wanted something that could never be, Clara. I didn't want you to get your hopes up."

But Clara could remember her pleading with her mother. Instead of not getting her hopes up, she'd lost all hope. There was a great difference, wasn't there?

"I never knew your reasonings," she whispered. "I thought you didn't want me to look better . . ."

"I never wanted you to be permanently scarred, Clara. You were my beautiful Clara, my youngest daughter." Her mother held both her hands. "You're right. I should have talked to you more. I should have explained myself. But it's not my way." With a helpless shrug, she met Clara's eyes. "Growing up, my parents never wanted me to speak out much. Your father was a good man, but he never encouraged me to spout my opinions either. I guess I got used to keeping everything inside."

"Maybe we could start over?" Clara asked. "Maybe we could both try to talk more?"

With a watery smile, her mother squeezed her hands. "I'd like that."

Feeling vaguely helpless, Clara gave this new way of communicating a try. "Um . . . I don't know what to do now about Tim. I don't want to leave you alone . . .

but I do want a life with him." She gazed down at her hands, not sure how her *mamm* would react to this kind of straightforward talk.

But her mother surprised her.

"I think I might have a solution. After our last conversation, I realized that I'd been intent on keeping you with me. Now I know you need some independence just like any other girl. So I wrote to your sisters and asked if I could live with them."

"What?"

"It's time. Besides, I think helping with the *kinner* is still something I can do. Then you could move back to this house, Clara. If you and Tim marry, he could farm this land."

She felt dizzy. "I don't know . . ."

"I know it's only fifty acres, but perhaps he could still help with Frank and Elsa, too." With a glint of humor, she added, "Something tells me that Joshua and Caleb aren't too eager to walk behind a plow."

"Mamm, I don't know if he'll want to leave his family."

"Even if he doesn't, I think I'll still go. It's time. Seeing Ty and Anson reminded me of just how dear each day is. We shouldn't spend each one in a shroud of self-pity. It's time to become a help instead of a hindrance."

"Do you think Ruth or Patricia will offer you a home?"

"Of course, dear." With a sly little wink, she said, "For all my faults, I certainly know how to use a smidgen of guilt to get what I want. This time, I applied a bit of that to your sisters. Actually, I really gave them little choice."

Clara found herself laughing with her mother. On a day that had started out to be one of her darkest ever, a ray of hope enlightened her way . . . shining more brightly than she'd ever dared to imagine.

Chapter 30

"You came back." Clara watched as Tim first peeked in her schoolhouse door, then seeing only she was there, stepped inside confidently.

He grinned. "I couldn't stay away."

The closer he got, the more her heart seemed to beat in double-time. Yes, she'd hoped he'd return from Indiana soon. And she had hoped that a visit to her would be on his agenda . . . but she hadn't really allowed herself to believe.

Believing in his promise would make her feel as if they were courting. And that was something that she didn't dare hope for.

"If you had hoped to see Anson or Carrie or Maggie, you missed them. The children are all gone for the day," she blurted. Even as she said it, she wondered why she even had. It was obvious that he hadn't come to see the students.

It had always been obvious that he hadn't ever stopped by school in order to see anyone but her.

"I know they're gone. However, I hoped you still would be here," he murmured, taking off his hat and setting it on the desk. Shaking his head slightly, he smiled a crooked grin. "And you are."

Hastily, she moved around her desk so he wouldn't think she was hiding behind it. But once she was standing right in front of him, she went speechless again. His eyes appeared especially golden with the sun streaming in from the open door. He looked as handsome as ever. His white shirt was obviously freshly pressed, and his brown trousers brand new.

He noticed her staring. Waving a hand, he shook his head again. "Sorry. Am I sweaty? It's a warm one out. Summer's almost here."

"No, you're fine. I mean, yes it is." When his eyebrows rose, she became even more flustered. "I mean . . ." By now she had forgotten what she'd even been commenting on. "I mean, it's good to see you. I was just going to write down some problems for the students' morning work."

"Ah."

She felt like a silly fool, standing in front of him. Scurrying over to the blackboard, she picked up the chalk, attempting to busy herself. "This will only take a few minutes. Or, um, I can wait to do my work if there was something you needed."

He looked her over. His lips curved a bit, like he was struggling not to laugh. "I don't mind waiting, Clara. What I need is worth it."

Oh! She turned her back to him and lifted her left hand to the board. Then completely forgot what she'd intended to write. What a ninny she was being. She needed to calm herself. And calm herself quickly.

Her pulse slowed a bit when he turned to the map of the United States, which now had thirty-seven postcards neatly pinned up across it. Seeing he was occupied, she quickly wrote out two math problems and a sentence in English for everyone to copy.

Behind her, he whistled low. "Well, those dancing girls are very bright indeed."

By now she'd become used to them. "Sometime I wish we'd gotten more postcards like that one," she said with a smile, finally summoning up her courage and walking to his side. "Somehow, the Mississippi River or the snow in Minnesota doesn't have the same excitement."

"I imagine not. I'm glad we can laugh about it now."

Remembering how awkward that lesson had been, Clara nodded. "Me too." Picking up her lunch bag, she said, "I'm all done here, if you want to leave. Or, um, talk."

"I want to do both. Care to walk with me by the creek?"

"I would like that."

"Then let's walk together, Clara."

His voice was tender and silky-smooth, warming her insides. Giving her hope. Holding on to that feeling, she moved to his side and let him escort her out the door.

Soon after they'd left the confines of the schoolhouse, he reached for her hand.

Their hands remained linked as they walked slowly away from the school and down the road. Up the hills surrounding the creek, and over a small bridge.

Soon, they were near the creek. By mutual agreement, they stood gazing at the view. "It looks a fair sight different now, doesn't it?" Tim asked.

"Very much so."

Though ten days had passed, the memories of the afternoon they'd searched high and low for Anson and Ty came flooding back, just as if the rain was still drenching their shoulders and the air was thick with worry and fear.

"Remember standing here?" he murmured.

"Oh, yes." It was where they'd walked unsteadily, frantically calling out for Anson and Ty, when all hope seemed to have been lost.

They walked toward the spot where the creek widened. Where three large rocks lay waiting for them.

Where she'd been on the afternoon they'd first met.

"You know, I don't think I'll ever be able to look at this creek without remembering that day."

"It was a scary one," she said. "I was so afraid we wouldn't find the boys."

"That was a special moment. But, I was talking about a different day. The day that we first met."

Ah. She remembered their first meeting as clearly as if it had happened only that morning. "I didn't know who you were. I thought you were teasing me when you asked if I had a sweetheart."

"I wasn't teasing at all. From the moment we talked, I knew I wanted to know you better."

"And . . . we have."

"I am grateful for that."

His words, so kind and loving, painted pretty pictures in her mind. For a brief second, she imagined being part of his life, forever. Of having a lifetime of pretty words.

"Clara, I went home to try to figure out our future. But I was wrong to have done that. My father reminded me that if I want a life with you, it should have been you who I told all my worries. I'm sorry for that."

"I didn't mind. I needed the time, too. Everything between us has felt like this river . . . choppy and full of surprises."

He bent down and ran three fingers through the placid water. "But sometimes it's also peaceful and perfect." He glanced up at her . . . offering a silent invitation.

She looked at him in wonder. Saw the truth in his eyes. Tim Graber did think of their relationship in those terms. As something full of promise.

"My mother and I talked," she murmured as she set her lunch bag down and knelt by his side. "She intends to move in with one of my sisters."

"Truly?"

With a wry smile, she said, "She says it's their turn. I, for one, am inclined to agree."

"Good for you."

"And good for her, too. We finally talked. Really talked. Timothy, I do believe she knows just how difficult it has been, taking care of her."

"What are you going to do?"

"Well . . . it's going to take some time for my mother to relocate, so I thought I might go live at Mrs. Miller's for a bit. She has a room above her garage. I think I might enjoy living in the middle of Sugarcreek, too."

"By yourself?"

"Perhaps." She nibbled her lip as she ran her fingers in the water. It was icy cold. "Living at Mrs. Miller's will be different, but I think it might be nice. After all, Joshua and Gretta have seemed to enjoy living over the store very much."

"I might like living in a place like that, too . . . until I started farming again."

"I don't know if you knew this, but my mother still owns quite a bit of land. Fifty acres."

"That's enough to farm," he said encouragingly. "Especially if someone had other work to do, say with his family's farm, too."

"Would that be something you'd ever want to do?"

"Would you let me?" Getting to his feet, he reached down for her hands and gently tugged. In an instant, she was wrapped in his arms. "Clara, would you marry me and live here in Sugarcreek? In a room at Mrs. Miller's . . . and then together, on your farm?"

This was a moment she'd always dreamed of. His words were so perfect, the setting so beautiful, she was afraid to believe it was happening. Afraid to believe it all couldn't be taken away in a heartbeat.

And so she questioned him, needing to be sure. "You wouldn't mind not going back to Indiana?"

Instead of minding her question, he linked his fingers behind her back and smiled. "I think my destiny lies here. During my visit my parents told me that they were ready to retire. Daed wants to sell the farm and travel some. He could have knocked me down with a feather, I was so surprised. They've never traveled anywhere."

"Perhaps it is time, then."

"When they're done, they want to get a little home in Sugarcreek so they can live near Frank and Elsa. That is, if I'm not going back."

"What about Ruby?" She didn't mean to sound coy, but she wanted everything settled between them.

"Didn't I tell you? She's already seeing someone else. Which is good, because I don't love her. I love you."

There it was. The three words she'd always hoped for, but had never dreamed of hearing. "I love you, too," she murmured.

"So, will you marry me, Clara? Will you be my wife?"

An answer had never been more easy to say. "Yes, Timothy. I will marry you."

"And live here in Sugarcreek with me?" he prodded.

"And I will live here with you."

Then, just when his lips were mere inches from hers, he murmured, "For happily ever after."

He gave her no chance to reply to that, for their lips finally met. Once, then brushed against each other again.

Clara felt his arms curve around her and hold her closer as his kisses became two and then three and then too many to count.

She kissed him back, his love making her feel like the most beautiful woman in the world. Just like a fairy tale.

Or something better. She felt new again. Renewed. Filled with hope and trust and love.

There, on the banks of a little creek right near her home. Right where they first met. Where she'd first dared to believe that dreams truly could come true.

Dear Reader,

Some books are just easier to write than others. Some mornings, I sit in front of my computer screen for an hour and barely get a single page written. Other times, I've had to stop when my fingers hurt because I've been typing so fast. I have to say *Spring's Renewal* was one of my favorite books to write . . . and one of the easiest. The reason is pretty simple . . . I fell in love with Clara.

There was something about Clara that made me dig a little deeper inside of myself in order to tell her story. Of course, I've always had a soft spot for a heroine in need, and for a person who continues on with a positive attitude, no matter what her circumstances.

Perhaps you know people like Clara. People who have quite a few unfulfilled dreams but are determined to make the best of things. People who don't complain but count their blessings. These are the kinds of people who inspire me. Who motivate me to count my blessings too and give thanks for God's grace.

Of course, this work of fiction could never happen without the help of many people. First, thanks to my editor, Cindy DiTiberio, who's given me the opportunity to write about the Amish and is always so kind and encouraging to me. She makes some of my most wordy, convoluted paragraphs actually make sense! I'd also like to thank everyone in the sales team at HarperCollins who do their best to make sure my books get into stores. You all are incredible and I'm so grateful for your enthusiasm.

Once again, I'd like to thank my agent, Mary Sue Seymour, who always listens to my worries like she has all the time in the world. Agents like that are priceless.

Thanks to my husband, Tom, for driving with me to Sugarcreek. And for cooking dinners and running errands so I can write. And for never pointing out that all people I talk about at dinner . . . are actually made up.

And, of course, I owe so much to the *real* Clara. Her patience and wisdom and kindness seem to know no bounds. Thank you, Clara, for letting me ask you dozens of questions . . . and then ask them again.

I love to hear from readers. If you're inclined, please visit my website, or visit me on Facebook! Thank you for picking up my books, for telling your friends about them, and for asking your library to put them on the shelves. I'm forever grateful.

With God's Blessings,

Shelley Shepard Gray

Questions for Discussion

1. Lilly's miscarriage and recovery was an extremely difficult period in her life. After two weeks, her mother finally encourages her to move on and go back to work. Was that what Lilly needed? What has helped you recover during times of grief and loss?

2. Perception of ourselves and how others see us is a key theme in the novel. Clara yearns to be seen as more than a woman who is scarred. She tries to show the dangers of judging others at face value by talking about the women on the Las Vegas postcard. Was this a fair comparison? How do first impressions play a role in our views on other people?

3. Why do you think Tim's relationship with Ruby Lee ultimately failed? Was it mainly one person's fault, or could the break-up not have been prevented?

4. Clara and her mother's relationship is multifaceted and complicated. As layers of lies are revealed, the underlying truth is almost as disheartening as the stories that were perpetrated. How did uncovering the truth help to heal their relationship? How might Clara's life been different if she'd been allowed to have that final operation?

5. Clara discovers that much of her mother's motivations were guided by fear. Fear of being alone, fear of being spurned because of her faults, fear of hurting her daughter further. How does fear play a role in our lives? Or, is it possible, to live fearlessly?

6. Anson's and Ty's disappearance brings the whole community together. Clara and Tim become closer, as do Lilly and Gretta. How do you think periods of stress help strengthen relationships?

7. As the series progresses, Caleb becomes more and more discontented with his life in the Amish community. Are these just normal adolescent feelings . . . or do you think his feelings can be justified?

8. Has Clara grown and changed at all during the novel, or has she simply finally gotten what she really wanted? Does it matter?

9. By the end of the novel, the Grabers and the Allens have forged their friendship. How have deep, meaningful friendships been nurtured in your life? Do all relationships mature over time, or through shared experiences? How can surviving a crisis bring people together? What friendships in your life have weathered a crisis or two?

Coming soon . . .
Book Three in the Seasons of Sugarcreek series

AUTUMN'S
PROMISE

"I'm pregnant," Lilly Allen's mother announced at breakfast. Calm as could be—just as if she was asking for someone to pass the bacon.

Lilly almost choked on her juice as she stared at her mother in shock. "What?"

"You heard me. I'm pregnant," she said again, her voice overly bright. "The doctor said I'm four months along. By Valentine's Day, we're going to have a wonderful new addition to the family."

Ty, all of ten, grinned. "Now I won't be the youngest anymore!"

Their mother laughed. "You sure won't. Now you'll be a big brother. I'm really going to be depending on your help, too." She looked at all of them. "I'm going to need all of your help."

"We already have a crib, don't we?" Ty chirped. "The one we bought for Lilly?"

Her mother's smile faltered. "Yes."

As Ty continued to chatter, Lilly felt her world flip on its side. Her mother was four months along? It was September first, which meant she got pregnant in May.

Right after Lilly had miscarried.

Waves of nausea coursed through her. Warily, Lilly looked her dad's way. He was eating his bowl of corn flakes like he didn't have a care in the world. As Ty kept chattering, she glared at him. "You knew about this, didn't you?"

Slowly, he set his spoon down. "Of course."

Her older brother Charlie scowled. "How come you two waited so long to tell us?"

With a helpless, almost sheepish look, their mom shrugged. "At first I just thought I had the flu. Then, well, I put two and two together."

For the first time in what felt like forever, Lilly stared at her mom. And as she did, she started seeing all the changes that should have been obvious. Her mother's cheeks were fuller, and her usually neatly tucked-in T-shirt was gone. Instead she wore an oversized button-down loosely over a pair of knit pants.

She should have noticed the signs. After all, she'd been in that same condition just a few months earlier.

Beside her, Charlie scowled. "I'm glad I won't be here to deal with it." Tossing his napkin on the table, he turned to her. "Lilly, you should have applied to college. Now you're going to have to take care of it."

"The baby," their father corrected.

"Whatever," Charlie retorted.

As their dad chastised Charlie, Lilly zoned them out. Her brother was right. She was going to be expected to help. It was inevitable.

She couldn't imagine a worse chore. The last thing she could imagine was being around a baby. Right now, it hurt to even see a baby in the grocery store. Or even on TV.

Now she was expected to be excited about living with one?

Abruptly, she stood up. "I've got to go to work."

"Right now?" Her dad looked at his watch. "You've got over an hour before you have to be at the Sugarcreek Inn."

"I told Mrs. Kent I'd come in early," she lied. "I'm, um, already late."

Her father got to his feet as well. "I know this is a shock, but I think once you have time to accept this, you'll see that it's really something to celebrate."

As the words sank in, Lilly looked toward her mom. For a moment, her mother looked vulnerable. Almost fragile.

Lilly knew she should say something to her. Anything.

But she couldn't. As it was, she was struggling to hold herself together. In fact, the only thing that was keeping her from bursting into tears were her nails digging into her palms. "It's not my fault I have to work."

"Please don't leave yet," her mother said, her face pale. "I think we should talk about this. Lilly—"

"There's nothing to talk about."

"Of course there is. I know you're still upset about—"

"Don't," Lilly interrupted, the pain inside of her making her voice hard. Clipped. "Don't mention that. Ever."

"But—"

"Let her go, Barb," her dad said quietly.

Before her mother decided to have some kind of heart-to-heart, Lilly set her plate in the sink, picked up her purse and keys from the kitchen counter, and raced out of the house.

Two minutes later, she was reversing out of her driveway and pulling onto the quiet state road that led to town. She hardly looked around her. The falling leaves in gold and bronze meant nothing. The cooler, crisp air with the hint of pine and apples failed to penetrate her awareness. Only pain surged through her as her eyes welled with tears that began to fall.

When her vision blurred, she pulled into an empty storefront's parking area and collected her thoughts. How could her parents be expecting a baby . . . just months after she'd miscarried her own?

And they'd looked so happy, too. *How could they be happy?* Her mother was forty-five years old! Charlie was twenty-one. Nobody had a baby when they had a twenty-one-year-old.

Except her parents.

Putting the car in park, she covered her face with her hands and breathed in and out slowly. She had to get a handle on herself. There was no way she could function if she didn't.

The knock on her window made her jump.

"You okay?" the Amish man said, looking through the glass at her and frowning.

Lilly nearly jumped out of her skin when she saw who is was. *Robert Miller.*

Robert, who came to the Sugarcreek Inn on a regular basis and always sat at her station. Who hadn't said
more than a handful of words to her the first five times
he came to the restaurant.

Who knew she'd had a miscarriage and had asked if
she was all right.

Who had volunteered to help look for her brother
during a horrible storm this past April.

And there he was, standing outside her door, just like
he wandered around Sugarcreek and looked in car windows all the time.

As his blue eyes continued to examine her, she nodded.
Perhaps then he would go away.

She wasn't that lucky.

He stood there, strong and still. Waiting for her to roll
the window down.

She did one better and got out of the car. Though she
knew any mascara she had on had long since washed
away, she looked at him directly and smiled. "Hi,
Robert."

"Are you all right? You've been sitting in here cryin'
for a good ten minutes."

"Has it been that long?" she murmured, not really
expecting an answer. There was no way she was going
to tell him about the latest development in her crazy,
mixed-up life. She hardly knew him.

Lilly decided to ask a question of her own instead.
"Why are you here?"

His face didn't even crack a smile. "You answer my
question first. Pulling over and crying is no good."

"I know. I'm just upset about something."

"Well, I can see that." He stepped closer. For a moment, she thought he was going to reach out and touch her arm. But he didn't. Instead, he folded his arms across his chest—mimicking hers—and murmured, "Sometimes talking about it helps."

"Talking won't help this problem."

"You sure?"

"Positive. It's something to do with my family."

Alarm entered his eyes. "Is someone sick?"

Lilly remembered hearing that Robert Miller had lost his wife to cancer a few years back. "No, everyone's healthy." She tried to smile. "It's just something to do with me, really. And I'll get over it. Now, why are you here?"

"This is my shop." He looked at her curiously—and with a hint of disappointment? "I thought you knew that."

Looking at the plain wooden building, decorated only by a beautifully carved sign, Miller Carpentry, Lilly shook her head. Honestly, she'd never noticed it before. And besides, Miller was a common name in Sugarcreek. It was common anywhere, actually. She wouldn't have had any reason to guess it belonged to him. "It looks nice."

"*Danke.* Me and my cousin started it four years ago, in honor of my twenty-first birthday. It's going good."

So he was twenty-five. She'd thought he was older.

For a split second their eyes met. Again.

But this time it wasn't concern and alarm that filled his gaze. No, it was interest. Awareness.

Unbidden, a flash of hope hugged her tight. Knowing that was the road to disappointment, Lilly squashed that feeling down. "I, um, need to get to work. I'm sorry I bothered you."

"You didn't."

She didn't dare reply. Just pulled open her car door and got back inside. If Robert thought she was being rude, then that was just fine.

Anything would be better than him guessing the truth . . . that for one brief moment, she'd been tempted to reach out to him for a hug . . . and hope he'd never let her go.

"Caleb Graber, you must stop being so lazy and fulfill your duties," his father said. "Now that Timothy is married, you need to do your part." Looking around the barn, his father scowled. "Why haven't you mucked out the stalls and watered the horses yet? It's already eight in the morning."

"I don't know."

"That's no answer."

Caleb knew it wasn't. But he also knew he couldn't tell the truth. The truth was that he was hung over. The truth was that the six pack of beer he'd drunk last night was making his stomach sour and the last thing in the world he wanted to do was rake up horse manure. Reaching for the rake, he muttered, "I'll do it."

Under the straw brim of his hat, his father's eyes looked him over. "*Gut,*" he said, then turned away.

As soon as he was alone, Caleb let go of the rake and then leaned against the barn. Closed his eyes against his pounding head. Wished he was anywhere else.

He hated his life.

"Still sitting around, doing nothing?" his sister Judith chirped.

He opened one eye. "Yeah."

"It won't help, you know," she murmured.

"What do you mean?"

Moving the basket of eggs to her left hand, she scowled at him. "I mean, that no matter how much you wish you didn't have to do things, it doesn't make responsibilities go away."

Judith Graber, the font of wisdom. "Can I wish you'd leave?"

Instead of turning away in a huff, she eyed him with disdain. "What's wrong, Caleb? Too much partying with your friends last night?"

"Shut up."

"You better get over that soon and grow up. We need you around here, you know. With Joshua busy at the store and Tim now farming Clara's land and ours, Daed has to depend on you."

"It's not fair that I have to do everyone else's chores just because they found something better to do."

Pure amusement lit her face. "Found something better? Caleb, Joshua and Tim got married."

He hated it when she made him feel like the dumbest person in the room. With a sigh, he turned away from her, filled a bucket with fresh water, and poured it into Jim's trough.

The horse perked up its ears and came to him for a pet. Caleb complied, rubbing the horse around his ears in the way Jim had always loved.

"You don't have a choice about your future, you know," Judith murmured. "Daed expects you to take over the farm since Joshua is in charge of the store. You might as well accept it."

Turning from the horse, Caleb angrily eyed his sister. "What if I don't want to?"

"Don't want to what? What are you talking about?"

"I'm just saying that maybe I don't want to work in fields and barns for the rest of my life."

"What else is there?"

"A lot."

"Not that I can see."

That was the problem with his family. They loved being Amish. They loved their way of life. They never contemplated anything else. Never longed for decent work, or meeting other people, or living other places.

Slowly, he said, "There're a lot of other things outside of Sugarcreek. One day, I aim to see it all."

Just a bit of her superiority slipped. "Caleb, what are you saying?"

For a moment, he was tempted to tell his sister everything. To share his dreams of escaping Sugarcreek and the endless rules that caged him in.

But he didn't dare. Judith would go tell his parents.

"Nothing. Leave me alone so I can get this done. And tell Anson to come out here and give me a hand."

"All right," she said quietly. "But I hope you know what you're doing."

He didn't. But that was okay. Anything was better than doing what was expected of him. Than staying.

All he had to do was wait just a little longer.

Then he could leave. Yes, just as soon as he was able . . . he was going to get out of Sugarcreek and go far away.

© Mary Lou Zinsser

SHELLEY SHEPARD GRAY is the beloved author of the Sisters of the Heart series, including *Hidden*, *Wanted*, and *Forgiven*. Before writing, she was a teacher in both Texas and Colorado. She now writes full time and lives in southern Ohio with her husband and two children. When not writing, Shelley volunteers at church, reads, and enjoys walking her miniature dachshund on her town's scenic bike trail.

DON'T MISS ANY OF
SHELLEY SHEPARD GRAY'S BOOKS

SISTERS OF THE HEART

HIDDEN
978-0-06-147445-3
(paperback)

WANTED
978-0-06-147446-0
(paperback)

FORGIVEN
978-0-06-147447-7
(paperback)

SEASONS OF SUGARCREEK

**COMING
AUGUST
2010**

**WINTER'S
AWAKENING**
978-0-06-185222-0
(paperback)

**SPRING'S
RENEWAL**
978-0-06-185236-7
(paperback)

**AUTUMN'S
PROMISE**
978-0-06-185237-4
(paperback)